villainous

Also by Matthew Cody

Powerless

Super

The Dead Gentleman

Will in Scarlet

— Supers of Noble's Green —

villainous

matthew cody

Alfred A. Knopf 🐎 New York

THIS IS A BORZOI BOOK PUBLISHED BY ALFRED A. KNOPF

All rights reserved. Published in the United States by Alfred A. Knopf, an imprint of Random House Children's Books, a division of Random House LLC, a Penguin Random House Company, New York.

Knopf, Borzoi Books, and the colophon are registered trademarks of Random House LLC.

Visit us on the Web! randomhouse.com/kids

Educators and librarians, for a variety of teaching tools, visit us at RHTeachersLibrarians.com

Library of Congress Cataloging-in-Publication Data
Cody, Matthew.
    Villainous / by Matthew Cody. — First edition.
        pages   cm
    Sequel to: Super.
    Summary: "Fourteen-year-old Daniel and his friends battle the Nobles of the new Noble Academy and attempt to defeat the Shroud once and for all." —Provided by publisher
        ISBN 978-0-385-75489-7 (trade) — ISBN 978-0-385-75490-3 (lib. bdg.) — ISBN 978-0-385-75492-7 (pbk.) — ISBN 978-0-385-75491-0 (ebook)
    [1. Supernatural—Fiction. 2. Superheroes—Fiction. 3. Supervillains—Fiction. 4. Mystery and detective stories.] I. Title.
    PZ7.C654Vi 2014
    [Fic]—dc23

                                    2013037497

The text of this book is set in 12-point HoeflerNew.

Printed in the United States of America
August 2014
10 9 8 7 6 5 4 3 2 1

First Edition

For James and Shirley Cody

Acknowledgments

Special thanks to my editor, Michele Burke, who shepherded this book through its ups and downs with her usual panache. Thanks to Karen Greenberg, Stephen Brown, and Nancy Hinkel for their wonderful insights and extraordinary patience. Thank you to my tireless agent and friend, Kate Schafer Testerman.

And, of course, thanks to Alisha and Willem for just about everything.

Prologue
October 14, 1934

He didn't want to come out, but he knew he couldn't stay in there all day. Eileen always said that when he locked himself in, he was only making it worse—giving the other children another reason to make fun of him. And it was hot and it stank, but then outhouses were supposed to stink.

Herman bit his lip as someone knocked at the door. He'd locked the latch but what if it was Bill Tyler? That boy told everyone about how he used to break into homes back in Philadelphia. He even claimed to have picked the lock on Brother Francis's door once, though Herman suspected that story was just bragging.

"Herman?" called a girl's voice from the other side of the door. "You okay in there?"

Herman breathed a sigh of relief—not a pleasant thing to do considering the generally poor quality of the air in there. It was only Eileen.

"I'm okay," answered Herman.

"You gonna be much longer?" she asked. "I gotta go."

"There's more than one outhouse," said Herman. Eileen knew that. She was just trying to get Herman to come out without saying she wanted him to come out.

Silence. Herman started to worry that she'd gone, that she'd gotten so frustrated with him this time that she'd finally given up. She wouldn't have been the first.

"Eileen?" he whispered against the slats of the door.

"Herman, why don't you just come out?"

She was still there. That was good, though he still wasn't about to come out.

"So this is where you been hiding," said Eileen. "You could at least find someplace that isn't so darn smelly."

He still didn't say anything.

"Herman, that was supposed to be a joke."

"I know what jokes are."

"Then you know it's polite to laugh when someone makes one, even if it's not very funny."

"Ha-ha," said Herman.

"Thank you," answered Eileen. "Now will you please open the door and tell me what happened?"

"It was that Jake Talbot," said Herman. "He's a bully."

"I heard you two had trouble."

"He chased me through the yard with a hickory switch. Everyone laughed."

Another silence.

"Herman, some of the other children are saying that you started it. They're saying that you put cayenne powder in his porridge."

"I didn't!"

"Well, somebody did. I saw the blisters on his tongue."

"It wasn't me," said Herman. "Swear it wasn't."

Eileen didn't answer right away, and Herman wondered what was going on in her head. Did she believe him? Lying came easily; it was something he did well. Maybe the only thing. The trick, he'd discovered, was that to make other people believe you, you had to believe in the lie yourself. If you could fool yourself, you could fool anybody, and at that moment Herman willed himself to believe that he hadn't snatched a bag of cayenne powder from Brother Leo's herb cabinet and poured at least half of it into Jake Talbot's morning porridge. And he willed himself to believe that he hadn't done all this because he'd seen Jake Talbot and Eileen holding hands last night after supper.

As he often did when things got bad, Herman found himself a lie that was better than the truth.

"Okay, then, Herman," said Eileen. "If you swear you didn't do it, I believe you. And I'll tell Jake Talbot that it wasn't you and to leave you alone. If he doesn't, he'll answer to me."

Herman grinned as he undid the latch on the outhouse door. His eyes took a moment to adjust to the glare of daylight. Standing there with the sun silhouetted around her like a halo, Eileen looked as bright as the sun herself.

He stared at her until he had spots in his eyes.

"You know you got to stand up for yourself," said Eileen. "If you didn't do it, then you should've stood your ground and told Jake that. I can't keep dragging you out of these fixes, Herman. I can't be your hero forever."

"I'll be your hero someday," said Herman. "Someday I'll save you."

Eileen smiled and they walked together back to the orphanage. A few of the monks had gathered near the front to look over the wares of a passing trapper. His was a familiar face around St. Alban's, a dirty fellow with an unkempt beard and patched-up clothes. From what Herman could tell, the trapper spent more time trying to convince the monks to buy knickknacks than actually doing any trapping. He always had a pouch of trinkets that he'd scrounged from who-knew-where, and occasionally the monks would find something in the pouch for the younger orphans to play with. Today he was trying to interest them in a ragged doll with hair the color of straw. One of her button eyes dangled precariously by a thread.

As Eileen led Herman past, the trapper smiled, tipped his coonskin hat at Eileen, and winked at Herman.

Johnny. That was his name. Johnny.

The inside of St. Alban's was arranged around a central cloister, the courtyard where most of the orphans carried out chores during the day. The children slept in the bunkhouse, divided into a room for the boys and a room for the girls. They took their meals together with the monks in the frater. There were nine of them right now. Nine unwanted children from all parts.

St. Alban's hadn't begun as an orphanage. The little monastery had been built in the wilds of the mountainside to escape the distracting trappings of civilization, even such meager trappings as could be found in the nearby town. But over the years, as more and more wayward children began appearing in the area—the sons and daughters of migrant workers too poor to feed them, or street children from Pittsburgh or Philadelphia who'd hopped a freight train but hadn't gotten very far—those lost children would eventually find their way to St. Alban's doorstep.

Right now five of the nine were gathered in the cloister looking at Jake Talbot's ruined mouth. Brother Leo was dabbing a wet cloth on Jake's blistered tongue and making concerned clucking noises.

Eileen guided Herman close enough that he could get a good look. Older than Herman by just a year, she already stood a good half a foot taller than the small boy. For several minutes, Eileen didn't move and she didn't let Herman walk away. She stood there with her hands on Herman's shoulders as the two of them watched Brother Leo tend to Jake.

Herman didn't know why they were watching this, as he'd successfully willed it that he hadn't had anything to do with it, but if Eileen wanted him to watch for some strange reason, then he was happy to do so as long as she kept her hands on his shoulders. She was gentle and Herman liked that.

People weren't gentle with Herman much. His mother might have been once, though Herman couldn't remember her very well. And the monks said that he had a brother somewhere although he couldn't remember him either. But Herman knew this: that real families were gentle with one another. They held each other, traded kisses and hugs. That made Eileen his family, the only family he knew.

She was his family, not Jake Talbot's.

Eventually, Eileen let her hands slide away, and with a pat on his head, she wandered off to collect the day's laundry for the evening wash. Herman drifted back toward the frater and the kitchen, ignoring the queasy knot of guilt that had tied itself up in his stomach. Maybe he could find something to take his mind off it. If Brother Leo was tending to Jake, maybe he wasn't keeping an eye on his herb cabinet. . . .

At dinner Eileen didn't sit with Herman, though he was pleased to see she didn't sit with Jake either. After Brother Francis said grace, the children dug into their meals, all except Jake. He was miserably sucking on a rag that he kept re-wetting with cool water from the pitcher.

After dinner the orphans marched single file across the cloister to the bunkhouse. The night was crisp and the stars shone brightly overhead. Herman saw Brother Francis and Brother Leo standing outside and pointing to a different spot of sky in the east. Herman squinted at it, and at first thought his eyes were fooling him because it looked like the sun was already rising. Only instead of being lit with a warm red glow, the horizon was a ghostly, shimmering green. He'd never seen anything like it. Herman wanted to stop and watch, but he was herded along with the other children indoors to their beds.

Herman's bunk was on the far side of the boys' room, and he wasn't halfway there when a shadow stepped into his path. No, it wasn't a shadow; it was just Bill Tyler.

"We know what you done to Jake," said Bill. A few of the other boys were standing behind him. They all wore evil looks. "Give me one good reason why I shouldn't knock your block off. Bad enough you're always skulking around, stealing other people's things. Herman the sneak. Herman the fink!"

Herman did try to think of a good reason why Bill shouldn't hit him, but he couldn't lie his way out of this one. And when Herman couldn't lie his way out of trouble, he had one other tactic that had served him well—he ran.

He was out the door before Bill had taken two steps. Out of the boys' room and through his secret exit—a loose floorboard at the end of the hall. Then past the backyard and all the way to his hiding place.

The outhouse was empty, as it always was (the seat in this

one was particularly splintery and best avoided). Herman closed the door and flipped the lock. Then he hugged his knees to his chest and waited. Bill would have to go to sleep eventually; then Herman would sneak into his own bed so that he'd be there when the brothers woke them for morning chores.

Herman waited for hours, until his own eyelids began drooping with sleep. When he finally opened the outhouse door, he was shocked to see that the sky overhead had changed. The stars had been swallowed up by a heavy blanket of storm clouds, but instead of lightning flashes, the clouds were lit with that sallow greenish light. It looked like the end of the world.

Herman was wondering if the other children were seeing this same sky, or if they were tucked into their beds asleep and unaware, when the air was rent with a tremendous boom. Before he'd come to St. Alban's, Herman had spent time in a mining town where he watched the miners use dynamite to blast their way into nickel veins, but this sound was ten times as loud as that had been. It set his ears ringing, and the clouds parted as a streak of green fire came hurtling from the heavens. It burned shadows into Herman's vision as it got bigger and bigger, a falling star set to collide with the earth. Truly, the end of the world.

It must've hit the cloister directly because the impact blew up such a cloud of dirt and fire that Herman was thrown into the back of the outhouse and the door slammed shut behind him. Once the cloud settled, Herman inched the door open and saw that the flames—green flames like the lightning overhead—had already begun to consume the frater. The kitchen was ablaze; the monks' quarters had been leveled in the destruction. The only building still standing was the orphans' bunkhouse, but the fires were already drifting that way.

Why weren't they running? Why weren't the children fleeing for their lives? But they couldn't, not without facing the rising inferno outside their front door. They were trapped in there and they would die. Eileen would die.

But not if Herman saved her. No one knew about the loose floorboard, Herman's secret exit. He could open it and lead them all out that way, through the back of the bunkhouse and into the safety of the woods.

Herman just needed the courage to step out of his hiding place and face the fire. He could do it. For Eileen.

He'd managed his first step when he saw a shape emerging from the trees. It was the trapper Johnny, and he was sprinting toward the burning orphanage. The front gate was aflame, so Johnny used the butt of his rifle to smash open a window high in the bunkhouse wall. Immediately, greenish black smoke came pouring out—the bunkhouse must have been filled with it. But Johnny didn't hesitate. He hauled himself up and through the shattered window, swallowed up by the smoke.

Seconds passed. Minutes. Whatever courage Herman

had summoned up to save Eileen had begun to falter as he watched the fires grow. It was too late surely. Johnny and the orphans would have succumbed to the smoke by now. There was no escaping it.

Herman's eyes stung with tears, but it wasn't from the heat or smoke. He was upwind of the blaze and spared the worst of it. His tears were for Eileen.

Then there was another crash as the bunkhouse's roof gave way and collapsed in on itself in a shower of glowing cinders.

"Eileen," Herman whimpered.

A moment passed, and the wreckage moved. The fallen timbers stirred and, unbelievably, rose. Johnny was lifting the collapsed roof over his head. His clothes were aflame but he didn't seem to notice. It was impossible. Ten men wouldn't have been able to lift that roof. Not a man alive could have withstood that heat.

Then she appeared. She wasn't alone—the other orphans rose with her, freed by Johnny and lifting themselves out of the burning wreckage, but Herman only saw her. Eileen floating up into the sky.

At first Herman thought she'd died and he was seeing her angel make its way to heaven, but she wasn't dead. She was glowing, and not with the green light of the fire but with a light all her own. She shone as brightly and as golden as the sun. She was flying.

• • •

"Mr. Plunkett? Mr. Plunkett, are you okay, sir?"

"Hmm?" said Herman, noticing the nurse's fat face for the first time. How long had she been standing there? "I was just thinking about something that happened to me a long time ago. Long, long time ago."

The young nurse was new here, but she'd already learned how to infuriate Herman with her chipper smile. She seemed determined to make up for her inexperience by becoming best friends with every patient at the Mountain View Home. But Herman knew there was no making up for inexperience. Experience counted for everything. At nearly a hundred years old, it had to.

"You've got just a little bit of Jell-O there on your chin, Mr. Plunkett," she said, and dabbed at his face with one of those dreadful wet wipes she always carried, the ones that smelled like a dentist's office. He knew he had Jell-O all down the front of his dressing gown as well and in his lap, but she either didn't notice or chose not to comment on that. He hadn't seen much use in cleaning it up before.

They'd parked his wheelchair at his favorite window, the one with the clearest view of the mountain, but though he stared at it all the time, he never really saw it. Not as it was today, in any case.

"Did you enjoy your morning paper?" the nurse asked as she tried to slip the newspaper away from where it lay clutched in his lap. But his fingers, swollen knuckles gone white, would not release their grip.

"Mr. Plunkett?" the nurse said again as she tried to pull

the paper from his hands. "Are you finished with the paper, because there are other residents . . ."

Ignoring her, he looked down at the paper in his Jell-O–stained lap. He'd been reading a story buried deep inside its pages. A small sidebar, listed under a regular section titled "Campbell's Curiosities." Herman didn't know who this Campbell person was, but his tastes usually ran toward UFO sightings and batboys. But not today.

"What's that you've been reading?" asked the nurse. She'd given up wrestling with him over the paper and now seemed to be trying a new tactic of feigned interest. He really did despise her.

"Oh!" she said, looking over his shoulder. "I love that column. So unusual! What's this one about? 'Astronomers Say Witch Fire Comet Returning'?"

She made a face. "Well, that sounds downright spooky, doesn't it?"

Herman turned and looked at her, and for the first time in a long time, he had a reason to smile.

Chapter One
Summer School

"Hey, kid! What can you do?"

Daniel took his time chaining up his bike before glancing over his shoulder. He'd been hoping that if he pretended not to hear them, they'd go away, but no such luck. A tour group headed by a man in a cheap plastic cape had crossed the street and were now standing in a semicircle around him. Their camera phones were already clicking as they snapped pictures. They didn't even ask if it was okay.

"What do you mean, *What can you do?*" said Daniel, although he knew full well what they meant.

"Do you *do* anything?" said a round woman who elbowed

her way to the front of the group. Her arms wiggled as she moved. "Anything special?"

Daniel considered what to say next. The morning was muggy already, and the sun burned hot and white in a pale sky. The heat and these tourists only worsened his mood, which was crappy to begin with. Even now, the fat woman looked flushed and sweaty from the heat, or maybe she was about to pass out from the possibility that he could be one of *them*. This was, after all, the town famous for being home to super-kids.

He could play with these tourists. He could say he had the power to erase the memory cards on their phones with a wave of his hand, or that he could read minds, and did they know that one of them was secretly in love with another member of their group? Those had worked in the past. But the best was always when he told them his power was a radioactive field that he called his *death zone*. It wasn't dangerous as long as you didn't look directly at him and wrapped yourself in tinfoil.

But it was too hot to mess with tourists today.

"I don't do anything special," he said. "I'm just a kid."

He could feel their disappointment as, one by one, they turned their backs on him. Then they continued walking down the street, busily deleting the pictures they'd snapped of Daniel before they'd learned that he was nobody important. Maybe they'd wander into Arnold Lebowski on his paper route, the boy who could turn himself into a human-shaped cloud. If he tried really hard, he could squeeze out a few raindrops for onlookers.

Daniel finished chaining up his bike and made for the opposite side of the street. He was a few minutes early today and decided to treat himself to something special. Lemon's Ice Cream Parlor and Doughnut Shop had been a fixture of downtown Noble's Green for nearly sixty years. It was a true family business that had weathered economic depressions, recent recessions, and globalization unchanged. But it had not weathered superhero mania.

As Daniel opened the door of the re-christened Happy Hero's Ice Cream Parlor—Home to the Superpowered Root Beer Float!—he was glad to hear the familiar chime of the old doorbell. At least that hadn't gone away. And the inside of the shop still smelled a little bit like what Daniel imagined heaven must smell like: powdered sugar and cinnamon. Standing behind the counter, wiping down the chrome tabletop with a rag, was elderly Mr. Lemon himself, dressed in a shiny silver tracksuit decorated with glued-on felt lightning bolts. Mr. Lemon had not developed any powers as far as Daniel knew, but that hadn't stopped him from cashing in on the town's newfound fame.

"Hey there, Daniel!" said Mr. Lemon with a smile. "What are you doing up this early on a summer morning?"

Ah, that was the question, wasn't it? Daniel figured he'd better get used to it, as this was going to be his routine for the foreseeable future.

"Oh, well," he said. "I'm taking a few summer classes. To get ahead, you know."

From the look on Mr. Lemon's face, Daniel could tell he did know. He knew that middle schoolers did not take summer classes to get ahead. It was called summer school, and if Daniel didn't pass it, he would be repeating the eighth grade.

But Mr. Lemon didn't embarrass Daniel by asking any more questions.

"Well, you'll need to get something in your stomach before you hit the books, won't you? I've got breakfast sandwiches that heat up real quick. Not half bad."

"Just a doughnut," said Daniel. "Jelly. And an orange juice. It's hot out there already."

"Looking for a sugar rush, eh? Well, I've got a fresh batch coming out of the oven right now. Be back in a second." He scurried off to the rear of his shop, the homemade antennae on his silver superhero cap wobbling as he went.

Daniel plopped down on a barstool to wait, enjoying the chill of the air conditioner. He held his arms away from his body to let the cool air work its way into his shirt.

Summer school.

For Daniel, it had turned out that keeping up with his studies had been a lot harder than he'd thought, especially when his nights were spent battling super-villains instead of studying. In the end, he'd just managed to scrape past his eighth-grade year with a miserable D in chemistry, but he'd flunked history, which was normally his best subject. His parents had greeted his report card with shock—Daniel had been an A and B student up until then. But to try to explain why his grades had plummeted would mean he'd have to tell them a whole host of secrets—about how when they'd moved to Noble's Green two years ago, he'd discovered a small group of super-children living in secret. About how he'd saved those children from their enemy, the power-stealing villain called the Shroud. And he'd have to tell them that he, a regular kid from Philadelphia, had caused the world-famous Blackout Event, when two hundred and three people woke up one morning and suddenly remembered that they could fly. Or breathe underwater. Or any number of wondrous and sometimes bizarre things. There were super-adults, but just as many were children and more were being discovered every day. He'd have to explain all that to his parents and hope they didn't lock him in his room until college.

It was easier just to go to summer school.

He wasn't worried. He knew that if he knuckled down and studied, he would pass with no problem. If he could finally focus on his studies instead of sneaking out every night to battle monsters, he might even earn an A.

"I threw a bagel with cream cheese in there—on the house," said Mr. Lemon, reappearing with a small white lunch sack. "A jelly doughnut is no kind of breakfast for a growing young man."

"Thanks, Mr. Lemon," said Daniel as he fished a couple of wadded-up dollar bills out of his shorts pocket to pay for the doughnut and juice. "And, uh, nice suit."

Mr. Lemon chuckled. "Oh, this ridiculous thing. Mrs. Lemon's idea, you know. Whole town's got the fever. Now if we could just get a photo of the chief eating a Lemon's doughnut! That would be the ticket!"

Mr. Madison, the floating fire chief, was the town's star resident. His smiling face graced travel brochures and billboards everywhere, and lucky tourists might catch a glimpse of his silhouette high in the sky, fireman's helmet and rubber boots and all.

"If I see him," said Daniel, his mouth full of jelly-filled pastry, "I'll tell him to stop by!"

The new school, built along the slopes of Mount Noble, was called the Noble Academy for the Gifted, but its title was a carefully crafted understatement. Its students weren't simply gifted; they were Supers.

The academy was the world's first boarding school for superpowered children, located right here in Noble's Green. In theory, it was a terrific idea. Staff the school with superpowered adults who could teach the kids to control their abilities, to use them to make a positive contribution to society. The advertising campaign was slick and seductive, with posters of beautiful children flying, like Icarus, toward the sun. Never mind, thought Daniel, that Icarus had flown so close that his wings had melted. That part of the story seemed lost on some people.

The best thing about the academy was that classes had already begun. Parents wanted help dealing with the hormonal daughter who could break every window in the neighborhood when she screamed, or the kindergartner who could make it snow over the toilet. Parents were desperate.

So, in effect, the academy was a combination of sleepaway camp and summer school for the Supers. Only their summer school was being held atop a mountain, like Olympus, while Daniel's was in a basement.

Being an ordinary fourteen-year-old, Daniel had a more traditional summer school experience. The middle school didn't bother to open up the entire building for the summer students, so "repeat" American history was held in room 207 in the lowest level, which during the regular year was used for biology. Inside, a human skeleton hung on a stand beneath the flickering fluorescent lights, and on a shelf behind the teacher's desk were rows of *things floating in jars.* All in all, the dangling skeleton and bloated, unrecognizable specimens made for a rather appropriate setting to kick off this new experience. All Daniel needed now was a black-hooded executioner to ask him for any last requests.

At that moment, sitting in that dungeon classroom, just

when Daniel's heart had sunk to its lowest, he felt someone flick him on the back of the head. Hard.

He turned around in his seat and found himself looking at an Asian American girl with straight black bangs cut close to her dark, almost black eyes. She had folded her arms across her chest, partially obscuring a T-shirt that read, in faded letters, IT'S NOT ME, IT'S YOU.

"Hey," said Mollie Lee, grinning.

"W-what . . . ?" stammered Daniel, rubbing the back of his head. He looked around her desk for the guilty weapon. It felt like she'd whacked him with a ruler.

"What are you doing here?" he tried again. Although he was glad to see a friendly face, her unexpected appearance threw him off. She often did that to people, using her superspeed to surprise them. Sometimes to hit them if she felt the occasion warranted. To most of the world, Mollie Lee passed by as a breeze and blur. And occasionally a whack.

"History," she answered, shrugging. "But I'm surprised to see you here. I thought you were, like, Rohan's brainiac twin or something."

"I'm not a brainiac . . . ," started Daniel. "But I fell behind last year. We had other things on our minds, you know."

Mollie nodded. "I had trouble last year too, and it's getting worse. I think I'm getting faster."

"Wow," said Daniel. He could hardly imagine Mollie being any faster than she already was. "Well, that's great, isn't it?"

"Except that I'm having trouble focusing on stuff for

very long. Teachers start talking and I just want them to hurry up already, and who can sit still and read a bookImeanwhat'stheuseofallthis . . . ?"

As Mollie talked faster and faster, her words became impossible to understand. Several of the nearby students looked up at the intercom, trying to pinpoint the source of the sudden buzzing in the room.

"Mollie! Slow down!" Daniel whispered.

Mollie stopped talking and gave Daniel a depressed sigh. She rubbed at her eyes with the palms of her hands.

"You see?" she said. "These days it takes everything I've got to not go into hyperdrive all the time. I don't have any energy left for American history."

"How were your other grades?"

"Not terrible," said Mollie. "Algebra and chemistry I can get and then move on, you know? At my own pace. I don't have to suffer through these boring lectures."

Daniel thought about this. He'd known that his friends were getting more powerful as they got older, but this was the first suggestion he'd had that this might not be an altogether positive thing. More power might be more of a curse than a blessing, especially when you were Mollie Lee and the world already moved in slow motion around you.

"When I asked what you were doing here," said Daniel, "I meant what are you doing *here*—the middle school? Don't you want to go to the academy with the rest of the Supers? If you can fly, who there's going to care about what you got in history?"

Mollie flipped open her textbook and began paging through it, studiously avoiding Daniel's eyes.

"I'm not going," she said finally.

"What? Why?"

Mollie stopped fidgeting with her book.

"We took a vote," said Mollie. "Rohan, Eric, Michael, and I. It was unanimous. We're not signing up for the academy."

Daniel was dumbstruck. Why not? What about the shining towers, the mountain air?

Mollie read the look of bafflement on his face correctly.

"I think it's creepy," she said. "You see those ridiculous posters?"

"Well, I admit they *are* kind of over-the-top. But aren't you curious about it?"

Mollie shook her head. "Nope. What are they going to teach me about my powers that I don't already know? I'll bet I know more about flying than any of their stupid faculty."

That was true, but Daniel had to wonder if someone up there might be able to help Mollie with her speed problem. Power-wise, none of the adults would be able to come close to Mollie or Eric. Most of the adults had been without full powers for decades, and when they finally returned, they were weaker than before. That's why they'd ended up with a floating fire chief rather than a flying one.

"I don't think it's a powers contest," said Daniel. "That's not the point of the school."

"You sure?" asked Mollie. "How do you know?"

"Well," said Daniel, hesitating. "The posters, I guess."

"See? Nobody knows anything about that place. It's all *Hey, are you having trouble getting your super-kid to clean up his room? Well, then, ship him off to us and you won't have to worry about it for the next seven years!*"

"Yeah, I guess the whole boarding school thing is kinda . . . British."

"Kinda."

"And Eric and Rohan feel the same way you do?"

Mollie nodded. "Michael too. They can take their super-school and shove it. I don't want to be sent off to a whole different school just so ordinary people can feel comfortable around me again."

Daniel cringed at the word *ordinary,* and Mollie, to his surprise, seemed to notice.

"You know I didn't mean—" she began.

"Don't worry about it," said Daniel, waving it away. By now, you would've thought he'd be used to it. "But I still think the academy's probably a good thing for a lot of kids. Most of them just got their powers back after years of going without, and they're having to learn how to use them all over again. And I've heard that there are even more who are developing powers for the very first time."

"I know. It's like, with the Shroud gone, everyone's suddenly a Super."

The Shroud. Just the mention of their old enemy made

23

Daniel's mouth go dry. For generations, the creature known as the Shroud had preyed upon the super-children of Noble's Green, stealing their powers and their memories. But all that had changed when Daniel revealed the Shroud's real identity to be old Herman Plunkett, the town's billionaire son. Powerless and defeated, Herman was now safely tucked away up at the Mountain View Home, hopefully until the end of his days.

"Mollie?"

"Hmm?"

"You guys . . . you're not doing this . . . I mean, you're not all doing this so that I won't be alone next year in school, are you?"

Mollie snorted as if he'd just claimed that the earth really was flat. "Keep dreaming!"

But when she said it, she didn't—or couldn't—look him in the eye.

That was the end of their conversation since a hush fell over the class as their new history teacher entered the room. He wrote his name on the board—*Mr. Smiley*. Daniel immediately picked up on the irony of the man's name, because one look told him that Smiley was as sour-faced a person as he had ever seen. His face looked built in such a way as to make it impossible to crack a smile. He was obviously even less happy to be here than his students were.

"So," Daniel whispered before turning back around in his seat to face their new teacher. "The original Supers of Noble's Green together again, that it?"

"You bet your butt," she whispered back.

And at that moment, Daniel's mood brightened—despite the grim classroom, and Mr. *Frowny* at the board, and the academy, and the sheer cosmic unfairness of school in the summertime. Because now he wouldn't be alone after all. Not yet anyway. He'd have Mollie, at least, to keep him company for a while longer.

"Mollie," Daniel whispered again over his shoulder. "I'm glad."

She didn't answer this time, but Daniel knew Mollie was smiling. He could feel it. It tingled, like a warm breath on the back of his neck.

Chapter Two
Fast as Lightning

Summers usually had a way of flying past, as one sunburned day blended into the next, and by the time school rolled around, an entire season had passed in a montage of beaches, picnics, and video games. Unless you happened to be trapped in Smiley's basement, that is. That classroom was the place where time slowed to a crawl and fun went to die.

Daniel had never been more thankful for Mollie than he was on those long days in summer school, and this included the many times she'd saved his behind. He could have handled getting beaten up by super-bullies, or left at the mercy of the Shroud, but enduring a summer alone in Smiley's basement was unthinkable. Since this history class was the only thing keeping them from repeating the eighth grade, Daniel and Mollie did try to keep their goofing off to a minimum. But Daniel finally got to see up close just how much of a struggle this was for Mollie. He'd always known that Mollie had trouble focusing on one thing for very long, and that she was super-impatient as well as super-fast, but Smiley's droning history lectures seemed especially difficult for her to follow. She missed the most important details because five minutes into a lesson she was already flitting through her book, rifling through the pages, or doodling pictures of Smiley with buckteeth and donkey ears with one hand while flicking Daniel on the back of the head with the other.

On one Saturday morning Daniel tried to explain all this to his father while helping him with some home repair and improvement, which in Daniel's house meant he got to hold the tools while his father did all the work. Even so, his dad listened patiently as Daniel laid out the tortures that awaited him every morning in Smiley's classroom, and his fears that Mollie wouldn't pass.

"Sounds like a form of attention deficit disorder," Daniel's father said as he straddled the roof with his legs and swung a hammer in one hand. Daniel's job was to sit in the open window of his attic bedroom and supply the requested tools. His father wouldn't let him come all the way out. He said it was too high up to be safe.

Daniel looked at the distant clouds in the sky, where he'd

flown with Eric countless times before, and thought, *Dad, if you only knew.*

"Has she been tested?" his father asked. "I mean, I know she's got those . . . powers of hers."

It was funny—the Blackout Event was half a year old and adults like Daniel's parents still had trouble even saying the word *powers.* They'd spent most of their lives telling their kids that they couldn't grow up to be superheroes, and that monsters weren't waiting for them in the dark. The world now knew that they'd been wrong on the first count, and having fought the Shroud, Daniel knew they'd also been wrong on the second.

"She thinks the powers are the problem," said Daniel. "It's getting harder and harder for her to sit still long enough to concentrate. And then sometimes she just crashes, like she's burned up all her fuel too fast and can't keep her eyes open."

"Well, if this teacher of yours isn't helping her, maybe she could use a tutor," said his dad.

"That's an idea," said Daniel. "But where would she get one?"

"Well, I was thinking— Ouch, darn it!" Daniel's dad stuck his thumb in his mouth after trying to nail it into the roof.

"You should watch your language, Dad," said Daniel.

"Yeah, and what made you such a smart aleck?" his father said, sucking his thumb.

"Good genes?"

"Hah. As I was saying, you used to be pretty good at history, when you weren't slacking off and letting your grades go down the toilet, that is."

His father was right. Daniel had actually enjoyed history, the great story of it all. It was just hard to keep up your grades when you were moonlighting as a crime fighter.

"So," continued his father, "I was thinking maybe *you* could tutor her. Be a good way to reinforce your own studies and help out a friend at the same time. Here, hand me another nail, would you?"

Daniel held out a box of nails for his dad to choose from as he pondered this idea. He couldn't quite picture Mollie having the patience for any tutor, much less Daniel. But then again, unlike their teachers, Daniel was very used to dealing with Mollie. He'd had to learn patience just to be her friend. In that way, Daniel was exceptionally qualified for the job.

"And voilà!" said his father as he stood a tall metal rod in the base he'd just nailed into the roof. It was long and thin, maybe an inch in diameter, but it reached up higher than the highest tree.

"What is it?" asked Daniel. "Some kind of antenna?"

"Lightning rod," said his dad. "With all the storms we've been having lately, I thought, Better safe than sorry."

Daniel looked up at the spindly metal spire and asked, "Just how is that supposed to protect us from a lightning strike? Isn't holding up a tall metal pole in a thunderstorm, like, a really bad idea?"

"It is," said his dad. "But a lightning rod on a house absorbs the strike. It controls the current and redirects it through there." He pointed to a copper wire snaking along the roof and down the side of the house. "The current follows the wire down and discharges harmlessly into the yard."

"Sounds a bit risky," said Daniel.

"It's a time-proven method. Provide energy with a path of least resistance—the metal wire—and that's where it'll go. Ben Franklin invented it!"

Daniel should have known. His dad was a bit of a nut when it came to Benjamin Franklin. Daniel's hero was the great detective Sherlock Holmes. His dad's was Ben.

"So now that I've helped you save our family from the thunder and lightning, can I go swimming with my friends later? They're meeting at the swimming hole."

"You finish this weekend's history homework?"

"Last night."

"Fine, go enjoy yourself," said his dad. "But give some thought to what I said about Mollie. Sounds like she could really use your help."

Chapter Three
The Swimming Hole

"**Y**ou came all the way out here just to fall asleep?" said a voice overhead.

Daniel squinted up at Mollie with one eye open.

"Not sleeping. *Chillaxing.*"

She snorted. "You sound like an idiot."

"*Whatevs.*"

"Oh my God, you're gonna get hit."

"All right!" said Daniel, propping himself up on one elbow.

Tangle Creek Bridge was Daniel's favorite secluded spot. Beneath the bridge the creek widened into a natural swimming hole, deep enough to dive. The water was cool, while the flat sandstones on either bank baked in the mid-day sun. Today, Daniel was stretching out across one of them. Fresh from a swim, he was enjoying the feel of the warm stone on his back as he let the sun dry his skin. Far from the town and its crowds, he would let this perfect day drive away all thoughts of summer school. That is, if Mollie would let him.

"Why aren't you flying?" he asked. "Thought you'd be dying for a bit of exercise after being cooped up all week with Smiley."

She sat down beside him. "Michael keeps showing off. Now that he's gotten his powers back, he's super-annoying."

"You mean *you* keep baiting Michael into racing you, and he keeps winning," said Daniel.

"Every time," said Mollie. "Like I said, super-annoying."

Mollie was wearing a pair of cutoff blue jeans over her swimsuit. The frayed edges had been stained green from the creek water, and she absently pulled at the loose strings as she spoke.

"Where's Michael now?" Daniel asked.

"Up there somewhere," said Mollie. "As usual."

Michael rarely came down. Thanks to the shroud, Michael had spent the last two years on the ground—his powers and memories stolen. Now that he could finally fly again, he seemed to be making up for lost time. Someone recently joked that if he could fall asleep on a cloud, he would, and when Michael had heard that, he paused for a moment, as if seriously considering whether he could pull it off.

"Have you talked to Louisa?" Mollie asked, still pulling at strings.

A butterfly in Daniel's stomach did a little flutter at the mention of Louisa's name. The two of them had shared a kiss last year, Daniel's first. Literally moments after that kiss, they'd been thrust into a new crisis, and there'd never really been a good moment to talk about what had happened. Saving the town had taken precedence over their young love lives.

But the crisis was all over now and they'd still not gotten around to talking about that kiss. Daniel had been given a slight reprieve when Louisa's family left for a summer vacation, but they wouldn't be gone forever. Louisa was a Super and a friend, but if she was going to be something more, then he would have to make up his mind about her, and soon.

"I haven't talked to her really," said Daniel. "She said she'd send me a postcard."

"I chatted with her the other day," said Mollie.

"Oh?" he said, trying to sound casual. "What'd she say?"

"Oh, you know Louisa," said Mollie. "Lots of cute boys on cruise ships apparently. She says that her mom wants her to sign up for the academy when they get back. Her and Rose."

"Wow," said Daniel. "Do you think they'll do it?"

Mollie shrugged. "Louisa's never been into the whole powers thing, so I can't imagine she'll want to. But if her mom pushes it, who knows?"

So Louisa might not be in school with them next year

after all. The thought of going to school without her made Daniel sad, but was that because he wouldn't get to see Louisa the friend, or Louisa the something else? Which one would he miss?

"So, Louisa and Rose are maybes," said Daniel. "Anyone else we know going?"

"Eric said that Sasha Knowles and Martin Baylor were already enrolled. And there's Simon—no one's heard from him in a long time."

Simon was the Super whom Daniel had failed to save from the Shroud his first year here in Noble's Green. Although Simon had his powers back now, he hadn't reconnected with his old friends the way Michael had. Granted, Simon was always kind of a jerk to everyone, but it still felt like a loss somehow. A failure that they hadn't been able to keep the Supers together—that their friendships had survived the Shroud, but might not survive growing up.

"Georgie's been asking about you," Daniel said, deciding that it was time to steer the subject away from would-be love interests and lost friends. "You should come by and see him."

"Aww," she said. "How is the little guy? He punch down any more doors?"

"No. Still nothing since the blackout."

"And your parents still don't know?"

"I can't tell them!" said Daniel. His little brother, Georgie, had displayed bouts of super-strength on definitely one occasion, and possibly two. But the only indisputable time had been in their final battle with the Shroud, which thanks to the super-villain's memory-stealing powers, his parents remembered nothing about. Daniel now found himself waiting for Georgie to do it again, hopefully with his parents around this time. It was like living with a stick of dynamite that threw temper tantrums.

"I guess he'll do something sooner or later," Daniel sighed. "I just hope he's not mad at me when it happens. Could toss me through a wall."

Mollie laughed. "That's so messed up."

"I know, but what else can I do? I guess I'll just let nature take its course, and someday he'll smash his tricycle into a little metal ball and that will be that. Then he'll be my mom and dad's problem."

For the next few minutes they just sat there on the rocks together and soaked in the sun. Mollie pulled her shoulder-length hair back into a small ponytail and looked up at the sky. Head tilted back, her bangs fell away from her eyes and the yellow sun lit up her face. She looked different somehow.

"Hey!" said Daniel, pointing at her.

"Hey, what?" said Mollie.

"You pierced your ears," he said, noticing for the first time two silver studs sticking out of her left ear, and a single one in her right. They glittered in the daylight, but the skin around them looked red and angry.

"Oh yeah," she said. "That."

"I didn't notice before with your hair down," said Daniel. "When did you do it?"

"Oh, I don't know," said Mollie. "Last week sometime." Then, as if retreating, she suddenly sank forward until her chin rested on her knees and her hair hid her ears. She sat like that, watching her toes as she wiggled them in the sunlight.

What to say next? Something was expected, and Daniel knew he should probably offer a compliment, but he was honestly a little shocked. It's not that the earrings looked bad; they didn't. But they didn't look like Mollie Lee. Sitting there in the sun with her hair drawn back and silver glittering in her ears, she had looked for a moment like a different girl entirely.

"Yeah, well, on second thought, maybe I *will* fly a little," she said after a moment, and before he could blink, she was gone. A speck high up in the sky.

He'd gotten it all wrong. By not complimenting the earrings, Daniel had insinuated that he didn't like them, which wasn't the case. They were mostly just surprising, but somehow Daniel didn't think that "Your earrings are surprising, Mollie," would have been any better than stunned silence.

If he couldn't manage to talk to Mollie about her new earrings without hurting her feelings, how was he ever going to manage talking to Louisa about the kiss? Girls used to be easy—they were just like boys, only cleaner. But in the last year or so, he'd felt the differences between the sexes widening into a vast sea, and every time he tried to cross the divide, he just ended up sinking.

Now he'd gone and hurt Mollie's feelings because he hadn't known the right way to compliment a few pieces of metal in her ears. But there wasn't anything he could do about it now. He might as well put it out of his mind and go for one last swim while there was still sun on this side of the bridge. Then he'd better put on some more sunscreen if he planned on staying much longer. Daniel never tanned, but he could turn lobster-red in no time at all if he wasn't careful.

As he moved around the creek bank, Daniel stepped gingerly along the hot sandstone, careful not to slip on the slimy rocks near the water's edge. He spotted Eric floating out over the swimming hole—not on the water, but hovering about a foot or so above it. He was following the tip of a snorkel that poked up out of the surface and traveled in slow circles beneath him. Eric had always been super-strong, but his strength had never had anything to do with his muscles. Now, however, with Eric's shirt off, Daniel noticed that in the last year his friend had developed a powerful, lean physique, and long summer days spent outdoors had tanned him to a deep nut-brown.

Daniel became suddenly quite self-conscious. The fluorescent lighting of Smiley's basement dungeon hadn't done anything to help his naturally pallid complexion, which, coupled with a seeming inability to put either fat or muscle onto his bony frame, left him with a thin, pale shape that might best be described as *wintery*.

It was a good thing that Louisa wasn't around after all.

Daniel watched as Eric did slow rolls in the air, lazily dipping his fingertips in the water and flicking the drops at gnats that were gathering around the shady spots near the shore.

Finally, Eric let out a long sigh. "Bored now," he said, and with a mischievous wave at Daniel, he began to slowly stalk the circling snorkel. The long breathing tube was still bobbing up and down slightly as the swimmer kicked along beneath the water, oblivious to the world above. Every now and then a flipper would break the surface.

With a wicked grin, Eric reached out and pinched shut the snorkel's breathing hole. For a few seconds nothing happened, but then the snorkel quivered and shook, and the flippers began kicking furiously as the swimmer appeared, sputtering and gasping for air. Rohan swam for shore, shouting curses at Eric.

Eric meanwhile had rolled onto his back, still floating in midair and laughing so hard that he had to hold his stomach. In that moment, he reminded Daniel of Peter Pan, who was content to spend forever playing and fighting in the sun. Daniel wished they all could be like the Pan and put off growing up indefinitely. No ear piercing, no summer school, no academy. Just *this*.

Rohan hauled himself up onto the rocks, where Daniel was waiting.

"He's such a little kid sometimes," said Rohan, spitting

out greenish water. Then he called over to Eric, "I hope a bee flies up your shorts!"

"He got bored," said Daniel. "How long were you under there?"

"I don't know," said Rohan. "A while. It's quiet down there. It gives me a break from everything."

Daniel nodded, understanding. Rohan's gift was that his senses were attuned to a superhuman scale. It was incredibly useful when one realized the full potential of what he could do, but it also meant that poor Rohan was constantly assaulted by noises and smells and other sensations that the rest of them weren't even aware of. It must be nice to escape it, if just for a little while.

Rohan poured out the water that had collected in his goggles. Then he pulled out his thick glasses, and Daniel watched his friend clean the lenses with his towel while squinting back at him. It was an ironic twist that the boy with super-vision needed glasses when his power wasn't kicking in.

"Where's Mollie?" asked Rohan.

"She flew off in a huff," said Daniel.

"What's she mad at you for this time?" asked Rohan.

"Oh, I don't know," lied Daniel. "Mollie things."

"Ah," said Rohan. "Those are potentially hazardous. Whatever it is, you'd better make up with her."

"What are you two talking about?" asked Eric, having finished his fit of hysterical laughter.

"Mollie's mad at Daniel," answered Rohan. "But it figures, with the two of them spending practically every minute together."

"Hey, it's no picnic," said Daniel. "Not Mollie, I mean, but the summer school part is about as much fun as you'd think."

"Yeah," said Eric, "but you two *are* together, like, almost every day."

"What's your point?" said Daniel.

Eric shrugged as if there was no point, but of course there was. Or else why bring it up?

"Eh, I'd get sick of Daniel too," said Rohan. "I'm already sick of him and I haven't been here more than a couple of hours."

"You should have stayed underwater, then," suggested Daniel.

"Better company down there," said Rohan.

The boys went on ribbing each other for a while, but through it all, Daniel's thoughts kept coming back to Mollie. He'd remembered what his dad had suggested, about offering to tutor her, and if he was serious about wanting her to pass history, then she needed his help. But Mollie always made things so difficult, and today was a prime example. They couldn't even talk about earrings without her flying off angry. Not to mention that if he agreed to do this it would mean devoting an extra hour or two every day after school to the books. It would mean even more summer hours lost.

Louisa. Mollie. Girls in general gave him a headache these days, and Daniel decided that the best cure would be to clear his mind of them entirely. And luckily he knew something that would work better than aspirin. He could just reach the bridge trellis without having to swim to it. Grabbing hold, he swung his legs over to the bottom rung and began to climb it like a ladder.

Daniel passed the jump mark, a spot arbitrarily designated by his friends as being a safe but fun place to do a cannonball into the pool below. He kept on climbing until he reached the very top, the diving platform. In reality it was just a few boards nailed to the trellis to provide a place to stand, but it served its purpose. Daniel took a couple of steps back from the edge, breathed in deeply through his nose, and smelled the water, the tang of fresh air, and growing things. And beneath it all, the tar of the road above him. Down at the bottom Eric was lying out on the rocks and Rohan had taken his snorkel back underwater. Daniel would have to be careful not to land on him.

He was just starting to prepare his dive when he heard a girl laugh behind him.

"Mollie—" he began, but couldn't finish, because he was interrupted with a rough push.

He threw out his arms to get his balance, but when he stepped out to steady himself, there was nothing except air beneath his foot, and he tripped off the high diving platform. Instead of cutting through the surface in a graceful dive, he hit the water flat on his chest.

It felt like he'd been slammed with a board. Panicked and disoriented by his tumbling fall, Daniel swallowed a mouthful of water as he sank. He tried to swim, to kick himself back to the surface, but he had trouble moving. He wanted to breathe, he *needed* to breathe, but he didn't even know which way was up.

Then someone else was there. An arm wrapped around his middle and he felt someone pulling him. He added his own kicks to theirs, and soon they'd broken the surface together. Daniel took a deep gulp of air. It felt like he'd never breathed before.

"Swim, Daniel!" someone was shouting into his ear. "I can't hold you up!"

Daniel looked over to see Mollie's sputtering face next to his. Her chin was barely cresting the water.

Then Eric was there hauling both of them out, his powerful hands grabbing hold of theirs.

The three landed on the bank in a heap, and for a few minutes no one said anything. Mollie lay on the rocks catching her breath while Daniel coughed up some greenish water. Rohan knelt nearby, and even Michael had returned from the skies. They all looked concerned.

Daniel peered down at his chest—there was no need to worry about a sunburn today; he was already bright red from where he'd smacked into the water. It hurt simply to breathe.

"What . . . ," he said, wincing with the effort of sitting

up. "What did you think you were doing? You could've killed me, Mollie!"

Mollie stared at him, her wet hair having come loose from its ponytail and now plastered across her face. It didn't hide her look of shock, however.

"Me? I was saving your life! What was that you did anyway, a belly flop?"

Daniel felt his blood rising. Maybe he'd been less than sensitive about her new fashion statement, but she really could have hurt him. Killed him even.

He pointed a finger in her face.

"You pushed me. Don't deny it, because I heard you."

Mollie blinked at him. "I didn't. I wouldn't. Not from up there. I'm not homicidal, Daniel."

Daniel looked to his friends. They were watching him with stares of outright disbelief. He glanced back toward the bridge, at the diving platform up top. Could he have just lost his balance? Had he mistaken a simple gust of wind for Mollie and missed his footing when he turned to look at her? But today was one of those summer days where the heat and humidity just hang over everything, unmoving. There hadn't been so much as a breeze across the water all afternoon.

"It wasn't me," said Mollie. "I promise."

"I . . . I heard laughing," Daniel said. "Before I fell, I mean. There was a strong wind, like someone was flying by me, and then a girl laughed, so I thought you were, you know, goofing around."

Mollie shook her head.

"Did you hear anything, Rohan?" Eric asked.

"No. I was underwater, though. All I heard were bubbles— Wait." Rohan had closed his eyes and put his finger over his mouth to signal quiet. He was listening for something.

"We're not alone," he whispered.

Then they all heard it. A girl's laughter echoing through the woods somewhere nearby. It was a mocking, ugly laugh.

"There's more than one," said Rohan. "I hear heartbeats."

Eric rose off the ground and peered into the woods. "Who's there?" he asked, but there was no answer.

"That's weird," said Rohan. "I can't . . . Huh. They're gone."

"Well, we can still catch them," said Mollie, and she jumped into the air alongside Eric.

"Wait!" said Rohan. "They're not running away. They're gone."

"Gone?" asked Daniel. "As in disappeared?"

Rohan nodded. "It was the strangest thing. I heard heartbeats beneath that girl's voice—several sets—and then nothing. . . . Hey, do you guys smell smoke?"

They didn't, but everyone knew better than to doubt Rohan's senses.

"I'll take a look," said Michael, and flew high into the sky.

While he was gone, Eric kept his eyes on the trees. "What do you think's going on?" he whispered to Daniel.

"I think . . . ," said Daniel, rubbing his raw chest. That would hurt for days. "I think we need to remember you all aren't the only Supers in town anymore."

"Guys!" called Michael, appearing once again over their heads. "We've got trouble!"

Daniel held on to Eric, and Michael lifted Rohan as they floated up above the trees to get a better look. Michael was pointing to a patch of forest near Mount Noble. A thick, curling tendril of black smoke was rising from the trees.

"Is that . . . ?" asked Daniel, squinting at the distant smoke.

"It's the tree fort," said Rohan, confirming Daniel's fears. "The tree fort is on fire."

Chapter Four
Those Kids

If not for all the recent storms, the fire might have eaten up a good portion of the forest, but luckily the moist undergrowth and low winds slowed the spread of the flames. The fire trucks arrived in time to contain the conflagration to the tree fort and a patch of the surrounding woods.

The tree fort. Generations of memories in a makeshift museum dedicated to the Supers, its collection made up of crayon drawings and yellowing comics, and it was all gone. Nothing was left but blackened nails and charcoal. The official report would lay the blame on teenagers shooting bottle rockets into the woods, but Daniel and his friends had their own suspicions. Someone had pushed Daniel off the Tangle Creek Bridge, and it was an awfully big coincidence that the tree fort should mysteriously catch fire the very same day.

But who besides the original Supers even knew about the tree fort? And who could have been at the bridge one minute, only to disappear the next? So far the sole clue they had was the laughing girl, and that wasn't much to go on.

In the meantime, the Supers began to rebuild, and Daniel became Mollie's tutor. Every day after school, Daniel would cross the street to her house and the two of them would recap what they'd learned in that day's lesson, while Mollie's mom kept them well supplied with snacks. Only this time he'd make sure to go fast enough that Mollie could keep up. It was kind of like reverse logic—he spoke quickly, never explained anything more than once, and never paused for questions. Mollie complained that even this was like watching a movie in slow motion, but at least she managed to sit still long enough to follow what he was saying.

They fell into a kind of routine, and one that wasn't altogether terrible despite their summer imprisonment. After about a week or so, Daniel even began to look forward to his study sessions with Mollie. The actual book work would be finished fairly quickly, thanks to Mollie's knack for speed, and then they'd spend the rest of the time sharing the Mr. Smiley jokes that they hadn't been able to in class.

Thanks to Daniel's afternoon tutelage, Mollie scored a solid C on the midterm, and felt confident that she'd manage to pass the final. Sitting still long enough to complete a final exam was always going to be tough for her, but at least it was doable. And what's more, she seemed honestly grateful for all of Daniel's help, and even offered to treat him to a movie one day after school. Mollie loved horror movies, not so much because she liked to be scared, but mostly because she liked to yell at the people in the movie when they did something stupid. This evening's selection was particularly gruesome, and Daniel had to close his eyes through much of it, but Mollie was happy to fill him in with her own narration:

"Now Jerk-Face is going up the stairs alone even though Bubble-Gum-Brain Girlfriend begged him not to." Mollie never bothered to learn the characters' names. It was more fun to make up her own.

"And?" Daniel asked, his face safely hidden behind his hands. "Is he going to get it?"

"Not yet," she answered. "Stupid Jerk-Face's flashlight just went out . . . and now he keeps on walking through the dark instead of turning around. GO CALL THE POLICE, YOU MORON!"

"Mollie, he can't hear you."

"Oh! Now he got it. Ew, ax to the head. And cut to Bubble-Gum-Brain Girlfriend calling up the stairs. No answer. She's trying the light switch, but it doesn't work, so she starts to climb the steps too. God, where do they find these people?"

"They're called actors, Mollie."

"This movie would be smarter if it starred monkeys."

"You chose it."

"THIS MOVIE WOULD BE SMARTER IF IT STARRED MONKEYS! Oh, she's dead now too."

Mollie's narration would usually go on until the credits rolled or they were asked to leave, whichever came first. The theater had been empty this evening except for them, so they'd stuck it out until the very end. By the time they walked out, Daniel felt queasy from all the soda and popcorn he'd ingested, and maybe a little bit from all the blood.

Outside the theater, they stretched as they peered up at the burnt sky. Late summer sunsets always managed to surprise Daniel. He enjoyed them, though, and the long days felt like such a victory after those dark Pennsylvania winters. He checked his phone—eight o'clock and the sun was just above the trees in the west. Easily an hour's worth of daylight left.

"I wonder what the others are doing tonight," said Daniel.

"No idea," answered Mollie.

"Didn't they say?"

"I didn't talk to them."

"Oh?" said Daniel. "I figured they'd want to see the movie too."

"I didn't invite them," said Mollie.

"Oh," said Daniel. Mollie didn't invite them. He'd just

assumed she'd sent them a text or something; it hadn't occurred to him that she might not even ask them along. Or why.

Huh.

Mollie took a deep breath and closed her eyes. "Wow, the air feels wonderful tonight, doesn't it?"

It did. The hot air still lingered, but as the sun sank lower, it was less oppressive. After they'd sat in the air-conditioned theater for two hours, the heat actually felt good. It made Daniel's skin tingle.

"You know," he said, "I've got my bike. So if you want to fly on home, that's cool. Bet it's a good evening for a flight."

"No, I'd rather walk with you."

"Okay."

It wasn't far from the movie theater to their neighborhood, maybe twenty minutes by bike, but if Mollie wanted to walk part of the way, Daniel wasn't going to argue. It really was turning out to be a nice night, and as long as he was home by his nine o'clock curfew, his parents wouldn't mind him taking the long way home.

"Daniel?" Mollie said.

"Yeah, Mol?"

"Have you talked to Louisa yet?"

At the mention of Louisa's name, Daniel bumped his shin against his bike pedal and nearly tripped. If he could manage not to crash over something every time somebody said *Louisa,* that would be a good thing.

"Uh, no. I haven't talked to her."

"She's been back for a week. Don't you think you'd better?"

"I will, I just . . . Hey, what exactly are we talking about?"

Mollie stopped walking and stood with her hands on her hips. "C'mon, Daniel, everyone knows what happened between you two last year."

Daniel resisted the urge to hop on his bike and flee. It would be useless, though. There was no outrunning Mollie Lee. "Everyone, huh?" he asked.

"Louisa's not one for secrets," said Mollie. "Plus, Rose has been telling everyone that you and Louisa are getting married."

"Oh my God!" said Daniel. "Is that what Louisa's been saying too?"

"Not exactly," said Mollie. "But you did kiss her."

"She kissed me! I mean, I guess it was more fifty-fifty, but still . . ."

"So, are you guys dating or what?"

"No! I mean, I don't really know. I guess. I don't think so."

Daniel concentrated on keeping his bike steady as he walked it along the gravel median—it gave him something to focus on. Everyone knew about the kiss, and they'd known for a while now. People were assuming he and Louisa were a couple. Daniel felt a deep flush spreading across his cheeks.

"So?" Mollie asked again. "What are you going to say to her?"

"I don't know!" snapped Daniel. "I honestly was hoping that if I left it alone, she'd forget about it and we could just move on. I mean it was only one kiss, right?"

"God, Daniel!" said Mollie. "You know, I thought those idiot boys in the movie were bad, but I'm starting to think they didn't do you all justice. Dumber than monkeys!"

"What's that supposed to mean?"

"You need to decide, Daniel, and it's got to be clear, okay? Are you two just friends, or are you more than that? She needs to know."

Mollie stepped in front of him, making him stop. She looked him in the eyes, her face unreadable. "And she's not the only one," she said. "So make up your mind, New Kid."

Then she was gone. One second there, the next nothing but a scattering of dust and wind blowing by. She didn't even say goodbye.

Fine, Daniel thought. If she wanted to fly home, why hadn't she done so earlier? He'd told her she could go after all.

But that wasn't why she'd taken off, and Daniel knew it. There was something else going on here. For some reason his relationship with Louisa was a huge concern for Mollie. Louisa was Mollie's friend, and maybe Mollie was just looking out for her, but Daniel and Louisa had shared their kiss months ago, so why wait until now? What business was it of Mollie's anyway?

Boys might be monkeys, but girls were from a different plane of existence, someplace where the rules of logic were backward. Bizarro world.

Daniel decided to get off the main road and bike through the center of town. He still had plenty of time before dark, and honestly he could use the long ride to clear his head. As he turned his bike onto Main Street, he saw the red flashing lights of a police car up ahead—an unusual sight for Noble's Green. A small crowd had gathered outside Mr. Lemon's soda shop. It was a mix of concerned-looking locals and a few tourists snapping pictures of the shop with their cell phones.

As Daniel pulled up, he saw what they were looking at. Someone had rearranged the neon letters above Happy Hero's Ice Cream Parlor! to spell *HI Poopy!*

Daniel started to laugh until he caught a glimpse of old Mr. Lemon standing off to one side, his face buried in his hands. Daniel biked a little closer and now saw that it wasn't just the sign that had been damaged. The whole front window of the shop had been shattered, and the street outside was littered with cartons of melting ice cream. Inside, stools were smashed, the counter was broken, and everything that hadn't been bolted down was overturned. The place looked like it had been torn inside out.

Daniel slowed to a stop. He thought about asking Mr. Lemon what had happened, but the man was in such a state that Daniel decided it was best not to bother him. Sheriff Simmons was talking to him, trying to get him to calm down.

"But, I'm telling you, I was only gone for five minutes!" Mr. Lemon was saying, his voice raw and cracking. "I left to deposit the day's till at the bank, and I heard this crash."

"Mr. Lemon," the sheriff said, in the same tone you might use on a hysterical child. "It had to have been longer than that. The extent of the damage . . . I mean no one could do that in just five minutes. . . ."

"Bet one of those kids could," someone said.

"Yeah," said another. "Who knows what they're capable of, really? Fly, do all sorts of crazy things."

Daniel couldn't tell who was saying what, but from the faces he knew that this was the sentiment of more than just one person. An ominous murmur was spreading through the crowd, and the sheriff took off his hat and scratched at his bald head thoughtfully, staring at the destruction.

Without waiting to hear more, Daniel turned his bike around and pedaled away as fast as he could. He'd just now heard a phrase he never thought would be spoken in Noble's Green. *Those kids,* someone had said. Not *our kids,* not like they were kids who'd been raised here, who belonged, and who were part of the town. They were *those kids,* the strange ones. The others.

Two little words, but they would keep Daniel awake with worry long, long into the night.

Chapter Five
The Junkyard

The next morning, Mollie was waiting for him outside the school, their previous day's argument apparently forgotten. Whenever Daniel showed up, there were several boys—the basketball players, mostly—waiting with her, but she never seemed very interested in more than just small talk, and the minute Daniel arrived, she'd break away from them and join him instead. Daniel had to grudgingly accept that Mollie Lee was a pretty girl, and if the boys hanging around her locker were any sign, she was getting prettier every day. She'd taken her tomboy habits and morphed them into a distinctive style with her sarcastic T-shirts and torn jeans. The earrings had led to additional pieces of jewelry, and she'd recently expanded her ensemble with several chunky silver rings. She looked ready for high school, whereas the best anyone could say about Daniel was that he looked a little less like a bag of unwashed clothes with a bad cowlick than he once did. But only a little.

But Mollie didn't seem to mind. Daniel had to wonder, if he was really honest with himself, whether he'd have done the same for her. If a gaggle of cheerleaders had wanted to walk Daniel to class, would he have said no, and waited for Mollie instead? He wondered sometimes whether he was half the friend she was.

When Daniel told Mollie about Mr. Lemon's shop, her eyes grew wide with interest. She wanted all the details and made him repeat them several times. The attack on the ice cream parlor and the tree fort fire had occurred one right after the other, and it looked like someone in town was having their own little crime spree. Mollie immediately began compiling a list of suspects.

"There are really four villains in this town, right?" she said, drumming her fingers on the locker next to Daniel's while he struggled to open his. He'd never gotten the hang of the combination lock.

"Four?" he asked absently.

"Sure. We've got Herman, of course, but he's locked in the sanitarium. And his Shroud powers are all gone, but that doesn't rule him out in my book."

"Yeah, but I don't think vandalizing an ice cream parlor

is really his style," said Daniel, jiggling the locker in hopes that it would miraculously shake open.

"Maybe not," said Mollie. "Then there's Clay and Bud. Busting up private property is exactly their style."

"They're the most obvious suspects. But if we are going to go with the theory that the girl at the bridge is involved, that makes it pretty unlikely it was Clay or Bud. Not exactly popular with the ladies, those two."

"You've got a point there."

"But you said there are four villains in Noble's Green. Who's the fourth?"

"Theo Plunkett, of course," said Mollie.

Daniel stopped fighting with his locker and shook his head. Theo Plunkett was Herman's sixteen-year-old grand-nephew, and while being a snob and a confessed car thief, Theo was not, in Daniel's opinion, a villain. He'd actually proved quite useful last year in their fight against the Shroud. Lots of kids would've run once they saw the things Theo saw, but he had toughed it out. Daniel thought of Theo as a friend.

"You've been listening to Eric," said Daniel. "He's always had a weird thing against Theo."

"It's not weird. Theo's a Plunkett," said Mollie. "Do you trust him?"

"I do," said Daniel. "He's a scoundrel, but he's no fan of his uncle, and again, why would Theo wreck an ice cream shop?"

"He stole his dad's Porsche and drove it off a bridge."

"The bridge was an accident. It's not the same thing."

Mollie shrugged. "Fine. But for the record, when you use the word *scoundrel,* it makes you sound like you were born in the 1800s."

"Okay."

"Just saying."

"So who does that leave us with?" asked Daniel. "Setting our mysterious laughing girl aside, Clay and Bud are our best bets so far."

"Yep," said Mollie. "So now what?"

"Now the game's afoot!"

"What's that supposed to mean?"

"It's something Sherlock Holmes would say when he started on a new mystery," said Daniel.

Mollie blinked at him. "Seriously 1800s. You should try a big walrus mustache and suspenders."

"Whatever."

"So, what's next? And enough with the dead-guy quotes."

Daniel had been giving their next move some thought, and unfortunately they'd gotten about as far as they could with theorizing and speculation. It was time to get out in the field.

"What are you doing after school?" he asked, returning for a second go at his defiant locker.

"I thought we were going to study?"

"Later," said Daniel. "I want to stop off someplace on our way home first."

Mollie grinned at him and pushed him out of the way

before giving the lock a twirl and stepping back as it popped open with a reluctant squeak.

"I'm your girl," she said.

Clay and Bud made their hideout in a neglected junkyard on the outskirts of town. Inside a rusting, hollowed-out old van they hatched their schemes to make Daniel's life as hellish as possible. It was also the one place they felt was secure enough to stash their petty stolen goods. That was the theory Daniel was going on, at least. He had a hunch that if Clay had done all that damage to the ice cream shop, he wouldn't have been able to resist taking a few mementos.

"I already agreed that it's a good idea to search their hideout," Mollie was saying. "I'm just saying that we could've used a better plan. Any plan actually."

Daniel stood staring at a long tear in the chain-link fence that circled the perimeter of the junkyard. This wasn't just a section where the fence had come loose, where someone might squeeze through. This was a boy-sized hole, where the steel links had been ripped apart like paper. This was Clay's work, and imagining the sheer strength it would take to tear the metal like that, Daniel began to wonder if Mollie was right. He wasn't exactly sure what he was expecting, but meeting Clay face to face on his home turf would be a bad idea.

"Let's just call this trip recon," said Daniel. "And if it

looks too dangerous, we'll come back another time. But if he's really not home, I wanna get a look inside his van."

Mollie had already scouted the area from the air and reported back that the junkyard looked empty from way up high, but she hadn't dared get close enough to be sure. If Clay and Bud were inside the hideout, then they wouldn't be visible from the sky anyway. Plus, Clay was known to throw junk at passing fliers who got too close. Anything would do—tires, toilet seats, the occasional car.

So here they were, with Daniel tiptoeing into the lion's den and Mollie right behind. And Mollie wasn't the quietest person he knew. If only she'd try to sneak more and stomp less.

"Have you thought about what we're going to do if they're home?" she asked.

"Haul them in for questioning?" whispered Daniel. "You be the good cop, I'll be the bad cop."

Mollie rolled her eyes and snorted. There was only one person in all of Noble's Green who scared Clay, and that was Eric. If Clay was here, interrogating him without Eric around would be suicide. And Daniel would be the only one without superpowers. In fact, if history was any guide, Mollie would probably end up having to save him. She'd pulled his backside out of enough bad situations already, what was one more?

Sometimes it seemed like he took Mollie on these adventures just to give her something to do.

As they walked beneath the stacks of rubbish, it occurred to Daniel that of all the great landmarks he'd discovered back in those first few months in Noble's Green, the junkyard was the one that had remained unchanged. Once mysterious and foreboding, Mount Noble was now home to a school. The Old Quarry had collapsed. Now even the tree fort was being rebuilt. But the towering skyscrapers of refuse here in the junkyard were as unchanged as the first time he'd laid eyes on them. Rusted-out cars, broken appliances, and more piles of unrecognizable junk leaned menacingly on every side, and when the wind picked up, Daniel imagined he could hear the creaking of metal as the stacks shifted and settled. One couldn't walk through this place without wondering what it would take to make the whole thing come crashing down like a line of dominoes. Not much, Daniel suspected.

It was a maze of garbage, complete with its own real-life Minotaur waiting at the center.

As they got ever closer to Clay's lair, even Mollie began to tread cautiously, taking care *not* to step on every soda can in sight. Daniel hoped that at last Mollie's instinct for survival might have kicked in. It would be nice to live long enough to have supper.

Their extra stealth was warranted, because they hadn't gone very far before they heard voices.

Daniel stopped and grabbed Mollie by the arm. Not daring to speak, he gave her a questioning look—could she have missed someone as she'd flown over? Mollie just shrugged. He hadn't been there a few minutes ago.

Wordlessly, Daniel tried to signal as best he could that she should wait here while he scouted ahead. Mollie responded with a considerably ruder gesture of her own, and pushed him forward.

He had no choice but to let her follow, and the two of them crept slowly and silently through the garbage. Soon, they came upon a familiar bend in the twisting maze of trash, marked by the smashed-up remains of a truck that Clay and Bud used for target practice when they were bored. On the other side of it, if Daniel's memory served, lay the van. They were close now, and the voices were clearer. Mollie crouched behind a pile of junk and put her finger to her lips, instructing Daniel to be quiet. As if he needed to be told.

"See. What'd I tell ya?" Clay was saying in his gravelly voice. Over the summer it had gotten even deeper, and what little boyishness it had once possessed was gone entirely. It was a man's voice now.

"You dragged us all the way out to a junkyard for this?" said another boy, a new voice Daniel didn't recognize. "Like I haven't seen beer before."

"Well, we can hide all sorts of stuff here," said Clay, sounding defensive. "It's private."

"I'll say. Who'd want to hang out here with all the rest of the garbage?" said another voice, a girl's this time.

"Yeah, well . . . ," answered Clay.

Mollie turned back to Daniel. He could tell they were thinking the exact same thing.

A girl.

"Hey," said the boy. "Where's the mutt? He go bounding off again?"

"He was here a minute ago," answered the girl. "Here, boy! Mutt, come!"

Daniel tugged on Mollie's sleeve and she glared at him, annoyed.

They have a dog! he mouthed. *Let's go!*

She tugged her arm back out of his grip and mouthed something that looked like *Not till I pee.* Daniel was terrible at reading lips.

But as she inched her head slowly toward the edge of the junk pile, he understood what she had been trying to say. She didn't need to *pee;* she wanted to *see* who Clay was talking to. Whoever it was, they were just on the other side of the junk pile, and there was little chance of Daniel and Mollie looking without being spotted themselves. She'd been right at the start—they needed a better plan.

Daniel reached for her arm once more, and again she tried to pull away but this time he refused to let go. They could circle around and get a look from the other side, where there was better cover. He needed her to listen to him.

She glared back at him and if she could have told him off, she would have, Daniel knew. But then something changed in her face as she looked, not at Daniel, but past him. She grew wide-eyed with surprise, or even fear.

When Daniel turned around, he was face to face with a boy a few years older than he, with dandruffy hair down to his shoulders, and pale, watery eyes. He was crouched in an almost feral position, perched on all fours atop the hood of the busted-up truck, and he looked ready to pounce. Though dressed in some kind of prep school outfit complete with blazer and tie, he was barefoot, his toenails long and yellow and sharp.

The strange boy leaned forward until he was inches away from Daniel. His voice, when he spoke, was surprisingly quiet.

"Bark, bark," said the boy softly, and then he smiled, showing them stained, pointed teeth.

Chapter Six
The Nobles of Noble's Green

The strange long-haired boy herded Daniel and Mollie out of hiding until they were standing in front of a new boy, who appeared to be smoking—a cloud of white haze seemed to perpetually linger about the boy's black-haired head—but he wasn't holding a cigarette that Daniel could see. Maybe his eyes were playing tricks on him.

"Guess we need some introductions, huh?" said the new boy. "I'm Drake, and you've already met Mutt. Must've smelled you two coming. Nose like a bloodhound, you know."

"Growl," said a voice behind him, and Daniel peeked

over his own shoulder to see Mutt crouched on the ground. Again, the boy named Mutt hadn't actually growled, he'd just said the word *growl.* Weird.

"Easy, boy," said Drake. "Heel. Guess he's more wolf than bloodhound these days." Like the others, this Drake kid was dressed in the same fancy prep school uniform. His hands were in his pockets and a smile was on his face, but nothing about him felt friendly. Daniel sensed the tension in the air, brittle and ready to snap.

"I'm Hunter," said another boy with dark skin and hair shaved so close he was almost bald.

"And that's Skye."

Unlike the three boys, the girl looked familiar. She was in her late teens, blond and pretty with too-white teeth, but she looked at Daniel and Mollie like they were two dirty strays who, at any moment, might jump up and muddy her clothes.

"Wait a minute," said Mollie. "You're that one with the show. That reality show . . ."

"Skye's the Limit," said Skye, breaking into a camera-ready smile.

"But your mom subs at our school, doesn't she?" said Mollie. "You're Janey Levine!"

"Skye's my stage name," said the girl, dropping the smile just as quickly. "To keep the paparazzi away."

"But you're on a reality TV show!" said Mollie. "You've got cameras with you everywhere."

"Yeah, yeah," said Drake. "There are no cameras here, so let's not get her going. If she starts talking about that stupid show, she'll never shut up."

Skye gave Drake a hurt look, but said nothing.

"Last," said Drake, "and probably least, is—"

"Clay," said Daniel, cutting him off. "We know each other."

Drake arched an eyebrow in surprise. "Friends of yours, Clay?" he asked.

"Daniel Corrigan and Mollie Lee," answered Clay, who was leaning against his van, glaring at the two of them with undisguised hate. Unlike the others, he looked miserable in his sport coat and tie, and he couldn't stop tugging at his shirt collar. "And, no, we're not friends. Not even close."

"Well," said Drake, "then that's the reason I haven't seen you two around the academy."

So these were academy kids. That explained the uniforms in July, but not what they were doing here. Clay had been so shocked at seeing Daniel and Mollie that he'd actually dropped the six-pack of beer he'd been showing off, causing two of the cans to explode and spray all over everyone. Skye called Clay a clumsy wad, and he blushed from the collar of his shirt to his forehead. Daniel couldn't imagine Clay being happy to see Daniel ever, but he was absolutely fuming now that Daniel had made him embarrass himself in front of his new friends—if that's what they really were. Daniel wasn't so sure.

"All right, Daniel and Mollie, now that we've all met," said Drake, "what are you two doing sneaking up on us in a junkyard?" As he asked the question, Daniel could have sworn he saw a little puff of smoke escape through the boy's nostrils, but again, he'd yet to light a cigarette.

"We were looking for Clay," answered Daniel. There wasn't a lie in the world that could explain why the two of them were skulking around in here, so Daniel didn't bother trying.

"Why?" snarled Clay. "You spying on me?"

"Don't be stupid, Clay," said Drake. "Of course they were spying on you. We just caught them doing it. What I wanna know is *why*."

Drake held out his hands, waiting for an answer. "So?" he said.

Mollie and Daniel exchanged looks. The situation hadn't turned overtly dangerous, yet. No one had threatened them, but then again Mutt and Hunter were uncomfortably close, standing on either side of them and conveniently blocking any escape. It was a tense situation that required finesse.

"You go first," said Mollie. "Why are *you* here?"

Finesse. Mollie's strong suit.

Drake studied Mollie for a moment, weighing how to respond. "Hot *and* hot-tempered," he said with a laugh. "I like it."

Mollie turned white, though whether this was from anger or embarrassment Daniel wasn't sure. Probably a mix of both.

"All right, I'll play along," said Drake. "My friends and I belong to a sort of club, and Clay here wants to join that club, so he was trying to impress us with beer he stole out of his daddy's fridge. See, it's against the law for *kids* our age to drink."

"I know that," snapped Mollie.

"Right."

"So, what's your club called?" she asked.

"We're the Nobles. Get it? The Nobles of Noble's Green."

"Hilarious," answered Mollie.

"Yeah, well, it wasn't our idea," said Drake. "Anyway, now it's your turn. Why are you here?"

Daniel thought he'd better take over before Mollie got them in any more trouble. He decided, once again, to go with the truth.

"Someone vandalized Mr. Lemon's ice cream shop," said Daniel. "We wanted to ask Clay if he knew anything about it."

"What are you?" said Drake, laughing. "Some kind of kid detective who solves neighborhood crimes? *Daniel Corrigan and the Case of the Ice Cream Vandals!*"

"Well, we just wanted to ask a few questions," said Daniel, and he hated the defensive tone in his voice. When Drake put it like that, it did seem kind of silly.

"And I guess that makes you his sidekick?" said Drake, winking at Mollie.

Daniel felt Mollie tense up, and he took her hand and

gave it a warning squeeze. They didn't need trouble. Not out here.

"Hey, Clay," said Drake. "You know anything about a busted-up ice cream shop?"

"No," said Clay.

"Well, there you have it," said Drake. "Guess you can go home now."

And just like that, Daniel knew that Drake was lying. The giveaway was just how quickly the conversation stopped. Drake had been enjoying the game up until then, taunting them and even flirting with Mollie, but now they were dismissed, fun time over. It had happened so fast that they had to be hiding something. Still, considering how outnumbered they were, Daniel thought it best to take Drake up on his offer. It was time to get out of there.

"Right. Let's go, Mollie."

Luckily Mollie was as ready to leave as Daniel was, but as the two of them turned to go, Mutt moved in front of them, pacing back and forth on all fours.

"Sniff, sniff," he said, staring at Mollie with those watery eyes of his.

"Uh-oh," said Skye with a fake smile. "I think Mutt wants to play first!"

"Growl," added Mutt, and he leaned forward on his hands.

"C'mon, Mutt," said Drake. "I told them they could go."

"But they're *peasants*," said Skye. "Mutt doesn't get to

play with peasants much, does he?" She was using a super-annoying baby-talk voice, as if addressing a puppy.

They couldn't go any farther. Mutt blocked the way out and Skye was now standing right beside Daniel.

"What do you mean, we're peasants?" asked Daniel, not taking his eyes off Mutt.

"You see," said Skye, leaning close to him until she was practically whispering in his ear, "we Nobles can do things. Amazing things. That's why we're, like, nobility. Born to rule. And peasants are everyone else. Like you, an ordinary little peasant."

Mutt crept up close and bared his teeth in a snarl. Mollie backed away.

Skye squealed. "Look at her face!"

Clay called over to her, "Hey, watch out! Mollie's not—"

Mollie moved so fast that if Daniel had blinked, he would have missed it. One second she was backing away from Mutt and the next she was standing behind him, her foot planted firmly on his backside. All it took was a little kick to send him face-first onto the garbage-strewn ground.

"Hey!" said Skye, but Mollie was already back at Daniel's side.

"Now we're leaving," she said.

But Mutt was up on his hands and feet again. He spit out a mouthful of garbage as he shouted, "Gonna get you for that!"

With a real growl this time, he lunged forward, leaping into the air like an animal. But as impressive as Mutt's speed was, he was no match for Mollie. She'd shoved Daniel out of harm's way and literally flown over Mutt's head before he'd even landed. Then she was behind him again, and this time she wasn't satisfied with a simple kick. She reached down, grabbed the back of Mutt's pants, and delivered what Daniel supposed was the world's first super-wedgie. Mutt's growl turned high-pitched and girl-like as his underwear was yanked up to his neck at super-speed.

Out of the corner of his eye Daniel saw the boy called Hunter start forward, his hands balling into fists. His eyes narrowed like he was concentrating on something.

But whatever he was preparing to do, he was stopped by Drake. "That's enough!" Drake shouted, and as he did so, a puff of smoke and fire escaped from his mouth and nose. Daniel hadn't imagined the smoke after all. Drake was some kind of fire-breather.

Hunter relaxed and Skye backed away, her head down and eyes staring at the ground. She looked like a child who'd just been given a time-out.

"Well," Drake said, regaining his composure, although wisps of smoke still trailed out of his nose. "If you're all done playing."

"I tried to warn you," said Clay.

"Shut up," answered Drake. "We're done here today. You two run along home before I change my mind."

Daniel didn't have to be told again. He grabbed Mollie's arm and the two of them ran for the broken fence. She let herself be led along, though she could've simply flown away at any time.

The last thing Daniel heard as they escaped the junkyard was Drake shouting for someone to help get Mutt free from his underwear.

Chapter Seven
The Unusual Suspects

"Academy kids, all of them," said Daniel. "But there is, like, zero information on the actual academy online other than press releases and their shiny new website. Luckily, we live in the age of the social network. Voilà!"

Daniel swung around in his seat and allowed Mollie to get a look at the computer. Onscreen was a picture of a teenager with coal-black hair, dressed in his lacrosse jersey and holding a trophy. He looked like he had an easygoing manner with just a hint of cockiness in his pose.

"'Drake Masterson,'" Mollie read over his shoulder. "Former student at Holy Cross—that's why we haven't seen him around before. Says he'll be in the tenth grade next year. He was captain of the lacrosse and debate teams."

"Now he's a hoodlum who hangs out in junkyards to score stolen beer," said Daniel. "I guess that's what an academy education will get you, huh?"

Daniel scrolled through Drake's profile on the computer screen. It had taken a while, with only a first name and approximate age to go on, but after searching enough social networking sites filtered by area, he was finally able to bring up this profile. Their new fire-breathing friend.

"Look there," said Mollie, pointing at the corner of the screen. On Drake's photo page was a group shot of what looked like a canoe trip. Drake and a bunch of his friends were in their life jackets, goofing off for the camera and making faces. A handsome African American boy stood next to Drake. He was smiling as he made rabbit ears behind Drake's back.

"That's that Hunter kid," said Mollie. "He's a lot better-looking when he smiles."

Daniel decided to let the comment about Hunter's looks pass unremarked. He sat back in his desk chair and rubbed his eyes. They'd been staring at the computer for hours now, scanning literally hundreds of profiles of kids in their area. Dinner had been a reheated frozen pizza on paper plates, devoured while sitting on the hardwood floor of Daniel's attic bedroom. They told their parents that they were working on a project for Mr. Smiley, but the truth was they hadn't touched their history books. With their final getting close, Daniel felt a bit guilty about that. Mollie in particular should be using this time to study, but then again he was as anxious to learn who these kids were as she was. Characteristically, Mollie told him not to worry, and that they'd hit the books extra hard tomorrow. As if this mystery could be solved in one day.

Daniel copied the picture of Drake and Hunter together and printed it out. He'd cleared the corkboard next to his desk of all his little comic strips and cartoons, and was now using it to assemble his own wall of suspects. Beneath each picture he'd written a name and a power.

"So, let's go over what we know so far," said Daniel, pointing to the photo of a girl in a red convertible. She was blowing a kiss at the camera. "We know Janey Levine, aka Skye. I haven't watched her TV show, but from what I've read online, she has some kind of telekinesis."

"She uses it to put on her makeup in the car. Twit."

"Then there's this Hunter kid, the *good-looking one*." The emphasis was for Mollie's benefit, but she didn't seem to notice. "No full name, but I think we can assume he went to Holy Cross with Drake, even though we don't know what he can do." Hunter got a question mark on his card where his power would normally be.

"That's two of them," said Mollie. "Still nothing on Mutt?"

"Nothing," answered Daniel. In place of a photo, Daniel had posted a blank index card with the kid's name on it. "You ever try doing a search on the name *Mutt*? It's impossible. We know he's, well, *animalistic* might be a good word, so we'll just write that down. Did you see those teeth?"

"Only too well," said Mollie. "So that leaves Drake."

"Yep," said Daniel. "Drake Masterson. Star student, sixteen years old, and I'm guessing their leader." Daniel pinned up the photo of Drake with his welcoming smile, the picture of a clean-cut Pennsylvania teen. Beneath that, he wrote, "Fire-breather."

"There they are," said Daniel. "Students of the academy. The Nobles of Noble's Green."

He'd arranged the photos in a cluster, and just off to the side he'd pinned up a picture of Clay, a scowling yearbook shot on which Rohan had once used a Magic Marker to give him missing front teeth and a unibrow. Beneath the defaced picture, Daniel wrote, "Super-strong, super-tough."

"We know Clay wants to join, but they didn't seem very impressed, so let's keep him close."

"What about Bud?" asked Mollie. "You think he's at the academy too?"

"If Clay's there, then I wouldn't doubt it. Bud doesn't do well on his own."

Daniel pinned up Bud's yearbook picture next to Clay's. It was slightly out of focus, as if the cameraman had rushed the shot.

Poor Bud, Daniel thought as he wrote "super-stink"

beneath the picture. The kid couldn't even convince the cameraman to get close enough to take a decent shot.

"There's our list of prime suspects," said Daniel.

"We're missing one," said Mollie.

"Oh, not Theo again! I told you I trust him."

"I'm not talking about Theo," answered Mollie, and she pinned up a blank card near the top of the board, on which she'd written a single word—*Shroud*.

"He's still alive," she said. "And I know you said vandalizing a store is beneath him, but as far as I'm concerned, he's always a suspect."

Mollie was right. It was foolish to ignore Herman, and potentially hazardous too. But while they couldn't ignore him, there was another danger to consider. The worst thing about Herman Plunkett, from a detective's point of view, was that with him around it was very difficult to even consider any other suspects. Daniel had made that mistake last year, when the Supers were being menaced by strange shadow creatures Daniel dubbed Shades. Herman was involved, despite the fact that he was presumed dead at the time. But the truth turned out to be more complicated, and though in the end Daniel was right about Plunkett being a part of it, he was certainly not the mastermind. The Supers found Herman helpless in his own secret lair, the Shades' prisoner. Those creatures turned out to be the manifestations of lost memories and powers Herman had stolen with his Witch Fire pendant, a piece of the meteorite that had burned St. Alban's to the ground. All the Shades had wanted was their freedom, but Daniel had been too obsessed with catching Herman to see the truth until it was almost too late.

Keeping an open, objective mind while Herman was on that board was next to impossible. The Shroud was a black hole sucking up all the light.

"Herman's powerless," said Mollie. "So, what do we write on his card?"

Daniel thought about this for a moment, then took up the black marker and wrote "Really, really evil" beneath his name. Yep, really, really evil. It was important to remember that.

Mollie had taken two more note cards and written "Tree fort fire" on one and "Attack at bridge" on another. Daniel tried to tell her that the word *attack* was a bit strong, but she wouldn't change it. He could have been seriously hurt, or worse, she said. So *attack* stood.

The only girl on the board was Skye, and naturally their suspicions centered on her. But if she was their mysterious laughing girl, how could she have learned about the tree fort in the first place? Another unanswered question.

Finally, in the center of the board Daniel pinned up a new article from the *Noble Herald*. The headline read, "Superpowered Delinquents Suspected in Vandalism Case." The article went on to say that because of the speed with which Mr. Lemon's shop was vandalized, combined with the sheer amount of destruction, the sheriff's department suspected that the culprits were "members of the town's superpowered population." Beyond that they had no suspects at this time.

Daniel stepped back so that he could take in the entire board. All the smiling faces staring back at him. Academy students, every last one.

The sheriff's department had no suspects, and Daniel had too many.

The next morning, Daniel was just finishing breakfast and arguing with Georgie over who'd get the last of the syrup for his French toast when Mollie appeared at the door, looking panicked.

"Have you all seen the news?" asked Mollie, not bothering to ask if she could come inside.

"Why no," said Daniel's mother. "Is something the matter?"

Catching the significant look that Mollie was giving him, Daniel hopped out of his seat and headed for the living room. Georgie snatched up the undefended syrup bottle with a shout of triumph.

The TV was already tuned to the local news, and as soon as the picture came on, Daniel saw it—an overhead shot of downtown Noble's Green. The camera was panning over the wreck of a building: windows shattered, doors missing. Several buses in the parking lot were actually overturned.

"Oh my," said Daniel's mother. "Is that the high school? What happened? Was it a tornado?"

"There weren't any storms last night," said Mollie.

Daniel looked back at the scene of destruction. One of the buses was a smoking, burnt-out shell. As the shot cut between the helicopter and a reporter standing in front of the rubble, a graphic flashed across the bottom of the screen:

"Superpowered vandals turn to rampage?"

At that moment they heard the shatter of a bottle breaking, and from the kitchen Georgie's voice.

"Uh-oh," he said. "Mom, can I have another syrup?"

Chapter Eight
The Scene of the Crime

Never had Daniel felt so slow. Since the high school was only a block away from the middle school, he had sped out of the house on his bike, hoping to get a chance to see the destruction up close and still make it in time for Smiley's class. Mollie, of course, had simply flown ahead. Daniel pedaled like he was competing in the Tour de France and still it wasn't fast enough. It felt like he was steering his bike through a swamp.

As he finally neared the school, he passed streets lined with news vans and crowds of gawking people, and it became hard to squeeze through them all. In a place the size of Noble's Green, the smallest things became newsworthy, and Daniel still remembered the controversy that had rocked the town last year when the council voted to put a stoplight on Main Street. Of course, everything had changed with the Blackout Event, and the town's fifteen minutes of fame had finally come. But as he passed the news crews, he saw the faces of the reporters and suspected that the story of the sleepy town of superheroes had already played itself out. Video segments on flying kids and profiles of the librarian who could breathe at the bottom of a lake were yesterday's news. The public was hungry for something fresh and exciting, and this attack on the high school would be just the thing. It was a new angle on the old story, full of scandalous possibilities — the dark side of Camelot. Even the crowd of camera phone–waving tourists looked like a pack of scavengers as they snapped pictures of the vandalized school. They'd come to Noble's Green hoping to catch a glimpse of a floating fire chief, but now were being treated to the superpowered destruction of public property.

"Hey," said Mollie, waving at him from a crowd of jostling onlookers. "Can you believe all these people?"

"This might be worse than we thought," said Daniel, panting. The ride had really worn him out, and Mollie was standing there without having broken a sweat.

The footage on television didn't adequately portray the extent of the damage, and for a moment Daniel actually wondered if his mom had been right — maybe a tornado *had* rolled through here. But once you looked closer, you could tell that this destruction wasn't the result of a random force of nature. It was deliberate. Every window was smashed, probably because nearly all of the desks within had been tossed through them. Someone had emptied each classroom, and the broken contents now lay scattered across the parking lot. The entrance looked like it had been firebombed, and the charred doors still dangled loosely from their hinges.

The headlines were right. No one without powers could have accomplished all this destruction in a matter of minutes, not without a small army. That was obvious now to Daniel, and to everyone who saw.

"Wow," said Mollie. "They would have to hit the high school."

"Huh?"

"What about the middle school? We've got a final coming up!"

Mollie's attempt at gallows humor was admirable, but they both knew that this was a very serious situation. The stakes of their own little investigation had just escalated.

"You know," said Daniel, "they say that criminals often come back to the scene of the crime."

"Why would they do that?"

"I dunno. Maybe because they get a kick out of seeing what they've done."

Mollie scanned the faces of tourists who were mouthing

Hi, Mom at the television cameras and holding up rock-and-roll fingers.

"You think one of *these* losers did it?"

"No, not really," said Daniel. "But keep your eyes open for anyone suspicious who doesn't look like a sightseer. Maybe we'll see Drake or one of his Nobles in the crowd."

Mollie nodded and went back to studying the faces. After a few minutes of useless staring, Daniel was just about to suggest they leave for summer school when he heard a commotion nearby. A group of onlookers were complaining loudly as a long black limousine with darkened windows rolled past them, obscuring their view and forcing several to leap out of the way.

The car came to a stop and out stepped two of the largest men Daniel had ever seen. Though both were conservatively dressed in neat suits and ties, they didn't look like any kind of businessmen. As they turned to scan the crowd, Daniel saw that one had a neck tattoo of a dragon that crept all the way up the back of his pale, shaved head. The other had dreadlocks tied into a tight ponytail, and he wore more rings in his ears, nose, and eyebrows than Daniel could count. Both men were so huge that their expensive suit coats looked ready to split against their broad chests.

They scanned the area for a few moments before walking to the back of the limo. Some of the tourists who'd nearly been run over stomped up to the limo, but when they caught sight of the two bruisers, they walked right on by.

The dreadlocked one kept an eye on the crowd as the man with the neck tattoo opened the back door of the car.

Out stepped a ghost. Daniel almost didn't recognize him at first. Gone were the sagging patchwork sweaters and dusty glasses Daniel had grown accustomed to. He used to think the old man looked like a turtle when he was playing the part of the aged artist, but when he dropped that disguise, he reminded Daniel more of a snake. Now, as the man stepped out of the dark recesses of the limousine, Daniel was reminded of an old silent movie he'd once watched with his dad called *Nosferatu*. The villain of the film, a thin black-clad vampire, had given Daniel nightmares for years. But that blood-sucking monster was nothing compared to this old man.

Herman Plunkett wore a long black coat that reached almost to his ankles, and despite the late-summer heat, he was bundled up to his chin in a dark silk scarf. The glasses he wore on his shriveled, liver-spotted face were thinner than his old plastic bottle frames, and these new ones had shaded lenses to hide his small, mean eyes. Though he stood taller than he had when he'd been playing the role of harmless invalid, he leaned heavily on a sturdy cane that he hadn't needed the last time Daniel had seen him.

Not that Daniel should have been surprised. He knew Herman well enough to realize that the oily villain would never stop popping up. The Shroud was gone forever, but Daniel had no illusions that that meant they were safe from

Herman Plunkett. Daniel had destroyed Herman's Witch Fire pendant, and with it all of the man's Shroud powers. But he was still dangerous, and always would be.

What was surprising, however, was seeing Plunkett out in the open like this. For years he had stayed hidden, choosing to strike from the shadows. He'd never been one to flaunt his wealth or power.

The bitter scowl on Plunkett's face as he eyed the crowd was matched only by the venom in Mollie's voice as she spoke to Daniel. "What's he doing here?" she said. "I thought he was locked up in the loony bin."

"It looks like he got better," said Daniel as he took a deep breath. He closed his eyes and forced himself to relax. He didn't want to give Herman the satisfaction of catching him off guard when he finally spotted them standing there.

"Ah!" croaked the familiar voice, one that sounded like a strangled bark. "Daniel Corrigan and Mollie Lee. Fancy meeting you here."

Plunkett was walking toward them, flanked by his two giant bodyguards. He was moving slower than usual, and really was leaning on that cane. From appearances he wouldn't be able to get around without it. But with Herman, appearances were always deceiving.

Mollie grabbed Daniel's hand and gave it a squeeze for reassurance. He didn't let it go.

"I hadn't expected to see you two here," said Herman. "But I'm glad nonetheless."

"We don't have anything to say to you," said Daniel. Bantering with the old man was pointless and sometimes dangerous.

Plunkett sighed heavily and peered down at them over the rims of his dark glasses. "I understand," he said slowly. Then, to Daniel's surprise, he turned and began hobbling away.

"Daniel was just saying how criminals like to visit the scene of the crime," said Mollie. "So fancy meeting you here too." Daniel gave her hand a warning squeeze. Didn't he just tell Herman they had nothing to say?

Plunkett stopped. "So you think this is my handiwork, then? That I've taken up vandalizing schools?"

"I wouldn't put anything past you," she said, and pulled her hand away from Daniel's. He should've known not to try to quiet Mollie.

"And what about you, Daniel?" said Plunkett. "What do you think?"

Daniel thought for a minute. "Not your style," he said.

Plunkett nodded.

"And you couldn't have," added Daniel. "You don't have the power anymore."

"Yes, you saw to that," said Plunkett quickly.

He took a halting step toward them, and nearly lost his footing. The man with the neck tattoo offered him a steadying hand.

"Thank you, Lawrence," he said.

Lawrence? The thug with the dragon crawling up his neck was named Lawrence?

"Would you believe me," said Plunkett, "if I told you that I really am glad to see you? That I've been both looking forward to this day and, to be perfectly frank, dreading it a little too."

"Would I believe you?" asked Daniel. "If I had any idea what you were talking about, no. I wouldn't believe you."

"Understandable," said Herman. "But still, I want you to know that my months at Mountain View, that time alone with my thoughts and . . . regrets, have changed me. For the better, I hope."

"He's weirding me out," whispered Mollie, but Daniel shushed her.

"I'm an old man, kids," said Plunkett. "And without the power of the Witch Fire pendant, I am finally looking at the inevitable—I will die soon. This cold, hard truth makes a man evaluate his life, the things he's done. . . . I told you once, Daniel, that all I ever wanted was to keep this town safe. But I, ah, may have lost sight of that somewhere along the way."

"Wait a minute," said Mollie. "Are you actually trying to apologize?"

"Would you believe it?" asked Herman. "Could you believe it? Could you find it in your hearts to at least accept the possibility that I've seen how wrong I've been all these years? That an old man's dying wish might at last be forgiveness?"

Mollie glanced at Daniel, confused, but Daniel kept his eyes on Herman. He couldn't say for sure, but from here it looked like those glassy eyes of his were wet with tears behind his shades. He was the picture of a broken old man, his walking stick quivering beneath the weight of his regret.

"Could I believe it?" asked Daniel, and now he summoned up his courage and took a step closer, ignoring Mollie's whispered warning not to. "No, Herman," he said. "I couldn't believe it. See, I did learn one thing from you—the difference between the truth and a lie."

Plunkett's pleading expression, the eyes brimming with tears—in a nanosecond they were gone, replaced by a sneering smile. "Well, at least our time together wasn't a totally wasted effort," said Herman as the mask of sadness slipped away from his face and his expression turned menacing. He shook off Lawrence's hand and took another step toward Daniel, but Daniel didn't retreat. The two old enemies were finally face to face, all pretense abandoned.

"The truth is," said Plunkett, softly enough to ensure only the three of them could hear, "I'd have Lawrence here tie the two of you up and drown you in the river like a sack of puppies before apologizing. I wasted everything on you, Daniel. I was foolish enough to think you'd see the truth of this place, the danger these children posed, but instead you've given us *this*."

Herman pulled back and swept his arm out toward the ruined school.

"Are you saying that's my fault?" asked Daniel, incredulous.

"Boy, this is just the beginning," said Herman, his voice rising again. "All that power in such young hands. Now unchecked, uncontrolled. A danger to us all!"

"You're lying," said Daniel. "Just more lies."

"Not this time," said Herman. "I thought you said you'd learned to tell the difference."

Plunkett turned his back on the two of them. "Come on, Lawrence. Let's go survey the damage. No doubt the school will come calling for someone to pick up the bill."

Then Lawrence with the neck tattoo helped Plunkett make his way toward the crime scene, while his dreadlocked partner cleared the way of onlookers, roughly and without so much as an *excuse me*.

Chapter Nine
A Super Crime Spree

"'A Super Crime Spree,'" said Eric, reading from today's edition of the *Noble Herald.* "'Deputy Gordon Lewis, new of the Noble's Green Sheriff's Department, came out of the popular local eatery Sam's Diner on Saturday evening to find his patrol car missing. "I have to admit it was pretty embarrassing calling in a missing vehicle report on my own cruiser," said Deputy Lewis. "But it wasn't half as embarrassing as where we found it!'"

"'It wasn't until seven hours later that the missing patrol car was found by Mrs. Ruth Rogers, of Briarwood. "I was out walking our Pomeranian Chow-Chow when I heard this ginormous splash from the backyard. Chow-Chow starts barking like mad and by the time I peek around the side of the house, all I can see are the flashing lights of that police car as it sinks into the Johnstons' pool. They are out of town like they always are in the summer, but I just know they will be heartbroken when they hear the news. They loved that pool, and Lord only knows what kind of shape it'll be in when they finally manage to get that car out. Wedged tight, I hear."'"

Eric looked up and shook his head. "This is what you wanted us to read? It's crazy."

"Just keep going," said Daniel. "Skip to the bottom."

"'In an effort to combat the recent rash of criminal activity,'" Eric continued, "'the City Council has voted in a new mandatory curfew for minors within the town limits. All minors are expected to be indoors or in the company of an adult by seven p.m. on weekdays and seven-thirty on weekends.'"

This time Mollie interrupted him. "Of course, they just assume minors are behind it all."

"You think they're wrong?" asked Daniel.

"No," admitted Mollie begrudgingly. "We all know who's behind it."

"Then let him keep reading. Get to the part about the academy."

"Let's see, here we go. . . . 'Mandy Starr, spokesperson for the Noble Academy for the Gifted, said that the school is responding to these latest incidents by making an effort to increase enrollment. "It's our belief that the best way to combat super-crime is a Super-education," said Ms. Starr. "The academy's expertly designed courses in ethics and civics are the best way to address the needs of our town's special youth population. And thanks to a generous donation from Plunkett Industries, we're happy to announce that all academy students will now be able to attend tuition-free while also earning an additional monthly stipend to assist their special needs and those of their families. All eligible families are encouraged to take advantage of our school's uniquely structured education model. Enrollment is ongoing, so it's never too late to apply."'"

Eric tossed the paper aside. "Long-winded, don't you think?"

"*'Uniquely structured education model'?*" said Michael. "What's that mean?"

"It means," answered Rohan, "they want to keep us out of trouble, and the school is willing to pay our families off with money to do so."

"All right," said Eric. "So those are the facts. At this point, I suppose we can officially call this meeting to order. First up on the agenda—now that Noble's Green has gone from the Safest Town on Earth to Crime Alley—what the heck are we going to do about it?"

Since the tree fort was still being rebuilt, Daniel's bedroom seemed as good a place as any to have this meeting.

It wasn't the same, cramming a group of super-kids into his room where his mom or Georgie could interrupt them at any minute. Daniel had never really recognized the true value of secret bases until now—they were little-brother–proof.

Something else had changed besides the location, and nothing demonstrated this more than who'd actually shown up for the meeting. Eric and Rohan were here, of course. Mollie and Michael. But Simon, whom no one had seen all summer, had refused the summons, and so had Louisa and Rose. Rose, only seven, wouldn't come without her sister, and Louisa had sent Mollie a message saying she had the flu. But Daniel thought he knew better. He'd been avoiding Louisa and now she was returning the favor. How had things gotten so complicated between them when they hadn't even talked in months?

But maybe that was the problem. They hadn't talked, which was mostly Daniel's fault.

"Well, unfortunately," said Daniel, trying to focus on the problem at hand, "ever since the high school was attacked, the town has been scared out of its wits. All these weird burglaries and stuff are just making it worse. The Supers have gone from tourist attraction to public hazard."

"I heard that there was a protest scheduled this week near town hall," said Rohan. "And the mayor's office has been flooded with calls and emails demanding he do something more. I guess sending everyone off to the academy is something more."

"What?" asked Mollie. "You're not defending them, are you?"

"No," said Rohan, calmly adjusting his glasses.

"I think Rohan's got a point," said Michael. "It's good to remember how we got here."

"I know how we got here," said Mollie. "Drake and his Nobles."

"We just need to catch them in the act," said Daniel. "Which has not been easy."

"They must have some really super-speeders in their group," said Mollie. "These crimes happen so fast and there are never any witnesses."

"Maybe that Hunter kid can go invisible like Rose," suggested Michael.

"Problem is, we don't know what he can do," said Daniel. "We don't really have enough intel on any of them. They spend all their time at the academy—when they're not tearing up the town, that is."

"Rohan and I have been thinking about that," said Eric. "And, well, no offense, but it looks kind of like you and Mollie have run out of leads."

Mollie started to argue, but Daniel waved her down. Eric was right. Daniel and Mollie had a wall of suspects but absolutely no evidence to connect them to even a single crime.

"What do you guys suggest?" asked Daniel.

"Now, hear us out," said Eric. "And don't say it's a stupid idea until you've had some time to think about it."

"Eric and I are enrolling at the academy," said Rohan.

"Wow," said Mollie after a moment. "I won't say that's a stupid idea because *stupid* is not a strong enough word for it."

"You see," said Eric, ignoring Mollie, "the way we figure it, there's no way to prove that these Nobles kids are behind the attacks unless we catch them doing something. But if we could get close enough, someone with super-hearing might eventually overhear them planning another attack. Or catch them bragging about one of the attacks that already happened. It's like you said, Daniel, we don't have enough intel."

"And it's not like we are going to stay. Once we get something on Drake and his friends, we'll quit and come back to school with you guys," said Rohan.

"Not if they stick you in some lab and brainwash you," said Mollie.

"Oh, not that black-helicopter stuff again, Mol," said Rohan. "Honestly . . ."

"You know what?" said Mollie. "Forget it. You obviously don't have a brain to wash."

"Will you two knock it off!" said Daniel, raising his voice and throwing up his hands. Sometimes having Rohan and Mollie in the same room was enough to make him wish he had just one superpower—the power to shut people up.

"I'll admit it's not a terrible plan," said Daniel. "But even though I'm not as freaked out by it as Mollie is, something about that place simply doesn't feel right. Look at their response to this crime wave—they use it as a recruitment tool. Creepy."

"Why just the two of you?" asked Michael. "I could come too."

"Spy work isn't teamwork," said Eric. "Two is already pushing it, but Rohan's the perfect fit for this kind of mission, and I'll be there to watch his back starting Monday."

"Wait a minute," said Daniel. *"Starting Monday?"*

"We already registered," said Rohan. "We didn't want to waste any more time."

"Stupid," said Mollie. "Beyond stupid."

"I have to agree with Mollie on this one," said Michael. "Why didn't you guys tell us before you decided to do something this crazy?"

"Because we didn't want you all trying to talk us out of it!" said Eric. "It's a good plan, and if Daniel was the one to suggest it, you'd all be, like, *Great idea!* and *Why didn't we think of that?"*

"He's right," said Daniel. "I don't see any other choice."

Mollie and Michael looked surprised, but the truth was that they couldn't be more surprised that Daniel was agreeing with Eric than Daniel was. But this time his friend had a point. Some of Daniel's plans in the past had been far crazier than this one, and yet no one had questioned him.

"We're not getting anywhere as it is," said Daniel. "If it *is* Drake and his Nobles, they are staying one step ahead of us. Meanwhile, the mood in this town is getting worse by the day. Everyone's scared and angry. That's a bad combo."

"See," said Eric, grinning broadly. "Good plan!"

"He didn't say that," said Michael. "He said we're just out of other ideas."

"So it's settled," said Daniel. "OPERATION PLEASE STAY OUT OF TROUBLE, ERIC AND ROHAN, begins Monday."

"C'mon, we'll be fine," Eric assured him. "I'm on the job!"

"Is it too late to change my mind?" asked Rohan. Eric gave him a playful punch that nearly knocked him off the bed.

"Hey," said Mollie, picking up the paper again. "What else did that article say? That Plunkett Industries had made a generous contribution to the school?"

"Well, that's Theo's side of the family," said Rohan. "They took control after Herman was declared missing."

"You know, it wouldn't hurt to reach out to Theo," said Daniel. "See if he knows anything about that place that could be useful."

Eric snorted. "Good luck. He's probably been too busy pursuing his own life of crime to pay attention to anyone else's."

"He only stole his dad's car," said Daniel.

"How many times?" asked Eric.

"A . . . few. But he kept it in the family." Daniel had to admit, when you put it like that, Theo did sound pretty unreliable. But though Theo was powerless just like Daniel, the young man did have one very special asset that could prove quite useful—his name.

"Look, let's not argue about Theo," said Daniel. "And if

you guys don't mind, Mollie and I have a final to study for. We can talk spy stuff later."

"I'm telling you guys—don't worry!" said Eric. "Rohan and I are the dynamic duo."

"Barf," said Mollie.

"Fine," said Rohan. "You two have fun hitting the books. Text us if you wrap up early."

They said their goodbyes and left—Eric and Michael through the window and Rohan through the front door. Once she and Daniel were alone together, Mollie heaved her history book out of her backpack and made a face.

"Can't believe those two," she said. "They're walking into that place totally blind, and honestly, I can't think of two worse spies in the world. Your little brother is sneakier than they are."

"Yep," said Daniel, tapping his chin with his pencil. An idea was brewing. "That's why I need to talk to Theo. Right away."

"Huh?"

"What are you doing tomorrow after school?"

"You know very well what I'm doing; I'm studying just like we always— Hey, what are you talking about?"

Daniel smiled as he picked up his phone and scrolled through his contacts.

"Thought we might see what Theo's up to. Maybe take a ride to someplace like . . . oh, I dunno . . . the Noble Academy for the Gifted!"

Chapter Ten
The Other Plunkett

As a private institution, the Noble Academy for the Gifted received its funding from a variety of wealthy individuals and corporations. Many patrons opened their wallets. (Who wouldn't want their name associated with the world's first school for superhumans?) But one family name in particular was responsible for over two-thirds of the school's endowment as well as donating the very land on which the academy was built.

"My dad offered to let Herman have the mansion back, but the old coot just stayed up there at the crazy house. Guess he liked the bingo nights."

Herman Plunkett's grandnephew Theo was sitting

behind the wheel of a brand-new night-black Jaguar. From the backseat (Mollie was riding shotgun) Daniel could see the gates of Noble Academy just up ahead. When he'd first climbed into Theo's car, he'd expected that "new-car smell" everyone talked about, but apparently that new-car smell wasn't so strong when your upholstery was Italian leather. That was a different smell altogether, and it smelled like money.

Several times over the past two years Daniel had biked up these very same mountain roads, and each time the trip had been fearful. The land that now belonged to the Noble Academy for the Gifted wasn't that far from the Old Quarry, which for years had served as the Shroud's secret lair. Generations before that it had been the site of the St. Alban's Orphanage, burned to the ground almost a century ago. That night a simple trapper named Johnny Noble rescued the orphans from the deadly fire, but something in the smoke had changed them all. That night long ago was when it all began, here in these very same woods.

As they stopped at the gate, Daniel craned his neck out the window to get a better look. He tried to picture what Eric might be doing here in a few days, doing loop-de-loops in the sky and showing off, maybe racing the other fliers. But all Daniel could see soaring over the school now were a few long-winged hawks, making lazy circles overhead. It looked as if they'd spotted prey somewhere in the woods nearby. Not an encouraging sign.

The brambles that Daniel had once hidden in, the

mountain trails that he'd explored were gone, and in their place was a long field of freshly sodded green grass. Where there had once been dense forest, there was now a cluster of buildings forged from glass and steel, a tiny metropolis built into the side of a mountain.

A polite security guard checked Theo's name off a clipboard, and then opened the gate for them to drive through. On the other side, the academy's walled campus sprawled out before them. The newly laid grass butted up against still-upturned earth, and the air smelled of fresh paint. The glass towers were adorned with gleaming white marble steps and polished walkways circling a giant metal spire in the center that reached taller than the tallest building. It was breathtaking. The mountain's forbidding north face was now a relic of history; this place was about the future. The symbol of an age where superhumans walked the earth.

"Wow," said Daniel.

"Mm-hm," answered Theo. "Plunkett Industries sank a big chunk of change into this place. You'll see our family name just about everywhere. I'm almost surprised they didn't name it the *Plunkett* School for the Gifted."

"That would have been ironic considering who your uncle really is," said Mollie.

"Yeah, but it would have driven Herman just crazy, don't you think?" said Theo, smirking.

They parked in a small lot marked VISITOR PARKING, and then set off on foot toward the campus. Waiting for them on the steps outside the front administration building was a smartly dressed young woman wearing blue-tinted glasses and cherry-red lipstick.

"Mr. Plunkett?" the woman asked, extending her hand.

"Theo. My dad's the real Mr. Plunkett." Theo shook her hand and returned her smile with one of his own, a charming grin that Daniel had come to envy but also distrust—it usually meant Theo was up to something. Although technically today they were all up to something, being here under false pretenses.

"I was so glad to get your message yesterday," the woman said, in a voice too chipper to be believable. "Any member of the Plunkett family is welcome here at any time! I'm Mandy Starr, PR liaison for the academy. As I was saying, we are, of course, terribly grateful to your family for their generosity. Why, I was just the other day talking about the last board of trustees meeting, in which I finally met your—"

"Uh, these are my friends," interrupted Theo. "They're really the reason I'm here."

"Oh," said Ms. Starr, blinking. "Pleased to meet you."

"Daniel Corrigan," Daniel said, offering his hand. He wished he could smile like Theo. His own smiles were always closed-mouthed and lopsided, and he realized too late that his hand was clammy.

"Mollie Lee," said Mollie with a wave, and immediately Ms. Starr began oohing and aahing over Mollie's hair, her choice of earrings. It was a real show.

"What was that about?" Daniel whispered to Theo. "Why'd you cut her off like that?"

"It's my dad," whispered Theo back. "He's this crazy flirt at those trustee things. I didn't want to hear another story about how he spent the whole meeting chatting up the pretty young PR person. Sorry."

Daniel nodded in understanding. No need to embarrass anyone. From what Daniel knew of Theo's dad, he was gregarious but hardly seemed the type who would flirt with women half his age. The man wore Bermuda shorts and black socks to work, for heaven's sake.

Oh well. It was just another example of how you didn't really know a person until you knew him.

"So, what brings you all to the academy today?" asked Mandy Starr. "I'm happy to give you the tour, but it might help if I knew what precisely you were interested in. It's a big campus and hard to take in in one afternoon."

"Well," said Theo, "I've always been curious, since it's so important to my family and all. Daniel's really just along for the ride, but Mollie here is a prospective student— Ow!"

Though it was too quick to see, Daniel knew that Theo had just gotten a super-fast kick to the shin.

"Eh, heh. Anyway, as I was saying . . ." Theo shot Mollie a look. "Mollie is a prospective student, and being a family friend and all, I thought it'd be nice to give her a personal tour."

"That's an excellent idea!" said Mandy with another

squeal of fake enthusiasm. Giving tours to new students was probably beneath Mandy Starr's pay grade.

"Here," said Mandy. "If you could wear these visitor name badges while we walk, and I have to ask you to refrain from taking pictures or using recording devices of any kind. Privacy issue, you'll understand. Now, as you may have heard, the academy serves grades K through twelve. As we go, if you have any questions, please feel free to ask."

While they toured the campus, Daniel watched as Mandy Starr switched into autopilot, ticking off the brochure-worthy facts about the new school. The materials used in the construction—reinforced titanium alloys and shatter-proof glass—would serve the special needs of their unique student body by preventing any accidental damage to the structures themselves. Every building had built-in sprinkler and foam fire systems, with redundancies in case of power failure. And on and on.

The first building they stopped at looked like a miniature stadium. A domed roof topped its tall circular base, and it was windowless as far as Daniel could see.

"Now in addition to providing the standard curriculum you'd find in any top-notch school, we also have a wide range of courses tailored to an array of special talents. What, may I ask, can you do, sweetheart?"

Mollie looked darkly at Theo, but he gestured toward Mandy Starr. "Well?" he asked.

"I'm a flier," said Mollie reluctantly.

"Oh, then we are at the right place!" chirped Mandy Starr. "And there's no need to be shy about it. We're all on the same page here."

Then Mandy Starr slid her blue glasses down to the edge of her nose, and for the first time they got a good look at her eyes. They were solid blue—no whites at all—except for the pupils, which were two twinkling red lights. She winked one glowing eye at Mollie and said, "Follow me and stay close."

Of course, thought Daniel. It would make sense that everyone who worked here had powers of some sort. Even the public relations lady. He wondered, idly, what she could do with those glowing eyes of hers.

She swiped the badge clipped to her lapel through a sensor panel next to the stadium door, which opened with a swoosh. It was all very science fiction, Daniel had to give it that.

Inside, the miniature stadium turned out not to be a stadium at all—it was a classroom.

Daniel recognized at once why this building had no windows, because they would have all been broken by now by the out-of-control small children hurtling through the air.

"Basic flight," said Mandy Starr. "Beginners' class."

Six small children—the oldest couldn't have been more than eight—were tumbling and flopping through the air as a frantic-looking woman wearing something like a baseball catcher's gear hovered near them. The kids were laughing as they ricocheted off the walls and ceiling, which had been padded with some kind of rubberized material. They looked like a group of kid-sized bouncy balls.

"The little ones aren't ready for open-sky classes—we wouldn't want them soaring off into the stratosphere now, would we? So we start them off in here until they learn control. We call it the Aviary."

Mollie snorted. For a girl who'd been flying since she was six, this was literally kid stuff.

"Who's that?" asked Daniel, pointing to the woman in the catcher's gear. She was trying in vain to slow the momentum of one little girl who was bouncing so fast the girl was turning a worrying shade of green.

"That's one of our flight instructors, Mrs. Moore. She ran a day care a few towns over, and lucky for us she woke up the morning of the Blackout Event and remembered she could levitate. Her experience with small children makes her the perfect instructor for this age group."

At that moment Mrs. Moore managed to bring the bouncing girl to a halt, but not in time. The little girl threw up all over Mrs. Moore's catcher's gear and onto the unfortunate kids who happened to be flying beneath her.

"Whoops!" said Mandy Starr, her thumbs dancing along her BlackBerry. "Let me send a message to maintenance, and we'll be on our way."

As they exited, Mandy Starr patted Mollie on the shoulder. "Of course, the Aviary isn't only for the little ones. We use it for fliers of all ages who just need that little bit of extra practice."

While Mandy Starr was looking the other way, Mollie made an "I'm gonna vomit" gesture behind her back. This woman had obviously made the assumption that Mollie was new to her powers, and she mistook Mollie's sullen quiet for shyness. Watching Mandy Starr try to coax Mollie out of her shell was almost worth the whole trip.

Next they observed part of a physical science class where the teacher lectured a roomful of bored tweens about the amount of pressure per inch standard household objects could bear. From the look of the reinforced steel desks the students were sitting at (a couple of which were still bent out of shape), Daniel suspected this would be a good class for Georgie someday.

Then they visited a sort of shooting range where some kids lobbed balls of fire, others ice, at brightly painted metal targets. Next was a swim class inside a humid gymnasium where the students and teacher didn't come up from the bottom for the whole time Daniel and his friends watched—at least twenty minutes. Eventually, Theo got bored and drifted away to check his email on his phone.

"Ms. Starr?" asked Daniel.

"Please, call me Mandy."

"Right, Mandy, are those kids all water-breathers?"

"Well, the teacher is—the town librarian, I think he was—but the rest vary. A few can breathe water, a few don't need to breathe at all, and at least one of them can turn herself into a fish, among other things. We're helping her expand her repertoire."

Daniel peered closely into the water. Indeed, there was a striped bass dancing in and out among the floating kids near the bottom.

"Chlorine-free pool, of course," said Mandy Starr. "No one wants to breathe that stuff!"

Daniel had to admit, the Noble Academy for the Gifted, at least at first glance, lived up to the hype. Classes were sloppy at times, and more than a few faculty members wore a look of constant panic as they instructed their students in disciplines that had never been studied in the history of humankind. Where else had there been a seminar on *reassembling loose particles after personal teleportation*?

Even Mollie came to be impressed in spite of herself.

They were admiring the view out of one of the common room windows, which had a really excellent perspective on the forest below and a track where super-speeders raced by in blurs of color among the trees, when Mandy Starr's Black-Berry began to buzz. Excusing herself, she scrolled through an email on her device with a look of increasing dread, then, with a real panic that broke through her fake politeness, announced that they'd have to cut the tour short today. Something rather urgent had come up.

She escorted them as far as the visitors' parking lot, all the while frantically typing away on her tiny keyboard and trying to jog along the walkways in three-inch heels. When they reached the parking lot, she gave a brief good-bye, and apologized to Theo for ending the tour so abruptly.

Theo was gracious and understanding and promised to tell his father just how accommodating she had been. This seemed to lighten her spirits slightly, before she sped back to the main building, her shoes clicking up the marble steps.

"What got into her?" asked Mollie.

Theo held up his smartphone. "While you all were admiring the fishpond, I used my dad's email to send her a message, flagged urgent, about the investors' dinner. My dad, of course, trusts that all the arrangements have been made and the academy is prepared to host a quiet banquet for twenty donors—tonight."

"There's no such thing, is there?" asked Daniel.

"Not that I know of," said Theo. "But Dad's traveling in Asia with Grandpa right now, so he won't even check his email till he wakes up tomorrow. I just hope she doesn't spend too much on the caterers. They're going to have lots of food left over."

"You're going to get so busted," said Mollie.

"But not until after we've had a real look around," said Theo. "C'mon, I'm sick of the brochure tour. Let's go meet some students."

They set off again back toward campus, but this time they veered away from the main path that Mandy had led them down. They passed a few members of the staff along the way, but seeing as Mandy Starr had been in too much of a panic to remember to collect their guest passes, no one questioned their being there. The campus looked about the same wherever they wandered: uniform glass buildings, walkways perfectly adorned with marble planters and benches. The only thing that stood out as unusual was the tall windowless spire Daniel had spotted on their way in. It stood at the center of the courtyard, and something about it bothered Daniel. He stared at it for several seconds before it occurred to him just what it was. There was a clear observation deck up top, but no doorway and no ladder.

They crossed to the other side of the courtyard to get a better look at the spire and found a fountain surrounded by students on break. Everywhere, teenagers lounged on the grass or sat on benches chatting, loose ties around their necks, sport coats slung over their shoulders. Most of the girls wore skirts. It was a prep school scene out of a movie.

"Hey, Mollie," Daniel said, looking at the students. "Over there."

"What?" said Mollie. "They look like morons."

"No," he said. "Not how they're dressed. Look harder."

Mollie squinted hard for a few seconds. "Whoa," she said.

It wasn't obvious at first, and if someone simply glanced at the courtyard while passing by, it would look just like a bunch of kids hanging out. But taking a closer look, Daniel noticed things, like the boy sitting on the edge of the fountain who was staring at the water, concentrating on it, and as Daniel watched, the water began to shimmer and shake. Eventually, it would rise up six or so inches, as though it had a mind of its own, and form itself into shapes: horses, a hand, a miniature Eiffel Tower. Each time the water took a new shape, the boy would wave his hand ever so slightly and it would fall away, only to re-form itself into something new.

No, the water wasn't re-forming itself. He was doing it.

"Do you guys know him?" Theo whispered, but Daniel and Mollie shook their heads no. Then Mollie pointed to a couple lying on the grass on the far side of the lawn.

"We know him, though," she said.

The boy was blowing smoke rings over his head, as tiny fireballs flitted in and out of his mouth. Every now and then, the girl on the grass next to him would reach up a finger and flick the smoke rings away.

"Drake," said Daniel.

"Jerk," added Mollie.

"Let's not get any closer. I don't want to be seen."

"Where are the teachers?" asked Theo. "Smoking can't be allowed on campus."

"He's not smoking," said Mollie.

"What?" asked Theo. "Then how's he . . . Oh."

"Yep," said Daniel. "Just like a dragon. Spooky, right?"

Before Theo had any time to answer, however, Drake called out, "Hey, Jack! Incoming!"

Then he took a deep breath and blew out a jet of bright orange flame. It arced over the kids' heads, but just as Daniel was afraid it would come down on someone, an equally long plume of water erupted out of the fountain and collided with it in midair. With a loud snap, the two elements exploded in a chemical reaction, bursting into a cloud of steam. Several of the students looked over at Drake and shook their heads disapprovingly as they gathered their things and fled the courtyard. The boy next to the fountain was wearing a huge grin. The girl on the grass clapped.

"Awesome, Drake," the boy was saying. "Awesome."

"Did that seem to you . . . ," Theo started to say, cocking his head toward Mollie.

"Totally dangerous and stupid and the kind of thing an idiot show-off jerk would do just to impress a girl and who cares who might get hurt?" Mollie asked.

"I couldn't have put it better," said Theo.

"I dunno," said a girl's voice from behind them. "I think he's kinda dreamy."

Daniel and his friends turned slowly around and saw Skye, Hunter, and Mutt standing mere feet away from them. Actually, Skye and Hunter were standing; Mutt was crouched down on all fours again. How the three had managed to sneak up on them was another mystery, but there they were.

"Hello, Skye," said Daniel. "Hi, Hunter. Hey, Mutt."

Oh well, thought Daniel. If he was going to get his butt kicked, he might as well say hello first.

Of the three of them, only Skye was smiling, but Daniel wished she wasn't. There was nothing warm about that smile.

"You two, I know," said Skye, her eyes moving over Daniel and Mollie and coming to rest on Theo. "You, I don't know."

Theo gave her one of his roguish grins, but Daniel noticed he was keeping his eye on Mutt.

"I'm Theo," he said, holding out his hand. "Pleased to meet you, eh, Skye, was it?"

But Skye was apparently immune to Theo's charm offensive. She shied away from his hand like it was covered in open sores.

"I don't know you," she said. "You one of us, or are you peasant folk?"

"What?" asked Theo.

"He's like me," said Daniel. "So I guess he's a lowly peasant."

"Hey!" complained Theo, but Daniel waved at him to be quiet.

"Thought so," said Skye. "Mutt here smelled it on him, didn't you, boy?"

"Yip, yip," said Mutt. "Pant, pant."

That boy really is disturbed, thought Daniel.

"So, what are you doing here?" said Skye. "Other than spying on us, again."

Theo opened his mouth to speak, but Mollie stepped in front of him and tapped her visitor's badge. "We're visiting," she said. "Is that a problem?"

"Not at all," said Skye, smiling prettily. "I was hoping

we'd run into you. In fact, Mutt here's been dreaming about a rematch."

"Anytime," said Mollie. "Hope he brought a change of underwear."

"That's it, girlie," said Mutt. "Keep it up."

"Whoa, whoa," said Theo, stepping in between them. "Why don't we cool it a bit, okay, buddy?"

"Let's just go," said Daniel. Theo was trying to be chivalrous, but he was going to get himself hurt. Mollie could at least handle herself, but Theo had no idea how dangerous these kids could be.

"Want me to go through you to get to her?" said Mutt. "Be happy to."

"Move, Theo," said Mollie.

"Look, just because I'm a Plunkett doesn't mean I'm a coward," said Theo.

"Wait a sec," said Skye, putting a hand on Mutt's shoulder to restrain him. "What did you call yourself?"

"Plunkett," said a new voice, and they all turned to see a tall man strolling down the lane toward them.

Daniel recognized the silver hair and close-cropped beard. And those vivid blue eyes that were at once so clear, yet ringed with lines and wrinkles. In some ways, the eyes looked older than the face. He recognized the man, but seeing him here in the school was such a shock that for a moment Daniel didn't believe his own eyes. He closed them, opened them again, yet it was still him.

"Theodore Plunkett Jr. is his name, to be precise," said the man. "I would have joined you all earlier, but I was swamped. I hope Ms. Starr's tour was educational?"

"Uh," said Theo, glancing at the others. "Yeah, yeah, it was great. And we were just headed back—"

"To the parking lot," said the man. "Which is that way." He gestured back the way he came. "Maybe you got turned around?"

The man looked all of them over, but took care not to make eye contact with Daniel. It wasn't surprising. The last time he'd been face to face with the man, Daniel had punched him in the jaw.

"Lester, don't slouch," said the man, and the boy Daniel knew as Mutt stood up straight while grumbling under his breath.

"Well, it's a good thing I came along when I did," said the man. "Because I'm on my way to the front and can show you all back to your car. If you're done visiting with these fine students, that is."

"Thanks," said Theo. "Thanks, Mr. . . . Sorry, I didn't get your name, sir."

"Apologies," said the man. "I'm Jonathan Noble, and I'm the principal here."

Chapter Eleven
Principal Johnny

"As Ms. Starr surely told you numerous times, the academy is the most technologically advanced school ever built," said Johnny. "And the spire there is a monument to that achievement."

Johnny was pointing up at the metal spire standing in the middle of the courtyard. It was easily as big around as a car, and taller than any of the surrounding buildings.

"If you look close, you'll see a platform up top. From there the whole town is visible below."

"But how are you supposed to go up?" said Theo. "Even if there's a stairway inside, there's no door."

"Exactly," said Johnny. "As a work of art, the lack of a door is supposed to be part of the aesthetic message. A tower that cannot be scaled by conventional means. Or at least that's what they tell me."

He smiled at them. "I think it's a bit silly myself."

Johnny was walking them back toward the parking lot, seemingly casual, but Daniel could tell he was keeping a sharp eye on them. They weren't going to get the chance to slip away a second time. He wondered if his own face betrayed just how shocked he really was at seeing Johnny again. And what must Mollie and Theo be thinking? To Mollie, Johnny Noble had been a legend—the first Super. To Theo, he was probably little more than a cheesy character from his crazy granduncle's comic books. But Daniel had met the man before, hero of Noble's Green in the flesh, and he still hadn't gotten over the disappointment.

"So are you the real Johnny Noble?" asked Theo. "I mean, the guy in the tights and all?"

Johnny laughed. "I haven't gone by *Johnny* since I was a much younger man. And I've never worn a pair of tights in my life. But, yes, I am the Jonathan Noble they named this town after. Now I'm the principal of this school. Funny how life turns out, isn't it?"

"Don't take this the wrong way," said Theo. "But why haven't I heard of this before? I mean, the academy would have no problem attracting students with the one and only Johnny Noble on the website."

Johnny sighed. "Yes. I'm told the board of directors feels just like you do, and I suppose it's bound to get out sooner or later. But for a while at least, I'd like the academy to be the story. Not me."

"The students don't know who you are? The staff?" Daniel said.

"They know I'm Principal Noble," said Johnny. "But most of the kids just think my name's a coincidence. And the staff has been good about respecting my wish for privacy."

Johnny looked Daniel in the eye. "I haven't lied to anyone, if that's what you're asking."

That was exactly what Daniel was asking. Next to Herman, there probably wasn't an adult alive who Daniel trusted less than Johnny Noble.

"Well, here we are." Johnny stopped outside the front building next to the parking lot.

"If you wouldn't mind coming inside for a few minutes," said Johnny. "I'd like to have a word with Daniel here."

Theo shot Daniel a look of alarm. They were already busted, caught trespassing on campus after they'd been asked to leave. But that didn't explain why Johnny Noble would want to talk to Daniel alone. Mollie snapped out of her shell shock at seeing Johnny up close. She hadn't said a word since Johnny had introduced himself, but Mollie found her voice now. "Don't go," she whispered to Daniel.

"It's all right," said Daniel. "You guys stay here and I'll be back in a minute."

"There's a reception area inside," said Johnny. "I'll show you."

The waiting room was stocked with expensive overstuffed chairs. On a tray table someone had left a few bottles of water and a bowl of fruit. It looked like they'd been expected.

"If you need anything else, just buzz that button over there and someone will come," said Johnny, gesturing to an intercom panel set into the wall. "I'd ask Ms. Starr to keep you company, but . . . she's got her hands unexpectedly full at the moment." Johnny paused just long enough that it was clear he knew exactly what Ms. Starr was doing and, more importantly, why.

Theo plopped down on one of the chairs and grabbed a banana. If meeting a century-old folk hero had fazed him at all, he didn't show it. Mollie, however, watched Daniel with an expression of clear worry as he followed Johnny out of the waiting room and into the hallway beyond.

They traveled through brightly lit corridors bustling with people. Most hurried past, mumbling hellos at Johnny and not bothering to spare Daniel a second glance. Despite the breezy, relaxed design of the place—the floor-to-ceiling windows, walls hung with brightly painted works of abstract art—there was a definite tension in these halls. Everyone was hurrying to and fro, and they had that overworked look that Daniel sometimes saw in his parents. He felt guilty for fooling poor Ms. Starr the way they did. Probably gave her an anxiety attack.

They stopped outside a tall office door marked PRIN-CIPAL, and Johnny stepped aside, allowing Daniel to enter first. The office had been designed with the same cheerful modernity as the rest of the school, but the effect was hampered in there somewhat by the shelves of dusty old relics and knickknacks—an antiquated typewriter with a few missing keys, a baseball yellowed with age, a dented infantryman's helmet. Johnny's office looked more like a flea market.

Johnny offered Daniel a seat, but Daniel didn't take him up on it. He wasn't planning on staying long enough to need a chair.

"It's a little cluttered for an office, but it helps me feel at home," said Johnny as he walked around the back of his glass-topped desk and eased himself down into his chair, smoothing out his suit coat as he did so. Sitting there, he looked strangely elegant, like a character from one of those old black-and-white detective movies. A man out of time.

"Come on, Daniel," he said. "Sit and hear what I have to say. And try not to throw any punches this time."

"Don't worry about that. I broke my hand last time I tried," said Daniel. His gaze came to rest on an old rifle mounted on a plaque behind Johnny's chair. The barrel was rusted with age and the wooden stock was blackened as if burnt.

"Strange thing for a teacher to put up in his office," said Daniel.

Johnny glanced over his shoulder at the gun and smiled. "Yes, it's gotten me a few looks, but I explained that it's a family heirloom and a part of history."

"Yours, isn't it?"

"I was carrying that rifle the night in 1934 when the Witch Fire Comet appeared over the mountain. I still remember every detail. I was coming home late after checking my traps. I remember what the sky looked like when it lit up with green fire. The trail of light as the meteor came crashing down to earth. And the screams from St. Alban's as the orphanage caught fire."

Johnny's eyes had grown distant, like he was seeing something Daniel couldn't, hearing things Daniel couldn't. His grandmother used to get that look sometimes when she'd talk about her childhood, about old friends dead and gone. Herman had that look too, when he'd first told Daniel his tale of the comet, of how a young Herman had been the only child to escape the fire that night unscathed, and unchanged, because he'd been hiding in the outhouse when the meteor hit.

Daniel's grandmother used to say that when you'd lived long enough, your whole life bore down on you, the good and the bad. It got so heavy at times, you just had to stop to catch your breath.

Whatever moment was weighing Johnny down passed, and his eyes focused once more on the here and now, on Daniel.

"You and your friends got curious about the academy, decided to do a little investigating, is that it?" he asked.

Daniel nodded.

"I should've been expecting that. Must be slipping in my old age."

Despite what had just happened, Daniel would never have described Johnny as old, not in the way his grandmother had been old—frail and sickly. Johnny was from a different era perhaps, but he was solidly built and moved with the grace of a young man in his prime. Still, if Daniel did the math, he figured Johnny was close to a hundred.

"So, Theo Plunkett, and the girl with you, that's Mollie Lee—the flier, right?"

Again, Daniel nodded. He didn't bother lying since he was pretty sure Johnny was asking questions he already knew the answers to.

"You don't look happy, Daniel, and I had thought that when you finally figured out that I was here, you might actually be pleased. Aren't you the one who scolded me last year for not getting involved?"

"Yeah," said Daniel. "But you missed your chance. All those years that Herman was preying on the kids in this town and you could've stopped it. You think you can make up for that by taking a job at the school?"

Daniel forced himself to look right into Johnny's eyes. There was something in that stare—a power that made Daniel keenly aware of just how small a person he really was.

It was hard to stare into the eyes of a giant and not look away.

Taking a deep breath, Daniel said, "The last time we talked, I told you to leave us alone. I meant it."

To Daniel's surprise, it was Johnny who broke their staring contest. Looking up at the ceiling, as if he could see past it and into the sky, he let out a tired sigh. "Do you know what this place is?" asked Johnny.

"We were told it was a school," answered Daniel.

"Oh, it's a school all right," said Johnny. "There's nothing insidious going on here, if that's what you were hoping to find. No secret labs. No sacrificial altar hidden away."

"You've been reading too many of your own comic books."

Johnny chuckled. "I never liked those. Herman's tales of caped heroes and masked villains never interested me. I've seen too much of the real world."

"So what?" asked Daniel. "Are you here to share your wisdom, then? Tell us all about *the real world*?"

"In part," Johnny said simply. "And to protect you from it."

Daniel nearly laughed in his face. "What do you mean? Protect us from who?"

Johnny stood up and walked to the window. His office overlooked the campus common, and beyond that were the verdant slopes down the mountain. It was a breathtaking view.

"I guess you've seen what's been going on down there in the town," said Johnny. "The incidents."

"You mean the attacks? Sure."

"It's exactly what I was worried would happen," said Johnny, and for the first time the smile dropped out of his voice. "I told you that the last time we talked."

"People are just getting scared."

"They're scared. And worse, they're jealous. It didn't take them long to go from 'Wow, they are amazing!' to 'Why can't I do that?' It's dangerous that there are so many of us."

"You sound like Herman."

"Well, even a broken clock is right twice a day," said Johnny. "But I'm going to try and help as much as I can."

"With this school?" said Daniel. "Was this place your idea?"

"No," admitted Johnny. "But when I heard what they were up to, I knew I needed to be here. If I can . . . control the out-of-control ones. Teach them to use their talents in a responsible way. Not to show off. Not to frighten people. Well, then, maybe we can avoid the worst of it."

"The worst of what?" asked Daniel. "Just what are you afraid will happen, exactly?"

Johnny studied Daniel quietly for a moment, as if weighing something about the boy. Finally, he slumped back into his chair.

"I've been alive for a long time, Daniel," he said. "In all those years my powers haven't weakened. If anything, they've grown. Changed."

"You healed me," said Daniel. "When I . . . broke my hand against your jaw. You used your power to heal me."

Johnny nodded. "I wasn't able to do that at first. It came with time. The point is, I've changed over the years, but as best I can tell, mankind hasn't. Fear is still the strongest emotion, and it can make people do terrible things if it's unchecked. All those years in hiding, I watched wars come and go, governments fall, and catastrophes wipe out thousands, but I chose this moment in history—now—to get involved. That should give you some idea of how serious I am about this."

Sometimes listening to Johnny was like listening to the class know-it-all who didn't realize someone had taped a KICK ME sign to his butt. Just when Daniel was about to be taken in by all that supposed wisdom, leave it to Johnny to remind him why he couldn't stand the man. He had such a self-important view of himself, of a person who'd spent the last century doing *nothing at all.*

"That's supposed to impress me?" said Daniel. "A list of all the times you *didn't* give a damn?"

For a moment, just a moment, a dark cloud passed over Johnny's face. Daniel had gotten to him, pierced that marble-hard skin with a little bit of truth telling. Good. Let him be angry. Anything to get rid of that arrogant smirk.

"You should watch your language, son," said Johnny. "You are in the principal's office after all."

"But I'm not your student," said Daniel.

"Look, Daniel—I'm here to teach. To help these kids

find their way so that people will have nothing *to* fear. But if it comes to it, I promise you this—no one will hurt these children while they are under my protection. They'd have to get through me first, and you and I both know that's a very hard thing to do."

Daniel looked at Johnny's face, trying to spot the lie there. But Johnny looked earnest enough. He probably believed it himself.

"You may hate me for letting the Shroud steal those children's powers," said Johnny. "And maybe you're right to do so, but ask yourself this—in all those years, did a single child die? And why not? You saw how unbalanced Herman had become, what he was capable of."

"Are you really trying to convince me that you weren't AWOL all that time? That you were some kind of secret protector?"

"I helped when I was needed," said Johnny. "Ask Rose. She watched as I saved your friend Eric's life."

It was true that in their first battle with the Shroud, Rose had hidden invisible while Johnny breathed strength back into Eric's wounded body. But Daniel had wondered, if Johnny was so all-powerful, why hadn't he simply stopped Herman himself? Last year he'd figured out the answer to that question. Johnny had been afraid the Shroud would steal his powers too. Johnny wasn't some mysterious savior helping from the shadows; he was a coward.

Now, thanks to Daniel, the Shroud was no more, and

there was nothing to be afraid of. Johnny was truly invulnerable at last. What courage did it take to come out of hiding now?

"I don't know why we're having this conversation," said Daniel. "You keep saying you're here to protect *us*. But I'm not even one of them. I'm not a Super."

"I think we both know that's not true. You've proved it, time and again." Johnny stood up. "You and your friends don't think you need me," he said. "But I can help. Mollie out there is, what, thirteen?"

"Fourteen."

"Growing up. And her powers, are they growing up with her?"

"How did you know?"

Johnny smiled. "It's not mind reading to guess that as their bodies are getting stronger, so are their abilities. I can help them control them, just like I'm already helping the rest of these kids. You tell them for me."

Daniel shrugged. Eric and Rohan would be there soon enough, but they would be none too happy when they learned that Johnny was a part of all this.

"Theo and Mollie will be wondering what's taking you so long," said Johnny. "I've pleaded my case, and I hope you can come to trust me, in time. The academy can be the answer to this town's problems. We can make it a better place. We can make the world a better place. I just wanted you to know, I really am one of the good guys, Daniel."

"Whatever," said Daniel. But as they walked to the door, he stopped and said, "Oh, about your students Drake Masterson and his buddies . . ."

"The ones you were talking to. Yes, what about them?"

"You've got your work cut out for you, Mr. Principal."

Chapter Twelve
Undercover

"**I**f I'd known he was the principal, there's no way I would've signed up," said Eric.

"It doesn't really change the mission," said Rohan. "We're going to be there to keep an eye on Drake and his friends. Johnny doesn't actually matter—"

"He matters to me," said Eric.

If Daniel disliked Johnny, Eric hated him. For most of his life Eric had idolized him as the first Super, the comic book hero of countless stories and Eric's own imagination. When Daniel had learned that it was all false, that the character of Johnny Noble was nothing like the real man, he'd felt disappointed, but Eric had felt betrayed. Another father figure had let him down, and Daniel knew that Eric had a thing about deadbeat dads. After his own father had passed away, there had been a string of men in his mother's life who'd promised to look after Eric and her, but each one turned out worse than the one before. He'd actually discovered his powers the day he threw one of them through a window.

"It's not too late to back out," said Daniel. "There's got to be another way to get intel on the Nobles."

For a moment Eric didn't speak, and neither did anyone else.

The three boys were sitting on the porch, waiting for Rohan's parents to drive Eric and Rohan up to the academy for their first day. The bags were packed, everything was set, but if Eric said the word, Daniel knew that Rohan would back him. He too understood how Eric felt about Johnny, and if his friend wanted to call it off, then he would call it off.

Eventually, Eric sighed and threw up his hands. "What's a spy mission without a few twists? But Johnny had better stay away from me, that's all I'm saying."

Rohan nodded and Daniel gave his friend a pat on the shoulder. He'd half been hoping that Eric would decide to call it quits, just because he didn't like the idea of them being up there without him, but then again he still wasn't any closer to catching Drake and his Nobles in the act. This could be their best shot at getting some evidence against them.

Rohan and Eric were dressed in their academy uniforms — white shirt, sport coat, and tie. With their ties loosened and coats slung carelessly over the porch railing, they looked like an advertisement in one of his mom's clothing catalogs. Young men of Oxford.

"And," said Eric, "have you seen the books we're expected to read?"

Apparently, they were done talking about Johnny, and Daniel was glad of it.

"He thought it was going to be all flying, all the time," said Rohan, nudging Daniel. "It is a *school*, Eric."

"Books!" shouted Eric. "I thought we were getting away from books!" He swept his hand dramatically over a stack of textbooks piled up next to his already full backpack.

"Sociology, Shakespeare. Oh, here's calculus. . . . *Calculus*, man!"

"That *is* a lot," agreed Daniel. He wondered if his book list for next year would look anything like that. He hoped not. He was having a hard enough time keeping up with one lousy history class, and the final was looming around the corner.

"And get this," said Eric. "We are not even allowed to use our powers on campus unless supervised by a member of the faculty!"

"Hey," said Rohan, pointing. "There's Mollie."

Daniel peered up at the sky but it was no use. Mollie would be traveling too fast for him to see, practically invisible to everyone except Rohan.

Sure enough, she appeared in the yard a second later, the only sign of her arrival the accompanying gust of wind.

"What are you guys wearing?" asked Mollie.

"What, this?" asked Rohan, and he took his sport coat off the railing and pulled it on, then began strutting up and down his porch like he was a runway model. A crest was stitched into the breast—a black mountain against a green field. Writing framed the top.

"Hey," said Daniel. "What's that say?"

"INTEGRITY, HONESTY, ACHIEVEMENT," said Rohan. "I would have gone with something other than *achievement*. I mean, *integrity* and *honesty* are qualities possessed by people, aren't they? But *achievement*'s not a quality at all. . . ."

As Rohan kept on talking, Mollie turned to Daniel and whispered, "I. Am. Never. Going. There."

"The uniforms are not so bad," said Rohan. He'd heard her. Of course he'd heard her. "I think they look smart."

"Smart?" repeated Mollie, shaking her head. "You're hopeless."

Mollie didn't see it, but Rohan gave Daniel a quick wink. In all the years that they'd been friends, she hadn't caught on that one of Rohan's favorite hobbies was to drive her crazy.

Rohan's mother called from inside, "Leaving in two minutes!"

"Oh, shoot! I'll be right back," said Rohan. "Forgot something."

Rohan hurried inside and the three friends were left with an awkward silence. Eric and Rohan were starting a new adventure today, one that Daniel and Mollie wouldn't be a part of.

"So, we'll check in every night by text," Eric was saying. "And while we try to get something on Drake, you two keep a watch on the town. We'll get them one way or another."

It wasn't much of a plan as plans go, but it was all they had. The Supers go undercover.

The door squeaked open on rusty hinges as Rohan's mother stepped out onto the porch. She jingled her car keys in her hand. "Time to go!" she said. "Oh, hello, Mollie. I didn't know you were here."

"Hello, Mrs. Parmar."

"Are you here to say goodbye?"

"Guess so," said Mollie. "Bon voyage."

Rohan appeared behind her, blinking at them as he wiped away tears. It took Daniel a moment to realize just what it was he was looking at.

After a moment of stunned silence, Daniel said, "Your glasses?"

"What?" said Rohan. "I got contact lenses."

"Doesn't he look handsome?" said Rohan's mother.

No one said a thing. They would have been less shocked if Clay Cudgens had just walked through the door with a box of doughnuts. Rohan without his glasses was just not Rohan.

"Come on!" said his mother. "We don't want to be late for your first day. . . ." Now Rohan's mother really was tearing up.

"Mom," said Rohan, embarrassed.

Daniel helped Rohan with his overstuffed backpack and grabbed a suitcase to take to the car.

"Superhero school," Daniel muttered.

"Hey, I just realized—why aren't you flying to school?" Mollie asked Eric as they followed Rohan down to the car.

"No powers allowed. The welcome letter specifically asked that all students report to school on the first day 'by traditional methods of transportation only.' Can you believe it?"

"Keep your eyes open, okay?" said Daniel. "And stay out of trouble."

"You bet," said Eric. "Always."

Daniel and Mollie waved as they watched the car pull away. They would need to hurry themselves if they didn't want to be late for Smiley's class. Well, Daniel had to hurry. Mollie could be there in minutes.

"What's going on with Rohan?" asked Mollie. "Contact lenses?"

"Things are changing," said Daniel. "No doubt about it."

"You think they'll be okay?"

"Sure," lied Daniel. "It's just a school. What's the worst that could happen?"

Chapter Thirteen
The Noble School for the Criminally Gifted

The clock on the wall refused to move any faster, no matter how much Daniel tried to will it to speed up. The sluggish minute hand barely ticked forward, and staring at it was giving Daniel a headache. If he kept looking at that preternaturally slow clock, he feared he'd burst a blood vessel in his brain, which, when he thought about it, might be a welcome relief from the boredom of Smiley's lecture on the Second Continental Congress. Mollie had checked out long ago, and was slumped at her desk, chin resting in her palm, eyes closed, and drooling. Daniel had been forced to kick her chair twice today when she'd started snoring.

Finally, just when he thought he couldn't take any more, he heard a sound sweeter than the trumpets of angels—the end-of-day bell.

As they streamed out of the classroom with the rest of the day's escapees, Daniel switched on his phone.

"I want to see if the guys texted yet. . . . Uh-oh."

"What?" said Mollie. "Something up?"

Daniel had four new messages from Rohan. As he scrolled down them, he saw variations of the same thing:

Emergency meeting @ new tree fort!
Gotta stop Eric!
Eric is idiot!
Come to tree fort when U get!!!

Mollie peered over his shoulder at the screen. "Looks serious," she said.

"Yeah," said Daniel. "Lemme go get my bike."

"No time," said Mollie. "From the school to the tree fort on a bike? You'll be there by dinnertime, maybe."

Mollie might've been exaggerating, but she was right that it wasn't a quick trip.

"Well, how do you expect— No. No! No way, Mol." Daniel knew that look. He knew what she was thinking and he didn't like it.

"Oh, don't be a baby," she said. "Forget your stupid male ego and let me fly you there. It'll take five minutes."

"It's not my ego," Daniel said, and loudly before he realized there were people still nearby in the halls.

"It's not my ego," he repeated, whispering this time. "It's that you have a habit of dropping me."

That wasn't strictly true. While Mollie had dropped him on a few occasions, it was usually over a large body of water and on purpose. Truth was, he did feel weird having a girl haul him around. Unlike Eric, Mollie wasn't super-strong, and the fact that an ordinarily muscled fourteen-year-old girl could carry him reasonably well was embarrassing. Especially when the girl started referring to him as "toothpick" afterward.

Quickly, Daniel ducked out of the school with Mollie at his heels. He dialed Rohan's cell phone and waited. It went directly to voice mail.

"You might not be able to get through," said Mollie. It was true that phone reception was spotty at best around Mount Noble, yet another of its mysterious qualities. Daniel was lucky he'd gotten Rohan's texts.

"Fine," said Daniel at last. "But let's find somewhere safe and out of sight to take off from. I don't want some tourist snapping a shot of you carrying me. And go fast, but not Mollie fast, okay? Last time I swallowed a bug."

With a quick prayer, Daniel wrapped his arms around Mollie and then the two were airborne. She'd been right, and the actual flight lasted mere minutes. As they sailed through the air holding each other, Daniel took in the view he never tired of seeing. Beyond the boundaries of their town, civilization gave way to green wilderness. A few roads cut through the forest and snaked their way up the mountainside. Somewhere in those woods was their destination—the new tree fort.

For the last minute or so of their flight together, Daniel decided to close his eyes and imagine he was flying alone. He heard the wind blowing in his ears; he felt it on his skin. He could almost pretend that Mollie wasn't there, except for the smell of lavender shampoo and cinnamon chewing gum—Mollie's scent.

Even after they'd touched down and Mollie had let him go, the Mollie *smell* still lingered. If he breathed deeply, it was there beneath the tang of the mountain pines. It worried him what he must smell like compared to her—probably closer to an old shoe. Daniel was trying to sniff-test his armpit without looking like he was sniff-testing his armpit when he realized that a strange silence had developed between them. They were hiking along the freshly cleared path to the tree fort, and Mollie hadn't once called him "toothpick." She was walking next to him—right beside him, actually—with her hands in her pockets and her thoughts someplace else.

They hadn't gotten very far, though, before she stopped. "Hold on a sec," she said, sniffing. "What's that?"

Oh no, Daniel thought. He did smell like an old shoe!

But then he caught a whiff of it too—a rotten odor being

carried on the wind from somewhere nearby. Only one creature on this earth could make such an unearthly stink.

"Bud," Daniel said. The fat bully's super-stench was unmistakable, but what would he be doing way out here in the woods near the tree fort?

Judging by the sudden look of worry on Mollie's face, she was thinking the same thing. What if Clay and Bud had found out about the new tree fort and ambushed their friends when they weren't expecting it? What if their friends were in trouble even now?

"Stayhereaminute," Mollie said, almost too quickly to hear.

"Wait, don't!" said Daniel, but he might as well have been talking to the empty air—she was gone before he'd breathed the first word.

Cursing under his breath, Daniel dashed up the path toward the tree fort. Mollie was rushing in without considering another, even more troubling, possibility. What if the bullies had somehow gotten ahold of Rohan's phone and sent that text themselves? She could be flying into a trap.

The tree fort was close enough that Daniel could just spot its outline through the woods—an unfinished structure half as big as their old tree fort. Nothing looked amiss, but then, if you were preparing to spring a trap, wasn't that the point?

Winded from the sprint uphill, Daniel reached the clearing beneath the tree fort. Mollie was nowhere to be seen, but Daniel thought he heard voices from up top. People were arguing.

A rope ladder dangled from an open trapdoor in the bottom, but he didn't have the necessary angle to see inside.

He could make out words now, and Mollie's voice raised in anger.

". . . out of your mind?" and ". . . right, you are an idiot!" and "Don't sit there, that's mine."

Those certainly didn't sound like cries for help.

Daniel was halfway up the ladder when Mollie's head appeared above him in the open trapdoor.

"Are you gonna take all day?" she asked. "My grandma could climb faster than that."

And like that, the memory of her smell, the feeling of flying together, his own worry for her very safety—they all disappeared. Mollie Lee was back to being an enormous pain in Daniel's butt.

He ignored her helping hand and hauled himself up the last few feet into the tree fort. The combination of woodland sprint and rope climb had left him a sweaty, out-of-breath mess. He rolled onto the floor and lay there for a moment—oblivious to the sawdust collecting in his hair. As he stared up at the ceiling, he realized the place still had only half a roof. What had begun as a project of passion had become an afterthought for most of them, with neglected tools and piles of unused lumber cluttering up the area. Daniel wondered, and not for the first time, if it would ever get finished. The Supers were no longer a secret, and maybe they'd finally outgrown their secret house in the woods.

The Bud stink was definitely stronger in here, and when Daniel lifted his head, he saw his friends standing or sitting around him. A few were holding their noses, and Rohan was wearing a swimmer's nose clip over his—Bud was kind of Kryptonite to a boy with super-smell. Eric was there in his academy uniform. Michael and Louisa and little Rose were present, though Rose kept blinking into invisibility. Right there and then, finding himself in the same room with Louisa for the first time in months, Daniel wished he could disappear too.

Lastly, in the corner, sitting on the ground looking miserable, was Bud. With his face flushed and his eyes all puffy and red, he looked like he'd been crying. His shirt was stretched near to bursting over his round belly, and his own academy tie was tied all wrong. It was strange enough seeing Bud without Clay by his side, but seeing him here in their tree fort was a shock.

"What's he doing here?" asked Daniel. "Did you guys take Bud prisoner or something?"

"Bud's not a prisoner," said Eric.

"And Eric's not in his right mind," said Rohan. "I think he's being mind-controlled. Oh, wait. No, he really is this stupid sometimes."

"Will you two knock it off?" said Louisa. "It's not

helping." She was leaning against the open window, probably to get as much fresh air as possible. She'd gotten a new haircut. Daniel started to wave a hello at her but realized she wasn't even looking his way, so he tried to save face by pretending to fix his own hair. An impossibility, of course. Daniel hadn't managed to get a hairbrush through that tangle of curls since the third grade.

"What's going on?" he asked as he pulled himself to his feet. "Mollie, do you know?"

"I'll let him tell you," she answered. Was it his imagination, or was she also avoiding eye contact with Daniel now too?

"Look, this is silly, you guys," said Eric. "I'm going to be late."

"Just you tell Daniel what you are going to be late for," said Rohan. "Since you won't listen to the rest of us, maybe he can talk some sense into you."

"What am I talking sense into him about?" asked Daniel.

"It took Eric one day to get into trouble," said Rohan. "One day!"

"It's a new record," laughed Michael.

"With the teachers?" asked Daniel. "With Johnny?"

"No," said Rohan. "With Drake and his Nobles. I think it's safe to say our cover is blown."

"That Drake's a real jerk," said Eric.

"We told you that," said Mollie. "And that's the whole reason you were going to the academy, to spy on him because he's a real jerk."

"Yeah, but he's like . . . a *super*-big jerk," said Eric. "Someone has to teach them a lesson."

"So you're the one to do it?" said Louisa. "Stupid, macho boys."

"Yeah," agreed Rose. "Stupid boys."

Daniel was surprised at the venom in Louisa's tone, and couldn't help but wonder if she was talking about someone else entirely, like him.

"It's not Eric's fault," said a hoarse voice from the corner. Everyone turned and looked at Bud as he wiped his eyes. "It's mine."

"That's not true," said Rohan. "You didn't do anything wrong, Bud."

"Okay, I'm lost," said Daniel. "Someone please tell me what happened. You're all mad at Eric, and Bud's now on *our* side. Is this some kind of parallel universe where we are all evil and grow goatees and stuff?"

Everyone started talking at once. Daniel held up his hands and shouted, "One at a time, guys!"

Surprisingly, they did as they were told.

"Rohan," said Daniel. "You first."

Rohan adjusted his glasses as he got ready to speak. His *glasses*!

"Hey," interrupted Daniel. "Where are your contacts?"

"Eh, I didn't make it past second period. Who can wear those things?"

Daniel smiled. At least one thing was back to normal.

"Anyway," continued Rohan. "You were right about

Drake and his Nobles. From the moment the first bell rang, that bunch started strutting around the academy like they owned it."

"They spent all morning making fun of the teachers behind their backs," said Eric. "I couldn't even focus on what anyone was saying because of all that snickering."

"With the exception of the Nobles, though, our morning was pretty awesome," said Rohan. "Did you know they have a molecular microscope in one of the labs?"

"Anyway," continued Eric, "by the time lunch rolled around, we realized that everyone gives the Nobles a pretty wide berth."

"The best way to deal with jerks is to ignore them," said Rohan.

"Says you," offered Eric.

"So they were at their table," said Rohan. "Laughing and making cracks about the cafeteria food and stuff, when, well . . ."

"I came in," said Bud, whining. "I walked into the lunchroom and Clay was sitting with them, with those Nobles. Clay and I haven't been getting along much lately, but we usually still sit together at lunch. This time, though, he was sitting with those Nobles and there weren't any other seats, so . . . I asked if I could sit there too."

"Clay said yes, then kicked Bud's chair out from under him as he was sitting down," said Rohan. "Trying to impress Drake and his buddies. Bud hit the ground, hard."

"Everyone laughed," said Bud. "Except you guys. The whole cafeteria laughing at me, and well, my power kicked in. I couldn't help it."

"That girl, Skye, got sick," said Rohan. "All over Drake's jacket. And that's when Drake lost it. For a moment I thought he was going to toast Bud right there, I really did."

They all looked over at Eric, who was suddenly very interested in a spot on the floor. Daniel could imagine what had happened next.

"And you stopped them, right?" said Daniel.

"No one else was standing up to those guys," said Eric. "And honestly, I was already sick of their crap."

For the first time since Daniel had seen him, Bud actually smiled. "I don't think Drake knows just how tough Eric is, 'cause they were getting ready to fight him right there. Clay knows, though. Even he backed away from that one."

It was weird, sitting there listening to Bud talk about Eric like he was his hero, after all those years of bullying.

"You were going to take on the Nobles by yourself?" asked Mollie.

"Rohan had my back," said Eric.

"Man, oh man," said Rohan.

"Where was Principal Johnny during all this?" asked Daniel.

"Never saw him," said Eric. "Not once all day."

Inside, Daniel started to seethe. Johnny had promised

that he was going to look after Daniel's friends at the academy, and yet the world's first superhero was missing in action. He wondered if he'd been duped yet again.

"Oh hey!" said Eric. "Guess who else I saw today."

"No idea," said Daniel.

"He's trying to change the subject," added Rohan.

"Gerald McNally!" said Eric. "You guys remember that kid? He was a couple of years ahead of us, big into school plays. He played Curly in *Oklahoma* and kept losing his cowboy hat."

"I don't know," said Daniel. "Must've been before my time."

"Well, it turns out he's one of us! The kid's got X-ray vision and nobody knew. All day long, teachers constantly had to tell him to keep his eyes on the board and off the other students."

"Jeez," said Daniel. "Turned out to be kind of a creep, huh?"

"Are you two done talking about the super–Peeping Tom?" Mollie asked. "Get on with it! Get back to the fight with the Nobles."

"There wasn't a fight," said Eric.

"Yet," said Rohan. "Tell them, Eric. Go on."

Eric hesitated, then, with a deep breath, said, "I told them I'd meet them after classes. I don't want to get expelled on my first day for fighting in the lunchroom. I mean, I'm not stupid."

Rohan snorted. "But you're dumb enough to sneak off campus to fight them."

"If you didn't notice you snuck off campus too," said Eric.

"Because of you!" said Rohan.

"Where?" asked Daniel. "Where did you agree to meet them? Here?"

"The junkyard," said Eric.

"See?" said Rohan. "First-class moron."

"And when?" asked Daniel, though he had a sinking feeling that he already knew the answer.

Eric looked at his watch. "In about ten minutes. We've got free time before the dinner bell."

Rohan began lecturing Eric again, while Eric tried to reassure everyone that he knew what he was doing and that he could handle himself even against five-to-one odds. Daniel felt like he ought to get involved, to talk Eric out of doing something this reckless, but he was distracted by another conversation that had started nearby.

While the boys were arguing, Mollie and Louisa had drifted off by themselves to the corner. Though he couldn't make out what was being said, it looked like Louisa was as frustrated with Mollie as Rohan was with Eric. Every time Mollie tried to get a word in, Louisa cut her off. At one point Mollie raised her voice, and Daniel heard her say, "I'm not the bad guy!" but the rest of the Supers were too busy with their own shouting match to notice. Then Louisa stalked away, leaving Mollie standing there looking stunned and alone.

Louisa was coming straight for Daniel. He worked up a smile. "Hi there."

But she didn't answer him, and she didn't stop. She just walked right through him. Daniel had seen Louisa use her phasing power before, but never to walk through a person, much less feel it happen to him.

It tickled.

"See you at home, Rose," said Louisa, and then she disappeared through the floor and was gone. And here Daniel had worried that she was upset with him for not getting in touch all summer, but what had Mollie done to make her so mad? He had to admit, it was nice not to be the one in trouble for once.

Daniel approached Mollie. "What's up with Louisa?"

When Mollie looked at him, her face was flushed, miserable.

"Hey, Mol," said Daniel. "What's wrong?"

Mollie shook her head and closed her eyes. When she opened them again, Daniel knew he was in trouble.

"Daniel Corrigan, you . . ."

She didn't finish. With something between a growl and a moan, she shoved him out of her way and stomped over to where Rohan and Eric were having their heated debate. Eric was in the process of explaining to Rohan what a little girl he was, and Rohan was comparing Eric to a less-than-average-intelligence Neanderthal.

"All right, you two," Mollie said as she wiped her eyes on her arm. Were those tears? "Eric, you said they wanted to meet you at the junkyard?"

"Yeah," said Eric, uncertain.

"Then let's go," she said. "Because I feel like hitting someone."

Chapter Fourteen

Supers vs. Nobles: Round One

That morning, if anyone had told Daniel that he would find himself in the middle of a superpowered gang war, he would have pulled the covers over his head and gone back to sleep. Now, as he looked at the faces of academy kids gathering in the junkyard, he wondered if it wasn't too late. Surely he could make it home by himself, lay his head upon his pillow, and forget that this insanity was even going on.

During the flight over, Daniel had wracked his brain for a convincing argument that might put a stop to all this and make Eric, or at least Mollie, see reason. Rohan wanted Daniel to try, but the truth was that he was just too distracted to be of much use. Louisa was mad at him because he was admittedly being kind of a jerk to her, but for some reason, so was Mollie. She hadn't offered to fly him this time — she'd grabbed Rohan and taken off without another word to Daniel. Michael carried Daniel, and Rose was with . . . somebody. It was hard to know for sure because she was invisible, but Daniel heard her giggling on the flight over, so he knew she must be around here somewhere.

Bud too had insisted on coming along because he wanted to "see the butt kickin'," therefore Eric was left with the unenviable task of carrying the super-stinky bully.

Louisa was angry with him and Daniel knew why. Heck, he probably deserved it, although in his own defense he would've pointed out that Louisa hadn't tried to see him all summer either. Why was he the villain in all this? But more baffling, and more hurtful, was the fact that he'd somehow ticked off Mollie too. Why was it so important to her what happened between him and Louisa? And what had Louisa and Mollie been arguing about anyway? Was it him? Had Mollie made the mistake of standing up for him?

"Women!" Daniel mistakenly said out loud. A large group of academy kids had turned up to watch the fight, and several were watching him now. Was it obvious that he wasn't like them? Did they think he was a *peasant* too? So while everyone waited for the Nobles to show up, Daniel drifted to the back of the crowd. Maybe he could just slip away and go home. Maybe his time would be better spent calling up Louisa and apologizing.

"Hey, Corrigan!" Daniel had just looked up to see who'd

said his name when he felt a shock against his butt. It felt like he'd sat on a live wire.

"Ouch!" he shouted, and looked to see a boy with spiky blond hair leaning against a dented old fridge and smirking at him, his academy tie fashionably askew.

"Hello, Simon," said Daniel.

When Daniel first met Simon, he'd thought the boy created his particular hairstyle with a ridiculous amount of hair gel, but he'd come to realize that the boy's hair looked like that because Simon was basically a human electrical conductor. It hadn't taken him long to become Daniel's least favorite Super because of his habit of jolting people for a laugh. But that hadn't stopped Daniel from trying to save Simon from the Shroud on his thirteenth birthday. Daniel had tried, and failed.

Even now that Simon's powers had returned, Daniel wasn't sure if the boy had forgiven him.

"I didn't know you were going to the academy. We were all wondering what you've been up to."

Simon gave a shrug that said he wasn't much interested in talking about what he'd been up to. But it was obvious—avoiding his old friends was what he'd been up to.

"So," said Simon. "You here to referee this little rumble or what?"

"No," said Daniel. "I don't really know why I'm here, to tell you the truth."

"My money's on Drake and his Nobles."

"You are really going to bet against your friends? I thought you were a Super too."

Simon chuckled. "Sure, back when there were only, like, seven or eight of us on the entire planet. But things have changed around here if you haven't noticed."

"What are you saying?" asked Daniel.

"Forget it," said Simon. "Let me just give you one piece of advice: This isn't your fight. You keep trying to save people when you should be looking out for yourself."

Simon cocked his head to indicate the other students who were standing around waiting. Some faces Daniel recognized; others he didn't. It was weird to think many of the older kids had shared the same school halls as he, and he'd never known they had once been Supers themselves. Others were experiencing their powers for the first time. Not all of them were academy students—not Michael, not Mollie—but wasn't it just a matter of time? Only one person here today really didn't belong, and that was Daniel.

Maybe Simon was right. Maybe this wasn't his fight.

"Yeah, you get it now," said Simon, reading his face correctly. "Not to be harsh, but you don't belong here, Daniel."

Simon turned and began making his way up to the front to get a better look. Before he disappeared into the crowd completely, he turned back to Daniel and said, "You know, I always hated the name *Supers*. You tell Eric that."

As Daniel watched Simon go, he saw that the Nobles had finally arrived. He climbed onto the hood of a busted-up

Model T—no doubt a beautiful car at one time—and watched as the crowd parted for the academy's self-proclaimed royalty. There was that kid Mutt leading the way on all fours, sniffing the ground as he went. Next came Skye, and the one called Hunter. Finally, in walked Drake.

Daniel looked over to where his friends were waiting. Eric, Mollie, Michael, Bud, and even Rohan. Rohan didn't want Eric to do this, and he certainly wasn't any kind of fighter, but he wouldn't abandon his friends either. A splinter of guilt pricked at Daniel for being this far away, far from the action, but something about this felt wrong. It had been something in Simon's attitude, in the faces of the kids watching—they were eager to see the fight. The Supers had stood up to bullies before, but this wasn't about that. When Eric defended Bud in the lunchroom, that may have been the right thing to do. But no one was in any immediate danger now. Eric wasn't defending anyone anymore. This was about pride, about turf.

And this was how they would handle it—by slugging it out in a junkyard? Had Daniel gone through everything— the Shroud, the Shades, losing his grandmother, and very nearly dying himself—to create a world in which might made right? Survival of the fittest? If the Supers went ahead with this fight they would be reinforcing Drake's twisted view of the world—that the rules didn't apply to you if you were strong enough to break them.

If the Supers fought now, they would lose either way.

His friends needed to walk away. Daniel came down off the car hood and began pushing his way toward the front, shoving kids twice his size out of his path in his desperation to reach Eric before the first punch was thrown. All he had to do was put himself between the Supers and the Nobles. His friends wouldn't risk hurting Daniel, and that would give him time to talk sense into everyone.

He'd been so focused on making it to his friends that he hadn't seen the thick-knuckled hand reaching for him until it was too late. It wrapped around the back of his neck like a steel clamp and hauled Daniel off his feet.

Clay! He'd forgotten all about Clay. Bud had said that Clay was still too afraid of Eric to face him, but of course he'd want to see the fight for himself. This was his junkyard after all.

"Not so fast, New Kid," said Clay, pulling Daniel close enough that he could whisper into his ear. "I hope you're not planning to break up the party."

Daniel tried to call out to his friends, but Clay wrapped his other hand over his mouth.

"Why don't you shut up for once?" Clay whispered, as he dragged Daniel back away from the crowd, away from his friends.

A pair of academy boys nearby had noticed what was going on, and looked ready to say something when Clay gave them a hard look. "You two ladies have a problem?" he asked.

The boys went as white as sheets and turned quickly away, pretending not to notice.

"Don't get too comfortable," laughed Clay into Daniel's ear. "This'll be over before you know it. Your friends don't have any idea what they're up against!"

Daniel struggled to free himself from the bully's grip, but it was pointless. He might as well be trying to wriggle free from a steel vise.

Clay dragged him back onto the hood of the Model T and turned him around. All he could do now was watch as a hush fell over the crowd. Eric and Drake walked toward each other until they were standing face to face. Each was flanked by his friends—Supers on one side, Nobles on the other. The air smelled of Bud stink, and Skye looked like she might be sick again. That was something at least.

"Well?" said Drake, loud enough that everyone could hear. "Are we going to have a staring contest, or are you going to do something?"

"I won't throw the first punch," said Eric. A tiny spark of hope kindled in Daniel's chest. It wasn't too late. *Walk away, Eric,* Daniel thought. *Be the bigger man and just walk away. Show them all it's possible.*

"How thoughtful of you," said Drake. Then he looked over Eric's shoulder at Mollie. "Hey, I remember you. You know I let you off easy last time, babe. You owe me one."

"Growl," said Mutt, prowling behind Drake like an animal on the hunt.

"Surprised your Mutt can still walk," said Mollie.

Now a real growl, low and guttural, rumbled out of Mutt's throat.

"Easy, boy," said Drake, shaking his head. "Not until I give the word."

Daniel couldn't believe it but the boy didn't look the least bit nervous. He might as well have been waiting in the lunch line for the special of the day for all he seemed to care.

"All right, then," said Drake. "Word."

Mutt leapt, and just as last time, Mollie moved out of the way so fast that she actually became a blur. But Mutt had learned his lesson and he wasn't leaping for Mollie. This time, he was going for Eric.

Surprised, Eric threw up his hands to protect himself as the feral boy tried to tackle him. Of course, tackling Eric was like tackling a brick wall. Eric looked more annoyed than anything else as Mutt clambered over him, but then Mutt reached with his fingers outstretched and clawed at Eric's face. From their last encounter Daniel knew that those fingers ended in sharp claw-like nails, but even so, Daniel had to wonder what kind of claws could possibly hurt Eric, who was nearly invincible to physical attack.

Indeed, Mutt scraped and gouged at Eric's face but left not even a scratch. Eric was swatting at Mutt like he would a buzzing mosquito, but the nimble boy managed to avoid his blows.

And through it all, Daniel saw what Eric did not. Mutt

hadn't hurt Eric, but he hadn't meant to. He was only distracting him while the real fight happened around them.

Michael had taken to the air, but so had Skye. On her TV show, Skye used her telekinesis powers only to move around small stuff, but she'd apparently been practicing because she lifted herself off the ground to meet Michael eye to eye. And a junkyard, it turned out, was the worst place to fight someone with her kind of power—everything in the vicinity was a potential weapon. With a thought, Skye threw a storm of junk at Michael. Old toasters shot past him with the speed of cannonballs. Rusted hubcaps flew through the air like spinning saw blades. It was all Michael could do to dodge the onslaught of airborne junk. A less talented flier wouldn't have been able to.

Seeing Michael in trouble, Mollie joined the fight and, in a flash of speed, hit Skye with a series of super-fast punches. The TV star let out a yelp as she grabbed at her now-bleeding nose and retreated. Mollie was just getting ready to pursue when a stream of fire cut between her and Skye. Using his flame breath to fill the air above with fire and smoke, Drake managed to drive Mollie and Michael to the ground, where they landed coughing and frantically trying to put out the tiny flames that had caught on their clothes.

Bud had disappeared behind a cloud of impenetrable stink as his instinct for self-preservation kicked in, and it was obvious that he would be as useless to the Supers as he had been to Clay. And it all happened in the few seconds it took Eric to free himself from Mutt's clutches. When the feral boy finally leapt away, Eric stumbled. Eric was left dizzied by the boy's frantic clawing.

So dizzied that he didn't see Hunter appear beside him. The newcomer reached out a hand and grabbed Eric by the shoulder. Just as Eric was getting ready to shake him off, the two of them vanished. There was no flash of light or noise of any kind. It was simply that one second they were there and the next they were gone.

Mollie patted out the last of her fires just in time to see Eric and Hunter vanish, but not in time to see the old garden hose sneaking up on her like a snake in the grass. With a mind of its own, it whipped itself around her, wrapping her up tightly and tying her to the fender of a broken-down pickup truck. Michael tried to pull the hose off her, but found himself pinned under a stack of tires that had ambushed him. Skye reappeared with a triumphant grin, despite her still-bleeding nose.

When Drake's smoke cleared, the fight was over. Hunter reappeared just feet from where he'd grabbed hold of Eric, but Eric was nowhere to be seen.

Rohan was the last man standing. Calmly, he wiped the soot off his glasses with his shirt. It wasn't bravado, Daniel knew. Rohan had to be scared, facing these Nobles who'd so quickly beaten his friends. But no matter how worried he might be, Rohan wouldn't show it. He'd been bullied enough over the years to know that the bullies enjoyed it more when you acted afraid. He could deny them that at least.

"All right," said Rohan. "You've won. Now let them go."

Mutt stalked closer to him, a wide grin exposing his sharp yellow teeth. He actually drooled.

"Of course we won!" said Drake. "We're Nobles."

He turned to the crowd of academy kids. "We're the future! Not those peasants down there in town, or the teachers telling us how to behave—no one can make us do anything we don't want to do, and soon enough, we'll be in charge."

He gestured to Mollie and Michael. "And this is what happens to anyone who gets in our way!"

"Fine, whatever," said Rohan. "Just let my friends go. And bring Eric back."

"Eric?" said Drake. "Hey, Hunter. You know where Eric is?"

Hunter laughed. "Oh, he's taking in the scenery."

A few of the other academy kids laughed too, although it was plain they didn't get the joke any more than Rohan did. But they were scared, and they wanted to make sure that the Nobles knew whose side they were on.

Clay tightened his grip on Daniel's neck, and pain rose up behind his eyes.

"See that?" Clay said. "The Supers are done. Finished."

"Those people down there," Drake was saying. "Doesn't matter what laws they make, what schools they try to make us go to. Doesn't matter if they live or die, because we are better than them! And the sooner you all accept that, the happier you'll be. You are better than they are. . . . And we are better than you!"

Then he walked over to Rohan and grabbed him by his tie. "You first," he said. "Bow to us. Bow to the Nobles and I won't set Mutt here loose on you and your friends."

Then he yanked Rohan's tie and forced the small boy down onto his knees, knocking his glasses off in the process. Mollie let out a shout of anger, but shout was all she could do. She was tied up tight.

All Daniel could do was watch and try to ignore Clay's nasty laughter.

"So," said Drake. "What do you say, kid?"

Still on his knees, Rohan picked up his glasses and put them back on. One side was bent higher than the other, but he didn't bother fixing them.

"What do I say?" said Rohan, blinking at Drake. "I say that if you could hear what I hear, you wouldn't be smiling."

"Aw, he's bluffing," shouted Mutt. "Lemme at them!"

But Drake narrowed his eyes and looked around. "What?" he asked. "What do you hear?"

Rohan shrugged. A gesture Daniel knew well.

"My best guess is . . . detentions. Lots and lots of detentions." And then he covered his ears with his hands.

"What are you—" But Drake didn't finish, because what happened next was impossible *not* to hear. A sound like thunder, like an explosion that burst eardrums. What little junkyard glass hadn't already been shattered did so now as Mount Noble was rocked by a sonic boom.

At first, Daniel thought it was Eric returned from

wherever it was that the Hunter kid had teleported him to. A figure came down from the sky and landed in the middle of the yard like a rocket, sending dirt and garbage flying everywhere. But when Daniel's ears stopped ringing and the dust had cleared, he saw that he was very mistaken. It wasn't Eric at all.

The principal of the Noble Academy for the Gifted straightened his tie and gazed out across the crowd of awestruck students. Although he appeared outwardly calm, his eyes flashed with anger—there was a green glow in the deep recesses of those ancient eyes. Eyes that ultimately came to rest on Drake.

"Would someone care to explain to me," said Johnny, "why you all aren't back at school studying?"

Chapter Fifteen
An Unexpected Hand

"C'mon, New Kid. We're getting out of here."

Daniel was being dragged through the junkyard clearing, hauled to someplace far away from the scene of the fight and from his friends. It had been easy enough for Clay to grab Daniel and run—all eyes were on Johnny at the time. The principal's sudden, and dramatic, appearance had been a shock to everyone.

It made sense that a small-time criminal like Clay could tell when there was about to be trouble with the law. He knew how to read the signs, and he knew when to make a run for it.

Unfortunately, he was taking Daniel with him. Daniel didn't know where, but it couldn't be anyplace good. He'd have asked, but Clay kept one hand firmly planted over Daniel's mouth to prevent him from calling out for help. Still, Daniel didn't go willingly. He fought and he tried to wriggle out of Clay's grip, even as the super-strong kid very nearly squeezed the breath out of him. Beyond fearing for his own safety, Daniel wanted to know what was happening to his friends.

"Stop squirming," said Clay. "'Cause you and me, we're going to have a talk."

They didn't stop until they reached a lonely corner of the junkyard Daniel had never seen before. Once, back in Philadelphia, Daniel's father had taken him to a cemetery to visit the grave of his grandfather on his father's side. As they walked past the grave markers looking for Daniel's grandfather, they wandered into an old section of the cemetery where soldiers were buried. Several graves there dated back to before the Civil War, and those gravestones weren't like the rest. Some were imposing crypts that looked more like stone houses than graves, while others were so small they looked like little more than flat stones in the grass. But what had struck Daniel the most was the age of the place, the sense of time that hung over everything like a cloud. Those graves belonged to another era, the whole place felt old, and Daniel couldn't help but think he was trespassing in someone else's world, the modern boy stumbling over history.

This lonely section of the junkyard was like that cemetery. The rusted-out cars here weren't shaped like modern cars—the corners were too rounded and they possessed none of the sleek curves of today's automobiles. Daniel spotted cast-iron stoves built for burning wood, and there was even what looked like the metal skeleton of a horse-drawn wagon. And like the old section of the cemetery, there was a feeling that Daniel didn't belong. The shadows were too dark, and everything was too old to be welcoming.

Clay carelessly tossed Daniel to the ground, and then started pacing back and forth beneath the stacks of antique junk.

"You know, the first time we met, I treated you fair," said Clay. "Since you weren't from around here, I thought you might be all right. Thought we might even be friends."

Daniel remembered. He also remembered that Clay's way of making friends was to threaten and laugh at them. Daniel had watched the way Clay treated Mollie and Rohan, so of course Daniel had sided with them. Now, however, was probably not the time to correct Clay's memory.

Luckily, Clay didn't seem interested in whether Daniel agreed or not. He just kept on talking.

"From that day on, you caused me nothing but trouble. Things were simple in this town until you came along."

Again, Clay's version of events was skewed in the extreme. The Supers of Noble's Green had been preyed upon by the Shroud until Daniel came along. Clay had even joined them, fighting alongside them the first time they battled the villain. But conveniently Clay skipped that part.

"You got everyone so confused that they didn't know which way was up! All of a sudden there's shadow monsters everywhere, and the next morning—boom!—everyone and his aunt Petunia has powers."

Then Clay stopped pacing. He turned slowly and pointed a long, calloused finger at Daniel's face. "You even got Bud so mixed up that he's wishing he didn't have powers anymore. We were a team, him and me, and you went and ruined that too!"

So that's what this was really about—Clay blamed Daniel for losing his best friend.

"If you care about your friend so much, you really have a weird way of showing it," said Daniel. "I heard about what you did to him in the lunchroom today, Clay."

It probably wasn't wise to antagonize Clay like this, but if Daniel was going to get beaten up, he'd at least like to get beaten up for something he really did, and the truth was he had nothing to do with the break in Clay and Bud's friendship—that was solely Clay's doing.

"Bud used to be able to take a joke! It's not my fault he got his panties all twisted and stank up the place."

Clay might have claimed that his "joke" was no big deal, but Daniel could see in his eyes that not even he believed his own lie. Clay knew what he'd done. He'd watched as a cafeteria full of students laughed at his only friend because of something he'd done just to impress a bunch of kids who thought they were better than him. Better than everyone.

"Now this stupid school," Clay spat, tearing his tie off and throwing it to the ground. "Drake and his stuck-up friends! And that principal. Ain't that a kick in the pants! Man, I know strength when I see it, and that old dude is *strong.*"

Clay took a step toward Daniel. "And here you are, mixed up in it all just like always."

"Clay," Daniel said, scrambling to his feet. Maybe he could get through to him. He was obviously upset about Bud, even if he didn't want to admit it. If Clay actually felt guilty about what he'd done, that might give Daniel an opening. "I don't know what you're thinking of doing, but let's talk about it, okay? You said you wanted to talk."

"Answers," said Clay. "I want answers, but instead of talking, you know what I think I'll do? Beat the answers out of you. More fun that way."

Daniel could run. Clay wasn't super-fast, and he couldn't fly (in fact, he was scared of heights), but where to run to? Clay had him cornered against a stack of old-fashioned iceboxes. The wood had been eaten away in places, and the holes stared down at Daniel like eyes. They were the only witnesses to what was about to happen. Eric wasn't here to save him this time.

"Bud came to us," said Daniel. "He came to the Supers because Eric stood up for him when you wouldn't. But it's not too late to get your friend back. You said it yourself: Drake and his friends think they're better than you. Bud doesn't. He's a real friend."

Clay cracked his knuckles, but he didn't come any closer. His tiny eyes were all scrunched up as if he was struggling with something painful. A thought perhaps.

"Did you talk to Bud—" Clay started to say, but before he could finish, there was a blue flash, followed by a sound like a whip crack, like lightning. Clay's whole body went rigid, his eyes opened wide in surprise. Then he collapsed, the air stinking of ozone and burnt hair.

"Well, well," said Simon, emerging from the shadow of one of the tall towers of junk. "I always wondered if Clay was vulnerable to electricity. Now we know!"

Daniel looked from Simon to Clay's fallen body and back again. He couldn't quite believe what he was seeing.

"You . . . you did this?" asked Daniel.

"Been practicing," said Simon.

Simon walked over and carefully nudged Clay with his toe. "He's out. Good thing too, 'cause after a shock like that, I think I'm gonna need a while to recharge."

Despite Simon's assurances that Clay was out, Daniel stepped carefully past him and quickly put several yards between him and the unconscious bully. He was relieved that Clay wouldn't be pounding him anytime soon, but on the other hand, Daniel had hoped he could talk his way out of it. And if Daniel had to choose between reasoning with a conscious Clay or running from an unconscious one, he'd always choose the latter.

"How'd you find us?" asked Daniel.

"I saw Clay dragging you out of there, and since hanging around didn't seem like such a good idea, I followed you."

"Did you see what happened next?" asked Daniel. "What did . . . Principal Noble do?"

"The last thing I saw was Drake hanging his head like a whipped puppy as Noble lectured him. No way was anyone gonna tangle with that guy. It's like Clay said, you can practically feel that dude's power. It's creepy."

At this, Daniel allowed himself to breathe a small sigh of relief. He'd been afraid that the Nobles might try to fight Johnny, and heaven only knew how that would go. Not even Daniel was really sure what Johnny was capable of, power-wise.

"C'mon," said Simon. "I don't mind zapping Clay when his back's turned and can't prove it was me who did it, but I don't want to be here when he wakes up."

That was the smartest thing Daniel had heard all day. He and Simon walked quickly past the ancient stacks of the old junkyard. For some reason Daniel didn't feel comfortable talking any more than they had to until they were well clear of it. Just like a cemetery, it felt wrong to disturb the silence.

"The way out's through there," said Simon once they'd reached more familiar ground.

"I want to go back to the clearing," said Daniel. "I need to see if my friends are okay."

"Are you nuts? If the Nobles catch you there, you're toast."

Daniel wasn't afraid of the Nobles now that Johnny was on the scene.

"I'm still going," Daniel said.

Simon shook his head. "You're something else, you know that? Why'd I bother saving your butt in the first place?"

"I was wondering the same thing, actually. Why did you?"

"I owed you, remember?"

Daniel did. "I figured you'd blame me for what happened," he said. "Because I didn't save you from the Shroud."

"But you tried," said Simon. "Even though I was kind of a jerk to you, you still tried. Even broke your arm trying, didn't you?"

Daniel nodded. He'd fallen out of Simon's window that night just after catching his first glimpse of the Shroud.

"Look, it's not like we're best buds now," said Simon. "You and Eric and all that do-gooder nonsense still make me want to puke, okay? But I owed you one for that night, and now I don't. We're even."

"So all that stuff you said back there," said Daniel. "All that stuff about not being a Super anymore, that was just talk?"

"Nope," said Simon. "I meant every word of it. Being a Super is worthless now. Drake showed everyone that. And you should still take my advice: This isn't your problem anymore. Leave it to the academy. Johnny will straighten those kids out. You just need to go home."

With that, Simon waved goodbye and headed for Clay's back door, the giant hole in the fence. Daniel walked in the opposite direction, picking his way through the stacks until he reached the clearing. As he went, he listened carefully for any sounds of movement. Who knew when Clay would wake up, and if he'd been mad before, he'd be furious now.

Daniel didn't want to think too hard about that possibility. He needed to check on his friends and get out of there as quickly as he could. But he knew even before he reached the clearing that he was too late. It was quiet—only the whistle of the wind blowing through the junk stacks. As he rounded the corner, the exact spot where Clay had grabbed him, he saw that it was empty. Whatever had taken place here after Johnny arrived, Daniel had missed it.

Footprints crisscrossed everywhere in the garbage-strewn mud, but eventually they all led off in the same direction, toward the front gate. The air here still smelled faintly of smoke, but all of Drake's fires had been put out. A few charred scraps of paper floated on the wind. There was no other sign of what had become of his friends, but Daniel suspected that if he followed those footprints, they'd lead him all the way back to the academy.

There was nothing more to be done here, and it was getting late. There was a trail near Clay's back-door entrance that would take Daniel on a shortcut through the woods and to home. He'd just started for it when he heard a new sound that could not be mistaken for the wind. He heard a girl, crying.

It was soft and muffled, like the sound you make when you cry into your hand or your pillow at night, and it was close by. But Daniel was alone. Unless . . .

"Rose?" Daniel asked cautiously. He didn't want to risk calling out any louder than he had to.

"Yeah," answered a small, sniffly voice from nowhere.

He was right. "What are you doing here?"

"They all left. After the fighting was over, they all left and they forgot about me."

"And were you invisible? Like you are now?"

"Uh-huh."

Daniel sighed. Of course she'd been left behind; no one had even been aware she was there. "You know, Rose, it would be really great if I could, you know, see you when I talk to you."

"Uh-uh. Don't wanna."

Daniel sighed again. It was pointless to argue. "Then can you at least tell me where you're standing? So I could face you?"

He nearly jumped when he felt a tiny hand give his arm a tug. She was right next to him.

"Great, thanks," said Daniel.

Rose was quiet for a moment. Daniel listened for the

sounds of anyone approaching. It wasn't safe to stay there for much longer, but he didn't want to scare off Rose again. If she got lost while invisible, it would be nearly impossible for anyone to find her.

"Daniel," she said.

"Yeah?"

"Why was everyone fighting?"

Daniel opened his mouth to say that Eric was standing up to bullies and that his friends were helping him. That the Supers were helping people like they always did.

In the end all he could say was "I don't know."

"I saw Johnny Noble, Daniel," she said. "I saw Johnny, and he took everyone back to the academy."

Daniel remembered that Rose had seen Johnny once before, back in the Old Quarry when Johnny had secretly healed Eric after his fight with the Shroud.

"Johnny looked real mad," she said. "He made that one kid bring Eric back from wherever he'd disappeared him to. Iowa, I think he said."

Well, at least Eric was back unharmed. Not like he had been in any immediate peril, apparently. Hunter might have been able to teleport him anywhere—over a live volcano, Antarctica. Iowa wasn't so bad.

"What's Johnny doing here?" asked Rose.

"He's . . . he's the principal."

"Huh?"

"C'mon, I'll explain everything to you, but we need to

get going. It's not a good idea to hang around here, even for invisible girls."

Eventually, Rose slipped her invisible hand into Daniel's, and the two of them snuck out through the back of the junkyard. There wasn't any sign of Clay, although whether this was because he was still unconscious or because he'd already fled himself, Daniel didn't know.

What he did know was that it had been a long day full of confusion and frustration, and that the only clear thing to do right now was to make sure Rose got home safe and sound.

The rest could wait.

Chapter Sixteen
Heartbreak

Daniel did make sure that Rose got home safely, but his courage nearly failed him when they reached her house. After all he'd been through that day already, the thought of facing Louisa again was almost more than he could handle. In the end, he figured it would be worse to have Louisa know that he'd walked her little sister home but had been too cowardly to actually see her to the front door. And maybe Louisa wasn't even there. Maybe Rose would just say goodbye and Daniel could slink away, pretending that his dignity was still intact.

But it was not to be. As soon as Rose opened the door,

she shouted, "Mom, I'm home!" followed quickly by, "Louisa, come see who I brought with me!"

Rose's mom appeared in the hallway, clutching a phone to her ear, her face pale with concern. "Rose!" she cried. "Where have you been? I've been worried sick!"

She had thrown her arms around her youngest daughter before remembering that she still had a phone to her ear, and said, in a considerably lower voice, "Oh, sorry, Sheriff Simmons. No, she's just walked in now. Yes, yes, I will. Thank you."

"Hi, Mom," said Rose.

Daniel saw Louisa hanging back at the end of the hallway, watching.

"Where have you been?" said Rose's mom, her relief swiftly turning to anger.

"Everyone left without me," said Rose.

"Rose, were you invisible?"

Rose nodded.

"Oh, Rose. How many times do I need to tell you—no one can help you if they can't see you, sweetheart."

"Daniel found me," said Rose. "He walked me home."

Rose's mom looked up at Daniel as if noticing him for the first time. "Daniel! Oh well, thank goodness for that! I feel like I should offer you a reward."

"Oh, don't worry about it, Mrs. Rodriguez," said Daniel. "It was on my way."

"Come on, then, Rose," said Rose's mom, shooing her

into the kitchen. "Let's get you something to eat. You must be starving."

Rose and her mother disappeared and left Daniel with Louisa. It was the first time they'd actually been alone together since the infamous kiss.

"Thanks for bringing Rose home," she said. "Mom was really worried. I'm in loads of trouble for coming home without her."

"No problem," said Daniel.

"Do you want to take a walk?" she asked.

"Oh, why?" Daniel said, feeling a warmth rise to his cheeks. "I mean if you want to."

Louisa made a face, and brought her hand up to her nose. "It's just . . . Have you been rummaging through garbage or . . ."

"Huh? Oh! We were in the junkyard!" After a day spent with Bud, and being tossed around the junkyard, Daniel could only imagine how he smelled. Actually, he didn't have to imagine; all he had to do was lift his shirt to his nose to get a whiff.

"Sure, let's walk," said Daniel, anxious now to get outside. No wonder Mrs. Rodriguez had taken Rose away so fast.

They stepped outside as Daniel apologized for the stink.

"Don't worry about it," said Louisa. "But I guess you probably should be getting home."

"Yeah. My parents kind of freak out these days if I'm even a minute late."

"I know the feeling. C'mon, I'll walk you down the block."

They crossed the Rodriguezes' immaculately manicured lawn in silence and turned onto the street. The street lights would be buzzing to life soon.

"So, did they fight?" asked Louisa. "Eric and Drake?"

"Sort of," said Daniel. "In the end it was Supers versus Nobles, thanks to Mollie leaping into it."

Daniel saw Louisa stiffen at the mention of Mollie's name. What was going on between those two?

"But Drake and his Nobles, they kind of kicked the Supers' butts."

Louisa looked shocked. "Is everyone okay?"

"I think so. Johnny showed up and put an end to it before it got too serious, I think."

"Wow," said Louisa. "How old is he now?"

"Gotta be nearly a hundred. But you'd never know it."

"Where's he been all this time?" said Louisa. "And why'd he come back now?"

"He's not what we thought," Daniel said. "He's trying to do some good, I think. At least I hope he is. But Johnny's no superhero. He's not a villain either. He's just a guy who happened to be in the wrong place at the wrong time."

Johnny had said almost those exact words to Daniel once before, and Daniel supposed he was finally coming to accept it. Johnny had been a real hero the night of the St. Alban's fire. He'd rushed into a burning building to save those kids, but did that mean he had to be a hero forever? Daniel wondered if anyone had what it takes to live up to that kind of expectation their whole life, especially when they lived to be a hundred.

But Johnny wasn't what either one of them wanted to be talking about. Not really. They walked together for a while longer before Daniel finally worked up the courage to apologize. In some ways, it was harder than facing down the Shroud.

"Louisa, I'm sorry I . . . haven't been around. Haven't called or anything."

"Okay."

"It's just that, we're such great friends, and I don't know if being more than that is a good idea."

Louisa surprised him with a laugh. "You are something else, Daniel Corrigan."

"Wha— Huh?"

"All this time, you've been avoiding me because you didn't want to be my boyfriend?"

"Well . . . Uh."

"Did I ever ask you to be my boyfriend?"

"No. I guess not."

"You're cute, Daniel. Cuter than you think, but here you are walking around telling everyone you're the world's greatest detective and you don't have a clue."

"Hey, I never said I was the world's greatest anything!" said Daniel. Then, "You really think I'm cute?"

Louisa took Daniel's hand in hers. "We, all of us, all the Supers, owe you so much. You stuck your neck out for us again and again, and I will always be thankful. But I gave up on the idea of us being more than friends months ago. I moved on, Daniel."

"But . . ." Although Daniel tried to catch up with what Louisa was saying, it wasn't working. His brain had gone sluggish on him. "But then why have you been acting all mad at me?"

Louisa let go of his hand, and did a very Mollie thing. She punched him. In the arm, and a lot more playfully than Mollie would've, but it still smarted.

"Hey!"

"I've been mad at you because you will barely look at me! We were friends before we kissed, and I was hoping we would be friends after, Daniel."

"Of course! No, Louisa, of course I want to be friends. That was exactly my point, I just—"

"—walked around for the last six months thinking I was pining away for you? Afraid to talk to me because you didn't want to break my fragile heart?"

"Eh, when you put it like that . . ."

"Promise me you won't be this thickheaded again, Daniel. Promise me that we are still friends, okay?"

"I promise."

"And promise me that you won't act like a wood post with the next girl you kiss."

"Okay. I guess."

Louisa took Daniel's hand again in hers, and this time, she shook it. "Settled," she said. "We're friends. Now I better get back."

"Okay."

Louisa smiled and began walking toward her perfect white house. She hadn't gone very far, though, before she called over her shoulder. "I hope you two know what you're getting into," she said. "You're both bordering on hopeless!"

You two? What was she talking about?

She left Daniel standing on the side of the street, happy that they were friends again, but more confused than ever.

Rohan had been right, and the fight in the junkyard had earned two weeks of detentions, plus probation, for every academy student present. Days passed and there were no more attacks, and Daniel began to think Simon might have been right about the Nobles—he should just let Johnny sort them out. For once, it looked like someone else would end up saving the day.

Meanwhile, if there was a soul left in Noble's Green who didn't know by now that Johnny Noble was the academy's principal, that person had to be living in a cave. After Johnny's flashy appearance at the junkyard, plenty of parents heard about Principal Noble, and it didn't take long for people to put two and two together. Every day the papers were filled with wild speculations about Johnny: Was this the original Johnny Noble, and if so, where had he been all these years? Why was he here now? Did he even have a degree in education?

Thus far, Johnny had turned down all interview requests, and the academy had made it very clear that the school was a reporter-free zone. Nevertheless, cell phone videos of Johnny began popping up online with the tag *Nobleacademy* or *Johnnylives*. But from what Daniel could see, they were all rather disappointing videos of Johnny telling students to run to class, or to put away their phones. It turned out that being a super-principal looked pretty much like being an ordinary principal.

Meanwhile, Mollie began falling behind again in Smiley's history class. Although she wasn't a student at the academy, and therefore Johnny couldn't punish her for her part in the junkyard brawl, she still seemed depressed. She and Daniel kept up their tutoring sessions when they could find the time, but Mollie's heart wasn't in it, and more and more of their study sessions ended with her shouting and Daniel getting bruised. All they did was argue.

Whether this was because of the pressure of the upcoming final or because of her fight with Louisa, Daniel wasn't sure. But he couldn't forget what Louisa had said, or at least what he'd thought she'd said. *I hope you two know what you're getting into.* Who? He and Mollie? Did Louisa think there was something going on between them more than friendship? That was absurd. That was ludicrous. That was . . . all Daniel could think about.

Without the Nobles to worry about, Daniel's mind needed something new to obsess over, and that new thing turned out to be Mollie.

What if? What if instead of hitting him all the time, Mollie kissed him instead? His kiss with Louisa had been nice, if a bit terrifying and sweaty, and he couldn't help but suspect that kissing Mollie would be even nicer. He thought about it—a lot. He thought about it when he was supposed to be writing down Smiley's notes from the board; he thought about it when he was yelling at Georgie for playing in Daniel's room without asking. His imagination was so preoccupied with the dream Mollie that it was always a guilty shock to see the real Mollie in person. Like a criminal with a secret, he became paranoid and worried that she might somehow read his mind and see all those thoughts—those kissing thoughts, those fantasies where he was the one saving her for once. And what would she think then? Something had happened between Mollie and Louisa, and maybe it had to do with Daniel, but then again maybe it hadn't. How was he to know?

In the end, and with only one day to go before the big final, Daniel put down his books and consulted the wisest person he knew. It was time for some love advice.

• • •

It was well past dinnertime when Rohan came online. It seemed detention at the academy was no laughing matter. Daniel had just finished spilling his guts to Rohan, and was anxiously watching the little word bubble on his computer screen for his friend's reply. He steeled himself for any number of possible reactions. It could be disbelief. More likely, Rohan would just laugh in Daniel's face and hit him with an array of snarky emoticons.

"So?" Daniel finally typed after a minute of watching the screen for nothing.

"So what?" came Rohan's reply. "So, how's detention? Terrible. Eric pouts while Drake passes notes to his idiot friends. Think they are drawing unflattering pictures of me to kill time."

"About Mollie," typed Daniel. He suspected Rohan was trying to give him a heart attack.

"Oh. Well, I think I've been waiting for this to happen since, like, that first day at the bus stop."

"Wait," typed Daniel. "This is a new thing!"

"No, it's not," came Rohan's reply. "Doesn't take super-senses to see that Mollie and you have something between you. Always have. By the way, this chat is boring boring boring."

Daniel ignored the last part. "So you think she likes me?"

"Ask her," came the reply.

"You crazy?"

"Nope. Man up. Ask her."

"Ask her?" Daniel said out loud. Was Rohan crazy? Had the academy driven him insane? What a stupid idea.

"Ask her!" he said again.

"Ask who what?" said a voice from outside the open window.

Mollie was floating there with her head cocked at Daniel like a confused puppy.

"Why are you talking to your computer?" she asked. "You on with Eric and Rohan?"

"What? No!" said Daniel, closing the chat window just as Rohan was describing the various ways that talking to Mollie might lead to kissing Mollie. Nope, no way Mollie could see that. Uh-uh.

Then Daniel powered down his computer for good measure.

"Okay," said Mollie. "What'd you shut down your computer for? Afraid I'd see your 'Nerdy Friends of Sherlock Holmes' website?" Mollie let herself in (through the window) and sat down on the edge of his bed.

"Ha-ha," said Daniel. "'Nerdy Sherlock' website. Good one."

"You know, that wasn't a laugh-with-you kind of joke; that was a laugh-*at*-you kind of joke. You're in a weird mood, aren't you?" She tossed a pillow at him, which Daniel barely managed to catch. He gave her a kind of shrug/nod. Staying nonverbal felt like the best strategy for the time being.

Mollie didn't bother to remove her backpack, which she had slung over her shoulder. She just sat there on the bed, watching him. He'd never really noticed before, but her eyes were so dark in this light. It made her look exotic.

Exotic? His brain needed to shut up.

Daniel tried to act casual, but he no longer had any idea what to do with his body. It was like an alien thing to him, awkward and ungainly. He stood up and tried to lean against his bookshelf, in the kind of cool, relaxed pose he'd seen Eric use so many times. Maybe it was because Daniel was still holding the pillow she'd tossed at him, or maybe it was just the fact that he would never be cool, but he ended up looking like a toddler sent to the corner, clutching his comfort pillow. His leg was starting to cramp, but he didn't want to change position again. He was fidgeting enough as it was.

"Daniel, seriously, are you okay?" she asked. "Why are you standing like that?"

"Just getting comfortable," he said as he shifted the pillow to his other arm. Why was he still holding that stupid pillow?

"Well, I wanted to ask you for a favor."

A favor? That was not what Daniel was expecting her to say. He'd hoped, in a wild fantasy-type way, that she was here to profess her undying love for him.

"Sure," he said. "What's up?"

With a sigh, Mollie dug into her backpack and produced a heavy, well-worn textbook. Doodles of a donkey-faced teacher decorated the sides.

"Will you help me cram for tomorrow's final?"

Chapter Seventeen
The Fire

He woke up the next morning still exhausted from their marathon study session. Over the course of one evening, Daniel had tried to recap weeks' worth of lessons, and it hadn't gone well. Daniel was distracted and Mollie turned impatient early on. She'd snap at him for going too slow; then when it came time to demonstrate that she'd understood, she'd miss a step and end up crumpling her paper in anger.

At first, Daniel found that sitting so close to her, sharing the same book, made it even harder to concentrate on what he was telling her. Those kissing fantasies kept getting in the way. But after she'd lobbed the book at his head in frustration for the fourth or fifth time, his infatuation turned to exasperation, and finally, aggravation. By the end of the evening he didn't want to kiss her so much as strangle her.

Worst of all, he genuinely feared she might not pass the test. She'd simply fallen too far behind to catch up now.

He'd woken up the next morning too late to bike to school and was forced to ride the slow bus instead. He half hoped that he might find Mollie waiting for him at the bus stop, just like old times, but she wasn't there.

When Daniel finally walked into Smiley's class, Mollie was already at her desk, and though she nodded at him as he walked by, they didn't say anything. Her mood didn't seem that out of place, however. There was an anxious pall over the entire class. Everyone knew what was at stake here.

Smiley set a timer and wrote "90 minutes" on the board. Then they were instructed to take up their pencils and begin.

At the thirty-minute mark, Mollie put down her pencil and walked her paper to Smiley's desk. Daniel had to stop himself from whispering *What are you doing?* to her as she gathered up her things. Any talking during the final would result in an immediate failing grade. Daniel watched her as she slung her backpack over her shoulder. Maybe she'd taken the test at super-speed? Maybe last night's study session had just needed time to sink in?

They made eye contact briefly as she headed out the door, and in that instant he saw that he'd been wrong. The tears pooling in her eyes told him everything. She'd bombed the test.

Mollie Lee wouldn't be going to high school next year with Daniel after all.

After Mollie walked out, Daniel very nearly didn't finish his own test. His instinct had been to run after her, to try in his awkward way to console her, but if he did that, he too would fail. He couldn't bear to see the disappointment in his parents' faces if that happened, and besides, he knew what Mollie would do if he did throw the test just to chase after her—she'd break his nose. Nothing would make her angrier than knowing Daniel had flunked history for her. She wouldn't see it as chivalrous; she'd see it as stupid. So he struggled with the last hour of the final and had to read most questions over more than once, forcing his brain to stop thinking about Mollie and focus on the task at hand. He was filling in the last answer when the bell rang. He hadn't done as well as he'd expected to, but he hoped he'd done well enough.

Although he knew she was long gone, he tore out of the classroom the minute the bell rang. In the halls he looked for her face among the crowds, a flash of silver earrings against black hair.

He made it to the parking lot, but of course she wasn't

there. Downhearted, he had just dragged himself over to the bike rack when he remembered that he hadn't ridden to school that day; he'd taken the bus. This realization came as the yellow bus was already pulling out of the parking lot, to deliver the survivors of today's finals like shell-shocked soldiers home from the war.

What a perfect end to a terrible day. Now he would have to walk the two hours it would take to get home from here, or call one of his parents at work. He was still trying to make up his mind when he heard a car pulling up behind him. A glance over his shoulder revealed a limousine rolling slowly his way.

Heads turned as the long black car came to a stop just feet from Daniel. He didn't move. He didn't try to escape, even though he knew who was in there waiting for him. To the contrary, he walked right up to the car, bold as could be. Herman Plunkett had picked the wrong day if he was hoping to intimidate Daniel. If he couldn't take out his frustration on Smiley or Mollie or his own awkward, foolish heart, then Herman would just have to do.

As Daniel approached, the back door swung open seemingly by itself, and he heard Herman's sandpapery voice.

"I was afraid we'd missed you."

Herman was alone. His black clothes disappeared against the dark leather seats, so that it looked like he was nothing more than a ghostly white head, floating above a pair of curled, arthritic hands.

"What do you want, Herman?"

"I want to give you a ride if you'll let me," he said. "Unless you're scared I will kidnap you. It's not too late to yell *Stranger danger,* you know." Herman chuckled at his mean little joke.

"I'd rather walk," said Daniel.

"Fine. Since we're done being polite," said Herman, losing all patience, "get in or I'll have Lawrence up there toss you in."

Daniel looked over at the driver's seat and saw a dragon tattoo crawling up the back of a bald head. Lawrence's eyes were watching him in the reflection of the rearview mirror.

"You'd throw me into your car in front of all these witnesses?" asked Daniel. There were at least twenty kids gathered around, struggling to get a good look inside the car.

Herman smiled and waved at them like some kind of movie star. "I'll do what I please," he said, still smiling. "You of all people should know this by now. Come on, my boy. I only want to talk."

If Herman had wanted to hurt Daniel, this wasn't the way he'd do it. Daniel believed him when he said he wanted to talk, but that was the problem. Sometimes with Herman Plunkett, talking was the most dangerous thing you could do.

Still, his anger over the test and over Mollie was making him feel reckless, and in the end Daniel's curiosity got the better of him, just as Herman no doubt knew it would.

He took a seat on the side opposite from Herman, as far away from the old man as he could possibly get without hanging out of the car.

"You have moxie, I'll give you that," said Herman. "Your grandmother had it too. Eileen wasn't afraid of anything."

If Daniel had known they were going to talk about his gram, then he wouldn't have gotten in the car. Everything Herman did was an affront to her memory.

Instead, Daniel pointed to the tablet in Herman's lap. The screen was a field of stars.

"Nice screen saver," said Daniel. "You taking up astronomy?"

"Old men need hobbies," answered Herman, closing the tablet cover.

"Or are you still searching for your comet?" Daniel asked. Herman had once shown him the paintings hidden deep within the caves beneath Mount Noble. The people who lived there long ago had a legend about a comet of green fire, the Witch Fire Comet, which appeared every few generations.

"When the comet last streaked through the sky over Noble's Green, it left eight children and one ignorant woodsman with godlike powers," said Herman. "Not like these floating firemen, or even your super-friends. Do you think the world's ready for that?"

Herman had a way of recasting himself as the hero in these hypothetical scenarios. Again and again he'd rationalized all the repulsive things he'd done as being in the service of some greater good. The old man had said goodbye to reality long ago.

"I think," said Daniel, "that you'd sell your soul for a chance to get your Shroud powers back, and I bet you stare at the stars every night just praying to see a glimpse of green light in the sky."

Herman's eyes narrowed and Daniel imagined he could see the hate glittering there, reflecting like a cat's eyes in the dark.

"You'd lose that bet," said Herman after a moment. "I don't stare up at the stars. I pay other people to do it for me."

Daniel laughed in spite of himself. In this at least, Herman was probably telling the truth.

"All right, Lawrence," said Herman, calling up to the front of the limousine. "And you, put your seat belt on. Lawrence drives like he just got out of prison. Which, incidentally, he did."

Daniel saw Lawrence glaring at them in the mirror as he put the car into drive, but whether that look was meant for Daniel or Herman he couldn't tell.

"I think I liked your old nurse better," said Daniel. He went ahead and buckled himself in, even though it felt a little bit like putting on his own handcuffs.

"I'm going to pay my dear estranged relatives a visit today," said Herman. "See about kicking those freeloaders out of my house."

"Shouldn't be a problem," said Daniel. "Theo's not crazy

about living there, especially since he learned what you really are."

"He's a Plunkett. He should get used to disappointment," said Herman. "But enough about my unsavory relations and phantom comets. How's your little investigation going? The Case of the Sabotaged Sweets Shop?"

Plunkett was openly sneering, his disdain for Daniel's detective work plain to see. But Daniel wouldn't take the bait.

"The ones who vandalized Lemon's shop also tore apart the high school," said Daniel.

"And you know who did it?"

Daniel looked Plunkett in the eye. "It's out of my hands."

"Then I'm no longer a suspect?" asked Herman. "You found another *bad guy*?"

"I think there are a lot of strange things going on in this town," said Daniel. "And I know you well enough to know that you are probably up to your armpits in most of them."

"Hah!" barked Plunkett. "I am no more responsible for those silly acts of vandalism than I am for the sudden and most inconvenient return of my arch-nemesis!"

Daniel gave Herman a look. With everything that had been going on, he hadn't stopped to think about what Herman might make of Johnny's return.

"Oh yes," said Herman. "The good Principal Noble. What do you think he's really up to with that school of his? Certainly you've wondered, haven't you?"

Herman leaned across the seat and took off his tinted glasses, as if he wanted to get a good look at Daniel. Once again, Daniel was struck by the old man's eyes. So clear, so bright, like Johnny's. Only something else showed there as well—something fearful. It was why the old man usually hid them behind a pair of dusty spectacles or tinted shades. Those eyes couldn't be trusted.

"Why is Johnny here?" asked Plunkett. "Why now, after all these years?"

Johnny was teaching. Or at least helping others teach. Daniel believed Johnny now, though whether it would work was another matter altogether. The important thing, Daniel guessed, was that Johnny was trying. And if he couldn't get Drake and his friends to fall in line, there was always Eric and Rohan. They might get some evidence on them yet.

Of course, Herman needed to know none of it.

"If I knew why he was here," said Daniel, "what makes you think I'd tell you?"

Herman steepled his fingers under his chin and grinned.

"Exchange of information," said Herman. "I'm aware you and Johnny had a talk, and I want to know what it was about. Tell me and I can give you the proof you seek regarding those unfortunate attacks."

So Herman was looking to bargain. He might very well have evidence against Drake. After all, he'd been compiling files on the Supers for years. But he could have a signed confession from Drake and Daniel wouldn't take it. Not from Herman. Not ever.

"Nothing happens in this town that I'm not aware of," said Herman. "You know that."

"Uh-huh," said Daniel. "Yet you don't know what Johnny and I talked about. Maybe we were talking about you?"

Herman's grin disappeared.

Yes, thought Daniel. *How's it feel not to have all the answers for once?* He'd just given Herman a taste of his own bitter medicine.

"Are you enjoying yourself?" asked Herman.

"I'm starting to," said Daniel. "Especially because I don't need your help with the vandalism. I know all about the Nobles and what they're up to."

"Nobles?" Herman said. "What are you talking about?"

Plunkett looked, for the moment, genuinely puzzled. Herman's feigned surprise was such a bravura performance that Daniel almost clapped. But they were interrupted as Lawrence called back to them.

"Mr. Plunkett?"

"Yes, Lawrence," said Herman irritably. "What is it?"

"You'd better see for yourself," said Lawrence.

With a sigh, Herman stabbed one bony finger at a button on the car door and the window slowly rolled down. They were approaching the entrance to Cedar Drive, the private street that led to the Plunkett estate. The mansion wasn't visible from the road, but the sky above was black with smoke.

"My house!" cried Plunkett. "Lawrence, drive!"

Lawrence turned the limo into Cedar on two wheels, and Daniel was very glad he'd taken Herman's advice about the seat belt.

As they sped up the road, Daniel pulled out his phone and dialed 911. He couldn't care less about Herman's home, but his friend Theo lived there.

He'd just finished shouting the address to the 911 operator as she calmly informed him that the fire trucks were already on their way. Lawrence stopped the car at the bottom of the driveway, but the mansion, or what was left of it, was unrecognizable. Its entire lower two floors were an inferno. Flames were licking up to the top floor, and so much smoke was billowing out that the air inside the limo already tasted of it. Nevertheless, Herman hauled himself from the car the minute they'd stopped, not bothering to wait for his man to help him. Daniel slid out the side and followed.

At once Daniel was beaten back by the wall of heat pouring off the giant mansion. He was amazed at how hot it was this far away, almost unbearable. He could only imagine what the temperatures were inside.

There was a sudden shattering of glass as a window on the top floor exploded, and a hand wrapped in a towel began waving frantically for help. Someone was alive up there.

Daniel looked around, as if he could find anything that could help him fight a massive fire like this. Where were those fire trucks?

"Lawrence!" shouted Herman, grabbing his man by the collar. "Get in there! You have to save them!"

"I'm not going in there!" said Lawrence. "You crazy?"

Herman took his cane in his hand like a bat. "My family is in there! My *only* family!" The old man swung the cane at Lawrence, but the big bodyguard hardly flinched as he was smacked across his broad shoulders. He was not moving.

Daniel took a few steps forward, but the heat was just too much. There wasn't anything he or Lawrence could do.

As he cupped his hands over his stinging eyes, he saw a shape in the grass, halfway between the car and the house. There was a person lying there, unmoving.

Daniel threw his arms over his face to shield himself as best he could from the heat and ran forward.

"Lawrence!" Daniel shouted. "Help me!"

Daniel's lungs burned as he choked on the smoke and he could hardly see for the tears stinging his eyes, but he kept his head down and made his way to the still figure—a plump man in a fireman's uniform, his chief's hat nowhere to be seen. Mr. Madison, the floating fire chief, was lying unconscious in the grass.

"Mr. Madison, wake up!" shouted Daniel, yet there was no response. His face was blackened with soot, but he was breathing. He had burns on his hands, and Daniel wondered if the floating fire chief hadn't tried to rescue whoever was still in there before succumbing to the smoke himself.

"Let me," shouted a voice behind Daniel, and then

Lawrence was at his side, trying to haul the chief's limp body onto his shoulders.

"He's heavy," said Lawrence. "Give me a hand."

In the end, Daniel wasn't sure he'd actually helped at all, but the two of them managed to get Mr. Madison atop Lawrence's back and run.

Clear of the worst of the smoke, they toppled together at Herman's feet, gasping for breath.

"Who cares about him?" said Plunkett, eyeing the fire chief with disgust. "Who'll save my family?"

Daniel looked back at the burning house, at the broken window on the top floor. But it was now empty. Whoever was up there had stopped waving.

Then Daniel's ears rang with a different sound, a familiar thunderclap, and while he watched, a hole exploded in the top floor of the house, sending flaming debris onto the grass below. Something had flown into the mansion, tearing a door-sized hole in the front.

It was as if the mansion had been hit with cannon fire. Seconds passed before another object hit the side of the house, shaking the already tremulous flaming timbers. Then a man came flying out of the house with a person cradled in his arms.

Johnny landed on the lawn next to Daniel and gently laid Theo's mother on the grass. She was coughing, filthy with soot, but alive. Tiny flames licked the edges of Johnny's suit coat, although he barely seemed to notice.

Eric burst out through another wall, carrying Theo. The young man was in worse shape than his mother, and he held a blistered hand to his chest, but when Eric tried to set him down, he grabbed Eric by the collar and pulled him close. Through hacking coughs and tears of pain, he whispered something into Eric's ear.

In an instant, Eric was flying back to the house, smashing his way once more into the raging inferno. Johnny started to follow, but Eric quickly reappeared carrying a shaggy, slobbery dog in his arms. Someone had wrapped a wet towel around the dog's head to help protect him from the smoke.

Theo threw his uninjured arm around the dog and in a hoarse voice said, "Good boy, Bernard. Good boy."

The fire trucks were coming up the drive just as the mansion started to collapse in on itself. It sent a shower of sparks into the sky, and they looked for a moment like a thousand fireflies taking flight.

"What's happened to Mr. Madison?" asked Johnny, bending down over the chief.

"I don't know," said Daniel. "I think he was first on the scene and tried to help."

The chief opened his eyes in between ragged coughs and struggled to speak. "Arson . . . ," he said. "Saw him running . . ."

He couldn't continue. Just breathing looked like an agony.

"The burns aren't serious but he's inhaled a lot of smoke,"

said Johnny. He gently scooped the fire chief up in his arms, lifting him as easily as if the heavy man were a baby. "I need to get him to a hospital."

"Can't you help him?" asked Daniel. He remembered last year when Johnny had used his power to heal Daniel's injured fingers—fingers he'd broken against Johnny's marble-like face.

"I . . . He's too badly hurt. I can only heal small things, remember?"

They were interrupted by the roaring of an engine coming to life, and they turned to see Herman sitting inside his limousine, one hand on the open back door. For a moment, Herman and Johnny locked eyes, and something inexplicable passed between them. Daniel wondered when was the last time they'd seen each other. Was it when they'd fought, over half a century ago?

Who knew what the two men were thinking now?

Without a word, Herman slammed the door and Lawrence steered the car away from the ruined house and out of sight.

"I have to go," said Johnny, and Daniel followed his gaze to see that news vans were right behind the fire trucks, and camera crews were unloading their equipment in a hurry.

Johnny sprang into the air with Mr. Madison in his arms, and then he was gone.

Daniel turned to Eric. "That was amazing."

"We were in detention when all of a sudden Rohan

jumped up from his desk," said Eric. His clothes were ruined and his face blackened, but he appeared unhurt. "He'd
heard the trucks, and he said that someone was calling for
help. Johnny didn't even hesitate. He told me to follow him
and took off into the sky. Right out the window—it was
awesome!"

"This is bad," said Daniel, looking back at the mansion
in flames. The firefighters were doing their best, aiming
their hoses at the blaze, but the house was lost. "People almost died. Theo, his mom. Good thing his grandpa is overseas with his dad."

"What do you think happened?" asked Eric.

"You heard the chief. He said it was arson."

"Yeah."

"It was Drake, Eric!" said Daniel. "It had to have been,
and he's gone way too far this time."

Eric blinked at him for a second and then said, "But,
Daniel, didn't you hear what I just said? I came from detention. With the Nobles. Every last one of them. There's no
way they could have done this."

Daniel had forgotten. The Nobles were serving detention together with Eric and Rohan. But if Drake's Nobles
didn't set this fire, then who did?

Theo and his mother were sitting inside an ambulance,
being administered oxygen from a tank. Bernard had his
head in Theo's lap, and his tail was still wagging, despite the
fact that he was now missing a few patches of fur. A TV heli-

copter was slowly circling the scene, capturing images of the destruction for the evening broadcast.

Then Daniel and Eric were surrounded by reporters shoving microphones into their faces, and they were trapped in the glare of lights as a phalanx of cameras descended upon them. It looked like they were about to become news.

Chapter Eighteen
Headlines

What amazed Daniel was not what was being said about the Supers, but how quickly the things being said had changed. On the six o'clock news, the Supers were being hailed as heroes. Every station broadcast images of Kid Noble (as they were calling Eric) and an as yet unidentified sidekick (that would be Daniel) who had saved the respectable Plunkett family from perishing in a fire. Although Eric and Daniel had declined to comment, there were enough dramatic images of the destruction that people started to create their own narrative—the town's most prominent family is threatened by a terrible fire, only to be rescued by two young people with remarkable gifts. It was a human interest story. Warm and fuzzy—an inspirational tale. It was, in short, exactly the kind of story that people were sick of.

By the time the ten o'clock news came on, the story had already begun to morph into something else. New details were emerging about the fire, and it was rumored that the floating fire chief was in intensive care after having spotted an arsonist at the scene. And at least one station was running with a story provided by an "inside source" who claimed that the fire had been the work of teenage delinquents, even though the chief hadn't gotten a good enough look at the perpetrator to identify his or her age. Nobody was accusing anyone of anything yet, but lots of questions were being asked.

By morning, the headline in the paper said it all. On one side of the page was a picture of Mr. Madison lying in his hospital bed, attached to tubes and his hands bandaged. (Daniel wondered how the reporters had gotten that particular shot.) On the opposite side was a grainy black-and-white picture of Eric and Daniel standing in front of the burning mansion. Across the top of the page was the banner headline:

SUPER-FRIENDS OR FOES?

Less than twenty-four hours, that was all it took for them to go from lauded heroes to suspected villains. That was all the time it took for a town to turn on its own. Daniel saw it first-hand at his own breakfast table. Last night his parents had been worried about their son, but also proud of him. Never mind that Daniel's story was full of holes (he told them he'd decided to stop by to visit his friend Theo, skipping the part about how he actually got there). And it didn't matter when he pointed out that Johnny and Eric had actually saved the Plunketts from the fire. When they said good night to Daniel, it had been with kisses of pride and tearful admonitions that he be more careful next time—he wasn't indestructible like his friend Eric, you know.

By morning they'd read the papers and called the editors to complain that their son wasn't one of *those kids* (there was that phrase again) and would they please stop using his image in their stories about them. It wasn't long before his parents were musing out loud if Eric might get Daniel hurt one of these days. The town had changed so quickly, and no one was really comfortable with that much power in the hands of people so young. Maybe Daniel should at least consider making friends more like him. Powerless.

It was easier, Daniel supposed, to defend their son by damning his friends. Parents always overestimated the influence peers had on their kids—as if they'd raised ciphers incapable of making up their own minds, of taking responsibility for their actions. Daniel had seen it so many times before, how someone's child, who was a complete angel, had "fallen in with the wrong crowd." Daniel thought it much more likely that their fallen angel hadn't fallen in with the wrong crowd; he'd just found the crowd that suited him best. He'd discovered his own.

But in Daniel's case, his own were good, decent kids, and now the town was trying to make them all out to be budding criminals. A match had been lit in the public's collective imagination, and their opinion of these super-kids was burning as fast as Plunkett's mansion. This "inside source" that everyone was quoting was just stoking the flames.

"It's Herman," said Daniel. "I know it."

It had been two days since the fire, and the charred timbers of Plunkett's ruined mansion cooled but emotions didn't. The papers were filled with dueling editorials, not about the guilt or innocence of the town's super-teens (that verdict had apparently come in) but what should now be done with them. Most argued that the early curfews weren't enough, a special school wasn't enough, and that the parents of these children needed to be more responsible for the actions of their kids.

There were more strident voices, who said that the parents of these super-teens were obviously overwhelmed, and that a small town like Noble's Green was not equipped to deal with superpowered criminals, regardless of their age. Lives had nearly been lost and the government had a responsibility to keep the law-abiding citizens of this town safe. Curfews weren't enough; a school wasn't enough. The Supers needed to go. Noble's Green didn't want them anymore.

Daniel was sitting with Mollie, Eric, and Rohan in the shadow of the Tangle Creek Bridge. Johnny seemed to be turning a blind eye to Eric and Rohan's little excursions off campus, but neither one of them wanted to press their luck. So they'd agreed to a short meeting at the swimming hole to compare notes. It was a throwback to simpler times.

Eric and Rohan had taken off their ties and tossed their sport coats into the grass. Neither of them seemed particularly worried about getting their uniforms dirty these days. Mollie sat on a rock and stared at the water. She wouldn't talk about the history final, and though they wouldn't know the results for a few days yet, Daniel felt like they both feared what the outcome would be. It made him angry, just as the ridiculous lies being printed in the paper made him angry. Angry and worried. This wasn't supposed to be the way this new world operated. Daniel had worked so hard to make it a place safe for his friends, and now they were practically fugitives in the eyes of the press. He wanted someone to blame it on, and there was one villain who fit the bill.

"I'm telling you, Herman is the one talking," said Daniel. "He's whispering to the papers, in the ears of his friends on the town council, probably the mayor too."

"Maybe," said Eric. "But that still doesn't explain who

torched his mansion. There must be someone else out there, someone no one knows about. Some kind of psychopath?"

"I just assumed that the laughing girl I heard that day was Skye," said Daniel. "But it could have been someone else. Someone we haven't seen yet, maybe."

"So you definitely think all these attacks are related," said Rohan. "I mean, maybe the Nobles did some of them, and maybe this fire was someone else."

"I dunno," said Mollie. "Seems awfully coincidental."

"Well, whoever it is," said Daniel, "the whole town is turning against all Supers, and fast."

"Plus, everyone now thinks you're my sidekick," said Eric. "How does the name Lil' Noble strike you?"

"Shut up."

"Or how about Super Junior?"

"This is serious, Eric!" said Daniel.

"I know it's serious, but we aren't helping ourselves by sitting here moaning about it." Eric stood up and began pacing back and forth, only he was pacing on the water. Daniel didn't know if his friend realized it or not, but he was floating several inches above the surface of the creek. Sometimes Daniel's friends took for granted the amazing things they could do. But not Daniel. Not ever.

"Then we should be out there," said Daniel, "looking for the person behind these attacks. If we're sure Drake and his Nobles couldn't have set fire to the mansion, then we need to look elsewhere. I'm still betting it's one of the academy kids. There are hardly any Supers left who aren't academy kids. Michael and Mollie, Louisa and Rose. That's it.

"Have you seen anything?" asked Daniel. "Anything even remotely suspicious?"

"Johnny's getting worked up about all the bad press," said Rohan. "He lectured the whole school on how important it is that we hold ourselves to a higher standard and blah, blah, blah. But if you mean anything criminal, no."

"Fine," said Daniel. "We start looking for another suspect. You two keep your eye on the academy; we'll keep digging down here. But I'm not forgetting about Herman. He's playing some kind of game in all this, I'll bet anything."

No one wanted to take him up on that bet. Everyone realized just how dangerous the old man was, whether he had his Shroud powers or not. But none of them knew Herman the way Daniel did. They hadn't had him in their heads. Last year Herman had used his Shroud powers to hack into Daniel's dreams and manipulate him into using the meteorite ring that stole his friends' powers on contact. Under Herman's influence, Daniel had nearly become the new Shroud himself.

Even today, even though both the ring and Herman's pendant had been destroyed by Daniel's own hand, whenever he dreamed of Herman, he'd wake up in a cold sweat and wonder *Was that really just a dream?* He could never be sure again.

As far as Daniel was concerned, Herman was guilty until proved innocent.

Daniel had hoped to talk to Mollie alone for a few minutes, but she flew away with Eric to scout the area just in case anyone had been interested in their meeting. He watched her soar off into the clouds beside Eric and found himself feeling both worried for her and a little bit jealous. Worried because ever since Smiley's final, she'd been quiet and hardly herself, and jealous because he knew whatever happened between them, he'd never be able to do what Eric was doing. He'd never fly with her. Not really.

He'd gotten a taste of that power when he'd accidentally used Herman's ring last year, and without meaning to, he'd borrowed Eric's powers. For a brief few minutes he'd experienced the thrill, the absolute joy, of flight. Now that he knew how he'd gotten the power, the memory made him sick. But it broke his heart too.

"I think I'm lucky that I'm not overly fond of heights," said Rohan, nudging Daniel.

Daniel tore his eyes away from the sky overhead and nodded. Rohan always seemed to know what he was thinking.

"Yeah," said Daniel. "I suppose so."

"Still," said Rohan, "she's not the type to go for the obvious hero. Strength, toughness, that sort of thing doesn't interest her. Eric accepted that a long time ago."

"Huh?" said Daniel. "Are you talking about . . . What *are* you talking about?"

"Mollie and Eric," said Rohan. "Didn't you know?"

"Know what?" asked Daniel. His pulse was pounding in his temples. It sounded like someone was beating his head against a bass drum. Were Mollie and Eric a couple?

"Relax," said Rohan, putting a hand on Daniel's shoulder. "You look like you're going to stroke out. I thought you knew, but Eric used to have a thing for Mollie. It didn't work out because she wasn't interested."

"Whoa," said Daniel. "I gotta sit down."

"You all right?"

"You just told me that one of my best friends is in love with the girl I . . . like. A lot."

"No," said Rohan. "I did not say that. I said he used to have a *thing* for her. A thing is not love."

"What is it, then?"

Rohan thought for a moment. "More than a crush, but definitely less than love."

"That's still terrible." Daniel put his head on his knees. If he threw up, he wanted to be closer to the ground.

"And you are missing the operative word in my sentence, I think. Eric *used* to have a thing for her. It's long over."

"Are you sure?" asked Daniel.

Rohan nodded. "Eric's not the type who lingers, if you hadn't noticed. Once it became clear that Mollie had eyes for someone else, he moved on."

"And when did that happen?"

"Oh, around about the time *you* moved to town," said Rohan, holding out a helping hand.

"C'mon," he said, and pulled Daniel to his feet. "They'll return soon and then Eric and I need to get back to the academy before anyone notices we're gone. And you"—he patted Daniel on the back—"you need to talk Mollie into giving you a ride home."

Chapter Nineteen
The Kiss

That night, Daniel couldn't sleep. Whenever he closed his eyes, he felt like he was on a boat out at sea, tossing back and forth until he was sick to his stomach. On the one hand, he feared for his friends. The mood of the town was going from bad to worse, and now it seemed that every little problem would soon be the doing of those dangerous Supers. When the temperature peaked at ninety-eight degrees, people would bet one of those Supers was controlling the weather. A faulty traffic light on Main Street would be flagged as a case of possible Super-related domestic terrorism.

The other part of Daniel's brain was selfish. It wasn't

worried about his friends or the town; it was worried about whether Mollie Lee from across the street would ever be his girlfriend. It was an anxious kind of feeling, bordering on happiness but not quite ready to commit. In his best moments, he felt buoyant, tingling from his fingers to his toes. He'd heard people say that being in love was like flying, and if this was it, then Daniel could tell them that they were right. He knew from experience.

At his worst, he wanted to pull the covers over his head and stay in bed forever with the shades drawn.

Mollie had suggested she and Michael do regular patrols of the town, in hopes that they might catch the vandals in the act. They were looking for a new suspect, but Daniel couldn't shake the feeling that they had all the information they needed right here in front of them. Herman, Johnny, the Nobles, and these attacks—he just needed the right clue to pull them all together.

That morning, as Daniel was out front looking for the paper (he did that a lot, since from his front yard he could also see Mollie Lee's house across the street), he was nearly knocked to the ground as someone grabbed him from behind.

It was Mollie and she was laughing. Or was she crying? It was difficult to tell.

"Is everything all right?" Daniel asked.

In answer, Mollie held up a slip of paper clutched in her fist.

"The final grades!" she said. "Did you get yours?"

Oh no, Daniel thought. He'd been dreading this moment, and frankly, if Mollie had failed, then he didn't really care what his own grade was. What would be the point?

"I haven't looked at the mail yet," he said awkwardly.

"I passed!"

"Huh?"

"I PASSED!" Mollie shouted again. "I got eighty-one percent, thanks to you!"

Then she was hugging him again and doing that laughing/crying stuff some more, and Daniel didn't have time to even process what she'd said because the next thing he knew he was kissing her.

He thought that it definitely ranked among the world's very best. It had to. This was a kiss two years in the making.

"Daniel and Mollie sitting in a tree!" said a little voice behind him. With a combination of reluctance and bright burning embarrassment, Daniel and Mollie pulled apart and looked down to see Georgie pointing up at them.

"K-Y-S-S-I-N-G," he sang.

"It's K-*I*-S-S— Oh, never mind," said Daniel. "Look, Georgie, why don't you run back inside, okay?"

But his little brother had already forgotten about the kissing, and begun hopping up and down and pointing at the street.

"Look, police cars!" Georgie cried with joy. "Police cars!"

A line of vehicles marked NOBLE'S GREEN SHERIFF'S DE-

PARTMENT was passing Elm, their red lights flashing. Was there some kind of parade going on? Then Daniel saw the news vans following the police cars. This wasn't a parade—something was happening.

Daniel looked at Mollie, but she was looking down at her phone, which was pinging frantically. Someone was sending her a flurry of text messages.

"Slow down a minute," she said to her phone as she scrolled through the beeping messages. That was something you never heard Mollie Lee say.

"What's up?" asked Daniel.

"It's Louisa," said Mollie. "She's sending me a link to . . ."

Mollie's face fell. She'd been flushed a bright red (as Daniel suspected he was too) a second ago, but as Daniel watched, all the color drained from her cheeks.

"Oh God," she whispered; then she held out her phone so Daniel could see the small screen too. "It's all over the Internet."

She tapped the screen and Daniel waited impatiently as the tiny black image spun and spun, loading.

"What is it?" he asked, louder than he'd intended.

"There," she answered, and a video began playing. It was shaky, a few minutes of footage recorded on someone's phone and from far away. But the picture was clear enough.

Drake was standing in the middle of the junkyard, surrounded by a crowd of similarly dressed students. Rohan was standing next to him, calm but obviously frightened. The scene was odd enough to look at, but then the boy started talking. Daniel cringed because he knew what came next. After all, he'd been there and he'd heard Drake's words.

"Of course we won!" the boy shouted. "We're Nobles."

And now he turned toward the hidden videographer, to the crowd of academy students. Flames and smoke escaped from Drake's nostrils as his face contorted with a kind of mad glee.

"We're the future!" he cried. "Not those peasants down there in town, or the teachers telling us how to behave—no one can make us do anything we don't want to do, and soon enough, we'll be in charge. And this is what happens to anyone who gets in our way!"

The video ended there.

Georgie was clapping and making siren sounds. "Policemen, Daniel!" he sang.

Daniel took Mollie's hand as they watched the police cars speeding up the mountain road. He knew exactly where they were headed.

Chapter Twenty
The Standoff

The police cars were making good time up the Old Quarry Road, but Mollie managed to overtake them, even with Daniel's added weight to carry. It was a strangely unreal feeling, to go from kissing Mollie in one instant to praying she didn't accidentally drop him to his death in the next. It didn't help that Mollie was flying with a recklessness that Daniel had seldom seen. He understood why—she wanted to get to the academy before the sheriff's men did. She wanted to stand next to her friends.

They landed rather roughly on the lawn just past the gatehouse, and Daniel skidded along the grass until his jeans had holes in the knees. A few academy students saw them fly in, and one ran out to greet them.

"Whoa, are you okay?" asked an orange-haired boy. Martin something or other, Daniel thought his name was. "Some landing!"

He was staring at Mollie like she . . . well . . . like she'd just fallen from the sky.

"Get Johnny. . . . I mean, go get the principal," said Daniel. "It's an emergency."

The boy nodded and started to walk back toward the campus, but still watching them over his shoulder.

"Can't you go any faster?" Mollie shouted. "He said it was an emergency!"

The boy nodded, then leapt into the air and flew off toward the main administrative building. That's right, Martin was a flier. Good.

Meanwhile, Daniel and Mollie sat on the grass and tried to catch their breaths. It was amazing how exhausting simply being carried could be when you were fearing for your life.

It wasn't more than a couple of minutes later when Johnny arrived.

"Daniel, what are you doing here?" he asked.

Johnny was standing before them, his arms crossed over his broad chest. Martin stood a few feet behind him, looking excited and concerned all at once.

"We came to warn you," said Daniel. "The police are

on their way here. We saw them driving up the mountain. They're coming to the school."

Johnny cocked his head. "The police? What do they want here?"

"Someone made a video that day of the fight at the junkyard," said Mollie, looking at the ground instead of Johnny. She'd been there; she'd been one of those responsible for the fight that day after all.

"They got Drake on video saying all that garbage about the Nobles being better than everyone," said Daniel. "Calling the rest of us *peasants*. Someone posted it online, and it's gone viral."

"The way it cuts off, it looks just like some kind of terrorist manifesto," added Mollie. "It's scary."

Johnny closed his eyes, but Daniel couldn't tell if the man was thinking or listening for something undetectable to their ears. If he was thinking, there wasn't much time left. Those cars would be here any second.

"Martin," said Johnny, his eyes flicking open. "Fly back to the main building and tell Ms. Starr to bring Rohan Parmar and Drake Masterson into my office and remain there with them. Everyone else stays indoors until I say otherwise, yourself included. You got that, son?"

"Yes, sir," said Martin, and he flew off back the way he came.

"Thanks for warning us," said Johnny. "I was afraid something like this would happen."

"What are you going to do?" asked Daniel.

"Let's go find out what Sheriff Simmons wants."

They walked together down to the gate and saw that a few deputies were talking to the security guard there. The deputies had pistols holstered at their hips; the guard had a clipboard. Two men were standing behind a semicircle made up of microphones and news cameras. The first Daniel recognized instantly as Sheriff Simmons, and the second, the rather round and baffled-looking mayor of Noble's Green, was talking to the reporters.

"I repeat that we are only here to question two persons of interest who were featured in the widely circulated video," he was saying.

"Can you confirm that the video is a terrorist recruitment tool?" asked one of the reporters.

The mayor addressed the question without looking directly at the questioner. He never took his eyes away from the camera. "We have no comment as to the nature of the video."

"What are the suspects' names?"

Sheriff Simmons leaned in and whispered something into the mayor's ear. "Huh? Oh yes, of course."

"The persons of interest," said the mayor, "are both still minors, and therefore we are not ready to give their names at this time."

"But you can confirm that they are the ones shown in the video?" said one reporter.

"And they are both Supers?" said another.

"No comment," answered the mayor. "Except that I assure the citizens of this town that there will be a full and thorough investigation into the claims made on that video and any connection to the recent rash of violence. No stone will remain unturned! And that includes this academy."

This was ridiculous. If the mayor hadn't wanted anyone to see these persons of interest, then why lead a caravan of police cars to the gate of the academy?

It was theater. All of this was theater, and apparently Johnny had had enough.

"Excuse me," said Johnny, stepping past the guard and walking directly into the mayor's impromptu press conference.

"Eh," said the mayor, startled by Johnny's sudden appearance. He quickly recovered, however, and gave Johnny a cold, accusing stare. "Ah. Principal Noble. If you will just show Sheriff Simmons and his men inside—"

"No," said Johnny.

The mayor had already turned back to face the cameras, a self-satisfied smile on his face, when he seemed to comprehend what Johnny had just said. But even so, he looked at Sheriff Simmons, as if needing confirmation.

"Did he just say no?" the mayor whispered.

The sheriff nodded.

"Now listen," the mayor said. "No one here wants to create a scene—"

"Yes, you do," said Johnny. "A scene is exactly what you're after. That's why you brought all these police cars just to question two boys. That's why every news van in town is here."

The mayor's face reddened as he poked a fat finger in Johnny's direction. "Out of respect for your long relationship with our dear town, I will pretend you didn't say that. But you must remember that I am the mayor and you are still just a principal!"

Johnny turned his back on the mayor and planted himself in front of the gate. As he did, the cameramen crouched low on their knees scurried after him like a pack of dogs.

"Do you have warrants? Because if not, this school is private property," said Johnny. "And I don't care how many stupid videos these kids make or what they say. This looks like a witch hunt to me, and I've seen a few in my time."

The mayor's face was red with fury, but when he spoke next, it was a whisper, just soft enough to be out of the reporters' earshot. "What if I have *you* arrested for obstructing justice?"

"Do you really want to try that?" Johnny whispered back.

Johnny folded his arms across his chest and looked out over the assembled reporters, the police, Sheriff Simmons, and the mayor. One by one, every person who met his gaze took a halting step back.

"This gate stays shut until I deem it safe to reopen," said Johnny, this time speaking directly into the camera. "The school's closed to visitors until further notice."

Chapter Twenty-One
Breaking News

The immediate effect of Johnny's announcement that he was closing the school to outsiders was silence. The birds and the insects of the surrounding forest had gone quiet. Even the wind seemed to be waiting to see what would happen next. Then the reporters erupted all at once, shouting questions at Johnny and yelling over one another to be heard. But Johnny wasn't interested in talking anymore. He turned around and started back up the sidewalk toward campus.

Mollie turned to Daniel and smiled. "Go, Johnny!"

Daniel nodded, but inside he wasn't so sure he agreed. What was Johnny going to do next—lock down the school?

He couldn't keep the police out forever. Eventually, they would come back with a search warrant or something, and then he'd either have to let them in or declare himself above the law. Imagine the town's reaction then!

"Daniel," said Johnny, "I appreciate that you two came up here to warn us, but I think you'd better be getting home now. You and Mollie."

"But what about our friends?" asked Mollie. "They think Rohan is part of Drake's gang."

"They're safe here with me. I won't let anyone come near Rohan."

"What are you going to do next?" Daniel asked.

"That depends on them." He glanced back at the police cars. "I hope that everyone will use this time to cool off."

"And what about Drake?" asked Mollie.

"What about him?"

"He's guilty!"

"Do you have any evidence to back that up?" said Johnny. Mollie, reluctantly, shook her head.

"We've been trying to connect him to the attacks," said Daniel. "At least some of them. But so far we've come up empty-handed."

"When you—or the police, for that matter—can present some real evidence that Drake or any of his friends are involved in these crimes, then I'll be happy to march them down to the sheriff's office myself," said Johnny. "But right now, all he is guilty of is saying stupid things on an Internet video. And fighting off school grounds—something that your friends had a part in too."

With this, Johnny gave Mollie a long look, and she seemed to shrink under his gaze.

"I won't have my students tried out there in the court of public opinion before any real charges are brought," said Johnny. "It's too easy to make us into scapegoats that way."

"Us?" said Daniel.

"Them," answered Johnny. "I'm talking about the students, of course."

Daniel wondered.

"Considering all the news vans out there," said Johnny, "it's probably best if you don't fly home."

Johnny walked them both over to the gate. The deputies had moved the reporters back to the edge of the road, where Daniel could see them preening themselves in their compact mirrors, getting ready to file their reports in time for the evening news.

The mayor had apparently gone home.

"Sheriff Simmons," called Johnny, and the sheriff approached the gate.

"I sure hope you know what you're doing," said the sheriff.

"Do you have warrants yet? Have any of my students been charged with any crimes?"

"No," the sheriff admitted.

"Then I know precisely what I'm doing," said Johnny.

"In the meantime, these two young people are not students of mine, and I'd appreciate it if you could see that they get home safely."

"That right?" asked Simmons, looking at Daniel and Mollie in turn.

"We go to Noble Middle School," said Daniel. "We were just visiting friends."

Sheriff Simmons stared into Daniel's face. "I know you, don't I?"

He did. Daniel and his friends had once been the objects of a townwide missing persons search that had caused the sheriff's department plenty of aggravation.

"Uh, don't think so," lied Daniel.

"Mm-hm," mumbled the sheriff. "Lewis!"

A deputy young enough to still have a chin covered in acne stepped forward. "Yes, Sheriff?"

"Give these two a lift home, would you?"

"Yes, sir."

"Go on, son," said the sheriff. "Maybe we'll get you back in time for supper. And, Lewis?"

"Yes, sir?"

"Keep an eye on your car this time."

The deputy's pimply face turned pink. "Yes, sir."

Daniel looked back at the academy one last time, hoping to catch a glimpse of his friends' faces at the windows, but the only person visible was Johnny, standing like a sentinel at the gate.

"C'mon, kids," said Deputy Lewis. "You don't belong here. Time to go home."

On the drive back through town, Deputy Lewis had to slow his car down because of the crowd of sign wavers gathered outside city hall.

"Can't these yahoos get off the street?" complained the deputy to himself as he blasted the siren at them.

Daniel craned his neck around in the backseat to get a better look. He remembered a time not too long ago when the streets had been crowded with tourists desperate to get a picture taken with a Super. Now they were filled with people waving signs that read WHOSE HOUSE IS NEXT? and SUPER-VILLAINS, GET OUT OF TOWN!

Daniel searched for any opposing protesters, maybe a few signs in support of his friends, but he didn't see even one.

Mollie talked Deputy Lewis into dropping them off at the entrance to Elm. That way they wouldn't have to explain why they'd been delivered home in a police car.

Daniel and Mollie exchanged an awkward goodbye. What do you say to each other when the day of your first kiss also happened to be the day the police came to take away one of your best friends?

Daniel's parents were in the living room with the

television on—an unusual thing for a Saturday afternoon. A breaking-news headline was flashing across the bottom of the screen, and Daniel saw a little house on a tree-lined street that he recognized right away. Daniel and his friends had sat on that front porch just days ago.

"We're outside the house of Mr. and Mrs. Parmar," said a very concerned reporter, "whose son, sources tell us, has been identified as one of the teens on the Internet manifesto. Fourteen-year-old Rowen—"

"It's Ro*han*," said Daniel. "Not Rowen."

"As a student of the Academy for Gifted Youngsters, Rowen undoubtedly possesses potentially dangerous powers, though the exact nature of those powers is still unknown."

"Turn it off," said Daniel. "Please."

Daniel's father reached for the remote, but Georgie was faster. He flipped the channel to a show about a red puppet dinosaur dancing with a stalk of broccoli.

Tears stung the corners of his eyes as Daniel pressed his hands to his temples. What was going on?

"Just breathe, honey," his mom was saying. "Just breathe." Daniel's father left the room.

"Aren't you going to ask me?" said Daniel, wiping his nose on his sleeve. "Aren't you going to ask me if what they're saying is true?"

His mom gently cupped his face in her hands and turned him toward her. "No," she said softly. "We don't have to."

His dad came back into the room, holding his car keys. "I'm ready to go. You'll call me if you hear anything new?"

Daniel's mother nodded. "And you'll be careful?"

"Of course."

Daniel looked at his dad. "Where are you going?"

"To city hall," he said. "We heard there was a protest happening down there, so a group of the parents are going down to stage our own protest—against what the mayor is up to."

Daniel's dad ruffled Daniel's already messy mop of hair and said goodbye. As he was leaving, the phone rang.

"Are you okay if I answer that, Daniel?" she asked.

"Yeah," said Daniel. "Can I go to my room?"

"You'll promise me you'll stay in for the rest of the day?" she said. "I'm serious, Daniel. Things are getting ugly out there."

"I promise," he sighed.

After giving Daniel a quick peck on the forehead, she got up off the sofa and answered the phone. "Yes, yes," she was saying. "We just saw them on TV. Have you talked to them to see if they're all right?"

Georgie had gotten bored with the dinosaur and broccoli show and began flipping channels until he came to a spunky blond teenager smiling at the camera as a variety of makeup products floated around her head. It was the reality TV show *Skye's the Limit*.

Daniel had never bothered watching it before, and now just seeing Skye's face made him sick to his stomach. She might be playing the ditzy blonde for the cameras, but Daniel remembered her at the junkyard, her cruel smile as she'd used her powers to bind Michael and Mollie up like cattle. He couldn't stand to be in the same room with her, even if it was only a screen of pixels.

He got up and started for the stairs just as she began arguing with someone about whether French was really a language or a kind of salad dressing. As Daniel turned his back on the TV, she exploded into giggles, laughing at her own fake ignorance.

Daniel stopped and slowly looked over his shoulder back toward the TV.

Georgie was reaching for the remote, clearly as bored with Skye as he had been with the dancing vegetable.

"Don't!" Daniel said. "Leave it on a second."

Georgie blinked up at his older brother, confused.

"Just for a minute, Georgie," Daniel said. He wanted to be sure.

She laughed again. A high-pitched giggle, vapid and mean.

There it was, the laugh he'd heard just seconds before being pushed off the Tangle Creek Bridge.

Chapter Twenty-Two
Threads

Daniel sat at his desk, eyes closed. He needed quiet to think, because that feeling had gotten so strong, that feeling that the clues were all there in front of him, waiting to be unraveled. He just needed to pull the right thread.

Janey Levine, aka Skye, had been at the swimming hole that day when he fell—that was for certain. And he didn't fall; he'd been pushed. He'd wondered how anyone could have gotten to him up there without flying, but you didn't need to fly when you could move things with your mind. When you could shove somebody off a bridge with a thought. Then she'd disappeared, almost as if she'd been teleported away.

And Daniel had seen Hunter teleport Eric thousands of miles in the blink of an eye. How many people could he take with him? Two? Three? Could he teleport enough people to set fire to a tree fort, or vandalize an ice cream shop? Enough to destroy a school?

Up until now, Daniel had been fairly convinced that Drake and his gang were responsible for the attacks on the ice cream parlor and the school, but he'd assumed those attacks had been random. Just Drake and his stupid friends causing trouble. But now he was sure Nobles had been at the tree fort and the bridge. Those attacks couldn't have been random. They had both occurred at the Supers' most secret places.

That day at the junkyard, Drake had acted like he'd never seen Daniel and Mollie before, but that had to have been a lie. They'd been watching the Supers for some time.

Just what were they up to?

Daniel stood and looked at the corkboard over his desk. He'd posted articles about every major attack, and now he took two note cards and added the names of two more. He wrote "Tree fort fire" and "Tangle Creek Bridge" and pinned them up on the board. Next, he took down the names of Clay and Bud from the list of suspects. Bud was certainly not involved, and Daniel had seen how dismissive the Nobles were of Clay. He doubted they'd even let him tag along on one of their crime sprees. For now he'd leave Clay off the board as well.

He grouped the Nobles all together, pinning them to

the board. Beneath Skye's picture he wrote "POWERFUL telekinesis." Under Hunter's picture he crossed out the question mark where his power should be and wrote "Teleporter." Then, using a spool of sewing thread he'd found in the kitchen junk drawer, he strung lines from the Nobles to the tree fort fire, the Tangle Creek Bridge, the ice cream shop, and the high school. The only event that he couldn't possibly tie them to was the fire at the Plunketts' mansion. There had been too many witnesses who saw them in detention at the time of the fire.

Daniel stepped back to take in the entire board, the web of connecting threads. With Clay and Bud gone, there was only one name still on that board not tied to any attack, and only one attack not tied to any name. It didn't make sense on the surface, but unless there was another unseen suspect lurking out there somewhere, there had to be a connection. Daniel closed his eyes again, trying to follow the threads in his mind—looking for anything that he might have missed.

The experience was not unlike that of flying. He felt weightless, and his heart pounded and his fingertips tingled. Quickly he grabbed a notebook from his desk and began writing. One image, one memory, per page:

> *Dad hoisting a lightning rod up to the sky.*
> *Drake standing in the junkyard, saying "Nobles of Noble's Green . . . it wasn't my idea."*
> *The "inside source" quoted in all the news stories, stoking people's fears.*

The Supers trapped inside the academy by a town stirred to anger.
   A field of stars.

And last, there was the memory of Theo stopping Ms. Starr before she could finish a sentence. He'd used his father as an excuse, but was that the real reason? What exactly had Mandy Starr been about to say? That moment had struck Daniel as wrong then, and he hadn't been able to let it go since.

He needed more space, but since he didn't have another corkboard, he tore down his SHERLOCK HOLMES AND THE HOUND OF THE BASKERVILLES movie poster and began pinning pieces of paper to the very wall itself. His mom would be furious, but he'd deal with that later. Right now, he needed to see them all at once.

Together, all the random memories he'd written down started to seem a little less random. He began rearranging them into groups—images that belonged with one another, explained one another in a way that would only make sense to him.

What was it Johnny had said to him up at the academy, when Daniel had reminded him that he, Daniel, wasn't a Super?

I think we both know that's not true, he'd said. *You've proved it, time and again.*

Daniel's detective work had saved his friends in the past,

and each time there had been a moment like this, a break-through when the clues snapped together in his mind. He couldn't stop it if he tried. It was a rush when it happened, and it felt like . . . well . . . like a superpower. Was that what Johnny was hinting at? Was he trying to tell Daniel that, like his grandmother and his brother, Georgie, he too was a Super and that he had been all along? That he was some kind of super-detective?

Daniel had dreamed about it. He'd wanted to be a Super so badly for so long, and for a brief time last year he'd been tricked into believing it was true. But now, as Daniel stood there staring at the board of suspects, at all those faces, he decided at last that he didn't care anymore. It didn't matter. Was a star basketball player a Super because he could jump higher than ninety-nine percent of the population? Because he could move so quickly that he appeared to defy gravity? Or the Olympian who could swim faster than anyone ever had before? Was she a Super? What about Albert Einstein, or Leonardo da Vinci or Rosa Parks or any of the other re-markable people who, through intellect or talent or just sheer bravery, had done something exceptional?

Daniel couldn't tell whether his knack for investiga-tion, his ability to catch connections others missed, came from a meteor that fell to earth nearly a century ago, or from reading too many detective stories, but he knew how to use it.

Standing back, he admired his handiwork. It wasn't

complete, his wall of clues, but enough of them now made sense that he was sure of one thing at least.

He walked over to the corkboard and threaded a line from the mansion fire to the last remaining name—Herman Plunkett.

"Gotcha," said Daniel.

Drake had let slip that the Nobles hadn't been his idea, but if not, whose was it? Herman's? He'd played dumb when Daniel had mentioned the Nobles by name, but then again Herman lied as easily as he breathed air. If he had put the Nobles up to the attacks, he'd have had the perfect tool to stir up antipathy against the Supers. Set a group of super-powered juvenile delinquents loose on the town and see what happens. And when Daniel started getting too close to the truth, Herman would've needed to do something drastic to throw him off the scent. A grand spectacle where Herman was the star—an attack on his own mansion.

When Herman showed up that day after the first attack on the school, he'd had two hulking bodyguards with him, but on the day of the mansion fire, Daniel had only seen one. Where was the second, the man with the dreadlocks?

Daniel thought he knew. After all, it didn't take super-powers to set fire to a house.

The "inside source" everyone was quoting had to be Herman too. By cleverly manipulating the fears of ordinary people everywhere, Herman had turned much of the public against the Supers. But why? What did Herman gain from it, other than making his enemies' lives miserable?

The one immediate effect of all this hysteria was that nearly every Super in town was now locked down in the academy with Johnny. Was that what Herman was after—to get all his enemies and potential enemies in the same place? If so, what was special about the academy? Why there?

Daniel had an idea, but he needed to know for sure. He needed to speak to Theo again.

He considered for a moment using the window. He could climb down the drainpipe; he'd done it before. He could sneak his bike out of the garage and be at Mercy General Hospital in an hour. That was where Theo was now, still recovering from the fire.

He could do that, even though he'd just made a promise to his mother that he wouldn't. He'd snuck out of the house many times before, always with the justification that what he was doing was important. People's lives had been at stake. But he'd never done it at a time like this, when he could see the worry and fear etched into his mother's face, on a day when so many parents in this town were afraid for their children.

Daniel chose the staircase instead.

The TV was, thankfully, switched off, and Georgie was playing with his trucks in the middle of the living room floor while Daniel's mother sat on a chair nearby, staring at the phone in her hand. She looked tired and anxious, and a million miles away.

"Mom," said Daniel. "I have to ask you a question, but I want you to promise you won't get mad."

Parents hated it when kids said that, Daniel knew. It was an assurance that, absolutely, what was about to come next was something worth getting mad about, but it forced them to act like they weren't angry. A dirty trick, but this was serious business.

Daniel's mother set the phone on the table and took a second to compose herself.

"All right," she said. "Ask me."

"And you won't get mad?"

"Daniel, just ask!"

Daniel took a deep breath to brace himself and asked:

"Can I get a ride?"

Chapter Twenty-Three
Mercy General

Daniel had been in this situation before, chasing one final piece of evidence, one last clue that would blow the case wide open. In past adventures he'd always been flying through the air with the Supers, or charging along hidden paths through the woods in a desperate race against time. But he'd never done it in his mother's minivan, going five miles below the speed limit with his baby brother belted in behind him.

He should've snuck out the window.

There weren't many moments in Daniel's life when he had regretted taking the honorable route, but this was beginning to look like one of them. And Daniel suspected that his mother was driving like someone's grandparent just so that she would have extra time to interrogate him along the way. He knew he'd been infuriatingly vague as to why it was so important to see Theo today, but she seemed to think getting out of the house was a good way to get Daniel's mind off his friends at the academy, and so she agreed. Even if Theo *was* a car thief.

But when he asked her to wait in the hospital parking lot for him, she shook her head and unbuckled Georgie from his car seat instead. She was coming too—she was determined to keep an eye on him. If she couldn't keep him locked up in one place, she would make sure that she was with him wherever he went.

Together, the three of them took the elevator up to the eleventh floor (after Georgie had accidentally leaned against the buttons for floors eight through ten). On the way to Theo's room, they passed the intensive care unit, where Mr. Madison was lying, still recovering from his own more severe injuries. Daniel was surprised to see a uniformed police officer sitting outside the unit, reading the paper.

"Hey, buddy!" said Theo as Daniel poked his head into the younger Plunkett's room. He was waving his bad arm, which was wrapped in a fresh bandage up to the elbow. The burns hadn't been too bad, thank goodness, and Theo looked more than ready to go home.

"Hello, Mrs. Corrigan," Theo added as he saw Daniel's

mom lurking outside his door. "It's such a pleasure to see you too."

Daniel's mother gave Theo a small smile and asked how he was feeling, after which she quickly excused herself to take Georgie to find a water fountain. Daniel's mother could only take Theo in very tiny doses.

Daniel watched his mother go. "She's like my own secret service," he said. "Won't let me out of her sight."

"You see all that academy business?" Theo gestured to the TV on the wall. The sound was off but the picture was of the locked-down academy. The images flipped back and forth between a news anchor and the closed school gate.

"I was there," Daniel said.

"Seriously? This has really gotten crazy." Theo held up his own copy of the *Noble Herald,* which had been sitting next to his untouched dinner tray. "All over the newspapers too."

"Yep," said Daniel. "This is really bad, Theo. You know, when Mollie was worried about that school, when she was spouting off all her crazy conspiracy theories, I thought she was just being paranoid. After all, the place had been built by my friend Theo's family, and surely if there was anything strange going on, my friend Theo would know about it, right?"

"Uh, right." Theo was licking his lips.

"You need a drink?"

"Yeah," said Theo. "Water pitcher's right over there. Should've offered some to your mom, come to think of it."

"I'll get it for you, Theo," said Daniel. "Just as soon as you answer one question. Who's running Plunkett Industries now? It's not your dad anymore, is it?"

Theo glanced around the room, as if someone might burst in any second and rescue him. Then he slumped back onto his hospital bed with a sigh. "Oh, this is stupid. Feel like I should be asking for my lawyer!"

Daniel walked over and poured water from the pitcher into a little paper cup, and handed it to his friend. Theo nodded thankfully as he drank.

"Just tell me the truth, Theo," said Daniel. "It's important."

Theo finished the water in one gulp, and crushed the paper cup in his hand. "Fine," he said, tossing the cup at the wastebasket and missing. "Three points."

"Theo!"

"Okay! After Herman reappeared last year, he reasserted his share in the company, and secretly bought out the rest. It was a hostile takeover, and my dad didn't even see it coming. Herman let us stay in the house as long as we promised not to make a big deal about it.

"I didn't tell you guys—I didn't want Ms. Starr to tell you guys—that Herman's in charge of the company again, because I was embarrassed. The truth is, we're totally broke. My dad made a lot of money but he ran up even more debt. Without Plunkett Industries we're sunk. There's no way we can keep up with what we owe. My dad's overseas trip with Granddad is just an excuse to look for another job.

"I'll have to sell my car for sure."

So there it was. What Mandy Starr had really been about to say that day was that she'd recently met the academy's chairman of the board—*Herman* Plunkett—but Theo stopped her just in time, and covered it up with a ridiculous story about his dad being some kind of womanizer. So Herman now controlled Plunkett Industries, a billion-dollar company, with all its connections and influence. Which meant . . .

"Herman built the academy," said Daniel.

Theo nodded. "He chose the spot, hired the architects, oversaw every last detail of its construction. He was weirdly secretive about it too. Now he runs the board of trustees. Dad says Herman rarely sits in on meetings, but he still calls all the shots."

Daniel had once compared Herman to a spider sitting in a web. It was a good metaphor for the old villain, who for years had sat back and manipulated the whole town into doing his bidding, waiting for any enemies to fall into his trap.

Now Daniel had found out that Herman had built that school on the side of Mount Noble to his own exact specifications, a secret project costing millions. Shining, magical, designed to be impossible to resist.

Herman had spun himself a new web.

"Thanks, Theo," said Daniel. "I was afraid you'd say that, but it's what I needed to hear."

"I'm sorry I didn't tell you earlier," said Theo. "But I didn't think it mattered. I thought Herman was pretty much finished with the super-villain stuff. Now he's just picking on his own family."

"I gotta tell you something else, Theo," said Daniel. "I think Herman's bodyguard set fire to the mansion."

"What? Why would he do that?"

"To win the public's sympathy, I think. To give Herman something really terrible to blame on the Supers. And to keep me from getting too close to the truth."

"But my mom and I almost died! If not for Johnny and Eric, we would have."

"I don't think Herman cared."

Theo shook his head. "I figured that since he couldn't be the Shroud anymore, since you busted that magic pendant of his, he'd be powerless to actually hurt anybody."

"His real power was never the pendant," said Daniel. "The Shroud wasn't our real enemy; it was always Herman the man."

"He's got everyone in his pocket, you know," said Theo. "The mayor, the papers. He owns just about everything in this town."

"I know. What I don't know is why he built the academy to begin with. Why does he want everyone there?"

"I don't think it's because he thinks children are the future," said Theo.

"I wonder if it has something to do with Johnny," said Daniel. "Herman acted like he was afraid of him, but after all these years, something has finally lured Johnny out into the open, and Herman built it. I wonder if Johnny knows."

Daniel shook his head. That earlier brainwave was spent, and now he was staring at the wall again.

"And that's as far as I get," said Daniel, rising. It was so frustrating to be this close to an answer that he just couldn't quite grab. "You get better, okay? You've been a big help."

"You'll figure it out," said Theo. "That's what you do, remember? Daniel the Detective!"

Sure, but would he figure it out in time? The clock was ticking, although what it was counting down to was still a mystery.

"Hey, could you do me a favor on your way out?" asked Theo. "Could you put this tray of disgusting food outside my door with my compliments to the chef? Gray meat and brown peas. It's making me sick just looking at it."

Daniel nodded and took the tray off of Theo's side table. It really did look terrible, like they were trying to make their hospital food live up to its reputation.

As he turned to leave with the dinner tray, his eyes glanced over the folded copy of the *Noble Herald*. The front page was the same one the cop had been hiding behind, only now Daniel could read the headlines clearly. Above a picture of the academy were the words "Super Trouble." Daniel groaned. The headline writers in this town were really getting lazy. Beneath that, in the lower corner, was a photo of

Mount Noble Observatory, with a much smaller headline that read "Unusual Comet Offers Local Stargazers a Show."

The dinner tray slipped from his fingers and clattered to the floor.

"Whoa!" said Theo. "Watch what you're doing!"

But Daniel wasn't listening. He ignored the off-color peas rolling every which direction, the spreading lake of milk soaking his shoes. He scooped up the fallen paper instead and began reading.

> Thanks to clear skies and unseasonably low humidity, careful stargazers will be treated to a once-in-a-lifetime experience tonight as a celestial anomaly, designated Comet B9-111, makes an appearance in the skies above Noble's Green. Famous for its unmistakable green tail and formerly ominous name, the newly christened comet was once . . .

The paper was shaking in his hands, making it hard to read, and Daniel realized he was trembling. With a deep breath he tried to steady himself and read on.

> As it passes near Earth's orbit tonight, modern scientists are anxious to get a good look at B9-111, an object that has long baffled astronomers.
>
> "We call it a comet, but the truth is, we're not really sure," said Professor Lewis Larson, director of the

Mount Noble Observatory. "People have been quick to label it a comet, I guess because that has a better ring to it than 'unclassified celestial phenomenon.' But after we get a look at it with our modern telescopes, we'll know for sure.

"Regardless, keep your eyes on the skies, because it's coming tonight!"

Daniel saw his father erecting a lightning rod on the roof of their house.

Daniel saw Johnny pointing and laughing at the metal spire standing in the exact center of the academy. Taller than any building, taller than the tallest tree, like a rod pointed at the sky.

And the answer was right in front of him, like a lightning bolt . . . like a comet.

"Oh no," breathed Daniel. "I know what Herman's planning, Theo. I've gotta go. I know what he's trying to do."

"What? Hey, wait!" shouted Theo. "What about the dinner all over my floor?" But Daniel was already halfway down the hall. People were giving him looks, a kid rushing through the hospital corridor, but he didn't care. He only slowed down when he passed the intensive care ward, but the cop was no longer there, so he full-out ran until he found his mom and Georgie, sitting near the water fountain.

Daniel was so breathless that he could barely get out the words. *We have to leave now. No time to explain.*

Johnny was wrong when he'd said that spire in the middle of the academy served no purpose. It had been built by Herman Plunkett, and as insane as he was, Herman never did anything without a purpose.

It wasn't art and it wasn't a mistake. It was a lightning rod aimed at the sky, and it was designed to attract just one thing.

The Witch Fire Comet was coming back tonight, and the Noble Academy for the Gifted would be ground zero.

Chapter Twenty-Four
Good Cop, Bad Cop

"I don't know how Herman's done it," Daniel was saying, "but I think that spire is designed to work like a lightning rod, only instead of attracting electricity, it'll somehow attract the Witch Fire Comet. The last time the comet appeared in the sky, a meteorite burned down St. Alban's. Tonight it'll hit the school. At least that's what he thinks is going to happen."

"The academy? But that's where—"

"Where most of the Supers are, yes! And Johnny! Herman's got them all trapped right where he wants them. The kids he despises, and the only person the Shroud ever feared. After tonight—boom!—all his problems solved."

"Daniel, slow down," his mom said. "Start from the beginning. What is a Shroud exactly?"

Daniel put his head in his hands. This was hopeless. They'd gotten as far as the car before she'd demanded he tell her everything. Why were they rushing out of the hospital? What had Theo said that upset him so? Just what was Daniel involved in?

He'd tried. He honestly had. He had tried to tell her everything, in a sort of Cliff's Notes version, but she'd understandably had trouble following along.

He realized early on that to explain everything, he'd have to start at the beginning, all the way back to that long-ago night when the Witch Fire Comet had appeared in the sky over Mount Noble—the night Johnny Noble and the first Supers had been born in the ashes of the St. Alban's fire. He tried to lay it all out for her, to describe how that alien meteorite had killed the rest of the adults and had changed Johnny and the children.

Because the Witch Fire Comet was coming back tonight, and if Herman was right and there was going to be a meteorite strike on the academy, many lives would be lost. Johnny and the Supers would be at ground zero, and the same comet that had given them their powers would take them away. In the aftermath of that explosion, they'd be at best powerless, at worst dead.

But there was still time to warn Johnny and the Supers. The hospital wasn't that far away from the academy. A ten-minute drive at most. Cell phone coverage was spotty up on the mountain, and Daniel hadn't been able to reach Mollie, but he'd already sent her several messages telling her that the academy was in danger and to get Johnny and the students far away. There was still time to save everyone if they acted now.

If he could only get his mom to cooperate. She was driving along the mountain road now, and soon they'd pass up their exit. Just one turn and they could be there within minutes.

"Really, Daniel," she was saying. "It all just sounds like . . . such a story! Even if you're right, and Mr. Plunkett is this Shroud person, how do you know what he's up to? This whole comet thing sounds crazy, I have to tell you."

"I know," said Daniel. "It is crazy, but that's how Herman thinks. There has to be a reason he built the academy in the first place, and I think this is it."

"And even if I did believe you," said his mother, "why would I want you closer to that academy when it looks so dangerous as it is—"

"Mom! Stop!" shouted Daniel, and his mother slammed on the brakes, squealing to a halt on the side of the road.

"Whoa!" shouted Georgie, clapping.

"What? Are you okay?" asked his mother. "Did I hit something?"

Daniel calmly pointed over his shoulder to the turnoff they'd just missed. The Old Quarry Road.

"Please, Mom," he said. "The academy's that way. My friends need me."

She looked at him, not saying anything.

It wasn't going to work, Daniel could tell. She wasn't

about to let her son get involved any more than he already was. He thought about making a run for it. He could hop from the car while they were parked here and head for the trees. It would take longer to cut through the woods on foot, but he knew the way, as long as he kept the road somewhat in sight. He could be there in half an hour. After dark, but at least he'd get there.

"Uh-oh," his mom said. *Uh-oh?* That wasn't the answer he'd been expecting.

Then he saw that she was looking in the rearview mirror at an approaching car, its red lights flashing as it slowed to a stop behind them.

"You have a taillight out or something?" asked Daniel. She certainly hadn't been speeding.

"He probably just wants to make sure we're okay," said his mother.

Daniel took his hand off the door handle. He could hardly make a run for it now with a cop standing outside.

The police officer got out of his car and crossed over to the driver's side door. He was shining a flashlight into the car even though it was only dusk. There was still plenty of light to see by.

Daniel's mother rolled down her window. "Hello, officer."

"Evening, ma'am."

"My son and I were just having a talk—well, an argument really—so I pulled over. There's nothing wrong."

"He your son?" the officer asked, gesturing to Daniel with his flashlight. From where he was sitting, Daniel couldn't see the officer's face.

"Well, yes," answered Daniel's mother. "These are both my sons." She gestured back to Georgie.

"Hi," said Georgie.

The officer ignored him and placed his hand on the door. "I'm going to have to ask you and your son there to step away from the car," he said.

"What?" said Daniel's mother. "Why?"

"Just cooperate, lady."

Daniel could see his mother tensing up, and he felt it too. Something was not right.

"Officer," said Daniel's mother, "why haven't you asked to see my driver's license?"

Daniel saw his mother's hand slowly drifting back to the ignition.

The cop didn't answer for a moment. Then he said, "Can I see your license?"

With one hand on the keys, she handed him her license, but when he reached down to take it from her, it slipped from her fingers. Daniel didn't have time to wonder whether it was an accident or on purpose, because as soon as the officer bent down to catch the falling license, Daniel got a glimpse of a dragon tattoo crawling up the man's neck.

"Mom!" Daniel shouted. "Drive!"

There wasn't any time for an explanation, but Daniel's

mother didn't need one. She twisted the key in the ignition, and the car turned over . . . and nothing happened. She gave it another try and the engine started to come to life, but by this time the tattooed-neck man had reached in through the window and grabbed the key from her hand, yanking it out of the ignition.

Georgie started crying.

It's me he wants, thought Daniel. *Herman sent him to get me.*

"Wait," said Daniel. "I'll go with you! Just leave my mom and brother alone. Lawrence, please." Daniel remembered that was tattooed-neck man's name: Lawrence. Together they'd saved Mr. Madison from the fire. Of course, that had all been a setup. Daniel was willing to bet that Lawrence's missing partner had started the fire in the first place.

"Get out of the car, kid," said Lawrence, and Daniel opened his door.

"Daniel! No!" said his mom.

"I'll be all right, Mom," Daniel lied, and he stepped out of the car.

He could hear his little brother crying and saying his name as his mom pleaded with Lawrence to leave them alone, but Daniel knew that wasn't about to happen. If he would just let Daniel's mom and brother go, maybe Daniel could find a way to escape. There was always a way.

He walked around the back of the car. Lawrence was standing outside his mom's door. One hand held her keys; with the other, he'd drawn his pistol.

"Give my mom back her keys and let her go," said Daniel.

"You're not in a position to tell me to do anything, kid," said Lawrence. "Go get in the car." He gestured to the police car and took a step forward.

One step, it turned out, was enough, because that put him directly in front of the rear door, where Georgie was crying, hysterical, calling Daniel's name, and kicking with all his young might. And with Georgie, that was a lot.

The rear car door popped off like a cork and took Lawrence with it. The keys went in one direction, the gun went in another, and Lawrence and the door went in still another.

Lawrence landed on the other side of the road, and it took him a few moments to wobble to his feet. Daniel could see that he was trying to wrap his brain around what had just happened, but it simply wasn't working. He couldn't process the fact that a four-year-old had just kicked a car door at him.

By this time Georgie had gotten out of the car. The seat belt hung uselessly over his shoulder, and little bits of white stuffing clung to the straps where he'd torn them from the seat. His face was wet with tears and red with little-boy rage. When he saw Lawrence standing on the other side of the road, he shouted, "You leave Daniel and my mommy alone!" and started reaching for another door.

"Wait!" called Daniel. "Not mom's car!"

Georgie paused; then he stomped over to the police car instead.

Lawrence seemed either too stunned to see what was

about to happen next, or just too stupid. But what was clear was he'd started looking around for his gun. He spotted it lying in the middle of the road just as Georgie reached the police car.

The first piece of Lawrence's stolen cop car that nearly hit him was a wheel. Not just a tire, but a whole wheel came tearing through the air and narrowly missed his head by inches. Next came a fender. By the time the rack of police lights went flying, Lawrence was fleeing headlong into the woods.

The police car was a wreck, but at last Georgie was calming down. Daniel's mother was whispering soothing words as she approached him.

"Just relax, honey," she said. "Everyone's all right now. Don't . . . don't tear any more cars apart, okay?"

Well, thought Daniel. *Now she knows.*

But there was no time to hang around and help his mother with Georgie. Herman wasn't going to be satisfied with eliminating Johnny and the Supers tonight. He obviously wanted Daniel out of the way too. Lawrence must've been following them, and with a sick, sinking feeling, Daniel wondered what had become of the sleeping cop outside Mr. Madison's room. He was ready to bet that this car belonged to him.

As long as Daniel stayed near his family, he was putting them in danger too.

Without saying goodbye, Daniel turned and snuck off into the woods. This was one last hike to the forbidden north face of Mount Noble. One last adventure to save his friends.

Chapter Twenty-Five
The Old Quarry

Daniel had been hiking for about fifteen minutes when he heard a voice cursing somewhere nearby. Daniel hunkered down low near the base of a tree and listened. There were footsteps, followed by another curse, only softer this time.

Risking a peek around the tree, Daniel spotted a familiar silhouette moving through the brush. Every now and again, Lawrence's big bald head would smack into a branch and he'd start up a fresh round of curses.

This was a surprise. Daniel had just assumed that when Lawrence took off into the woods, he was headed back toward town. But here he was, blundering through the forest, apparently intent on the same destination as Daniel—the academy.

But he was having a harder time of it than Daniel. Lawrence didn't know these woods, and between the setting sun and all the noise he was making, Daniel could easily have outpaced him without being seen or heard. He'd reach the academy long before Lawrence.

But why was he here?

He watched as Lawrence took something out of his pocket. Daniel couldn't see exactly what it was in the dark, but he did catch a flicker of light, like a tiny flashlight being switched on and off again. Or a cell phone.

He was using the light of his phone to find his way.

Daniel decided to follow him. While he was in a hurry to reach the school and warn Johnny, he didn't want to lose sight of Herman's thug. Daniel needed to know where he was going.

They continued through the woods up the mountain, and Daniel kept a safe distance from him. It was easy, because whenever Daniel thought he'd lost Lawrence in the dark, all he needed to do was wait a minute before Lawrence's cell phone would light up again like a beacon in the woods.

After a while, Daniel started to get the feeling that they were drifting away from the direction of the academy. The road was no longer visible, and they seemed to be moving laterally instead of vertically up the mountain. They must've wandered too far in the wrong direction and passed the academy. It lay somewhere behind them in the woods.

Daniel chided himself for following the bodyguard in the first place, and was just about to turn back and abandon Lawrence for being lost when he spotted a bit of gravel through the trees. It had to be the Old Quarry Road. That was lucky. If he followed that road, it would wind its way down the mountain and to the academy. But if they'd hiked far enough up the mountain that the Old Quarry Road had turned to actual gravel, then that meant that they were near . . .

He hadn't been back in over half a year, and he'd hoped to never set foot in that place again. The university had established a permanent camp there to study the caves, but Daniel had no interest in their findings. He'd seen it all before, and the memories of what he'd found still haunted him.

He stepped out onto the lonely stretch of road and peered into the darkness up ahead. He could see the light of Lawrence's cell phone, a pinhole in the dark. It was the last place Daniel wanted to be right now, but if Lawrence had come all this way, then there had to be a reason. As quietly as he could, Daniel made his way up the road, feeling as if each crunch of gravel echoed beneath his feet. It always seemed unnaturally quiet in the Old Quarry.

The pit loomed before him, a great gaping chasm, a dark gash in the side of the mountain. The moon had risen, and gave just enough light for Daniel to see that the scaffolding erected by the archaeological team still stood against the sheer walls, but all signs of the base camp were gone. This place looked as eerily abandoned as when Daniel had first set eyes on it over two years ago. Of course. Herman had control of Plunkett Industries again, and this quarry belonged to him. One of the first things Herman would've done after regaining his company would be to cut off the funding for the archaeological project intent on digging up his secrets. He would have done it quietly, and by spreading around a lot of money. Daniel bet that every scientist working here had found himself unexpectedly flush with grant funds and a one-way ticket to a new job far, far away. For many long years the secrets beneath the Old Quarry had belonged to Herman alone, and he wanted them back.

Daniel spotted Lawrence's light down near the bottom, and he began to descend the steep, rocky path after him. Daniel couldn't risk any light of his own for fear of being seen, so he had to rely on the moon to find his way. Was it his imagination, or did the light have an unhealthy tinge to it tonight? Daniel took one last look up at the sky before making the treacherous descent. Was that a sliver of green in the distance or just his imagination? There might not be much time left.

The way down was harrowing, but not truly as dangerous as Daniel had feared. The scientists had built a switchback road into the side of the quarry to haul their equipment down to the bottom, and it was wide enough that one could walk it and not worry about teetering over the side. Still, there were a few heart-stopping moments when Daniel stumbled on a bit of loose dirt, and he tried to keep from imagining what it would be like to fall over the edge. Was he high enough that the fall would kill him right away, or would he simply break every bone in his body and lie there helpless and alone?

It was with these comforting thoughts roiling around in his brain that he finally set foot on the bottom. The quarry floor was mostly clear of debris, the ground littered only with the occasional soda can or wrapper left by some careless graduate assistant. Daniel looked for Lawrence, but he'd lost track of him on the way down. The last he'd seen, the bodyguard had been shining his light along the edge of the far wall.

With no other options, Daniel groped his way through the dark until he found the wall. No Lawrence. And with no light to see by, it was impossible to tell what he had been looking at.

There. Daniel felt the grainy dirt wall give way to cool rock. An opening there too, maybe three feet wide. The Shroud-Cave.

Once, this cave had been protected by a heavy rolling door that hid Herman's secret lair from unwanted guests. Then that door had been broken in two by the Shades when they turned Herman's lair into his own prison. Now it was gone entirely, and the cave mouth beckoned.

Daniel had never liked the fact that cave openings were called mouths. Why, then, would anyone in their right mind want to walk into one? But there was no use turning back now.

He hadn't gone more than a few feet before it got so dark that he couldn't see his own hand in front of his face. He'd have to risk a light; otherwise, he'd be stumbling around in the absolute pitch blackness of the cave. So, by the light of his own cell phone, Daniel set out on his third exploration of the Shroud-Cave.

The cave used to lead to an inner chamber that had glowed with its own green luminescence, but that eerie light had died with the Shroud's powers. Now the heart of Herman's old lair looked more like a workroom. There were lengths of tape scattered about the chamber, and small wooden pallets stacked up here and there that had been left by the scientists who'd come back this far to study the cave paintings, but all signs of the Shroud were gone. His mural of lost children, the throne-like chair—gone. Lawrence wasn't here, so he must've continued on deeper into the caves.

As Daniel stepped gingerly through the chamber, he spared a few seconds to look at those ancient cave paintings again. The Witch Fire Comet could still be seen clearly on the wall—a big, burning ball rendered in whatever passed for paint those centuries ago, threatening the stick figures below. The mural revealed that the comet had visited this mountain once many years before St. Alban's, and it had brought about the destruction of a whole tribe of people. The few survivors recorded the tragedy here in these caves, which had remained secret for hundreds of years until Herman discovered them.

History was about to repeat itself if Daniel didn't hurry.

Daniel left the chamber behind and followed the tunnel for what seemed like forever before noticing that the rock walls had given way to metal. He'd crossed from a natural cave into a man-made hallway, and the glow of artificial light could be seen up ahead. He powered off his cell phone light, and moved cautiously onward. Eventually, the hallway ended in a spiral staircase of metal, leading up. From above, Daniel could see a bluish fluorescent light spilling down and hear voices.

As stealthily as he could, Daniel climbed the stairs, which ascended into some kind of underground bunker. The walls were solid concrete, and fresh air was being pumped in through vents somewhere near the ceiling. A metal door was set into one wall, and a computer console was set into another, surrounded by a number of monitor screens showing images of what looked like the academy grounds, as well as a section of the tunnel he'd just come through. With a start, Daniel realized that if anyone had been watching the screens, they would have seen him coming, but it soon became obvious why no one was paying attention to the screens — they were all too busy scolding Lawrence.

Herman was standing a few feet away from the console,

leaning heavily on his cane and flanked by his bodyguards. Daniel was pleased to see that the dreadlocked bodyguard's hair had been burnt down to charred stubs, and one side of his face was covered in angry-looking blisters. It appeared that setting the mansion fire hadn't gone quite as planned, probably because of Mr. Madison's unexpected arrival.

Lawrence stood before Plunkett with his head down like a puppy being threatened with a rolled-up newspaper.

". . . not only did you set off every alarm, stumbling through the tunnel like that," Herman was saying, "but you didn't even manage to get the boy?"

"I told you," said Lawrence pathetically. "It was the little brother. He's one of them! Tore apart a car and nearly took my head off!"

"It would have been your most expendable asset," said Herman. "Now keep your voice down." Herman turned back to the bank of screens. One showed the bottom of the stairs, where Daniel had been climbing oblivious to the hidden cameras just moments ago. "I see you neglected to shut the doors behind you as well."

"I get claustrophobic," said Lawrence.

Herman sighed. "It doesn't matter. It's nearly time for you two to go anyway, and I'll deal with Daniel Corrigan later. Come morning, he won't be a problem."

"But how are you going to do it without us?" asked Lawrence. "I told you, that little brother is tough, and you're not . . . well . . . I mean—"

"What?" said Herman. "You mean I'm feeble? Too old and weak to deal with a boy and his family?"

"Let me handle it," said the one with the burned face. "I'll torch the house. They'll be ashes by morning."

Herman seemed to be considering the offer while Daniel held his breath. He couldn't let them set fire to his house. If that was the plan, then Daniel would have to give himself up just to keep his family safe.

"No," said Herman, and Daniel let out a quiet sigh of relief. "No need for that. Get back to the safe house, the both of you, and wait for further instructions."

The bodyguards turned and started walking, not toward the far door but back toward the stairwell. Daniel was caught between them and the tunnel. He could try to back down the stairs, but then he'd be walking right in front of Herman's cameras. If he stayed crouched on the stairs, the bodyguards would literally stumble over him.

Although he was trapped, that didn't mean he needed to be caught. He just hoped that Mollie had gotten his messages. It was up to her now to warn Johnny. Daniel's answers, he knew, lay in this room.

Standing tall, he stepped away from his hiding place on the stairs just as the rubber sole of his sneaker squeaked against the concrete floor.

Real heroic entrance, thought Daniel. *Might as well be wearing clown shoes.*

Herman spun around in his chair, and for an instant,

the look of complete shock on the bodyguards' faces was enough for Daniel.

But Herman, at least, quickly recovered, even as his two thugs stood there with their mouths hanging open.

"I really should have known," said Herman, grinning. "Well, don't just stand there in the shadows, my boy. Come out into the light, and let's finish this chess match once and for all."

Chapter Twenty-Six
Knight Takes Pawn

When the two bodyguards did finally come to their senses, they grabbed Daniel roughly by the arms and hauled him forward.

"No need for that, gentlemen," said Herman. "Really, two of you to hold a scrawny kid?"

Lawrence, in particular, seemed reluctant to let Daniel go, and he added a little shove as he did it.

"So you followed Lawrence, did you?" asked Herman.

"No way," said Lawrence. "I would've seen him!"

"Lawrence," said Herman. "This will go easier if you keep your voice down and don't interrupt me."

"No money is worth this," Lawrence mumbled, scowling at both of them.

"Yes, I followed your man," said Daniel, "but I should've known to look for you here."

"Is that so?" asked Herman.

"I'm guessing we are directly under the school, right? You built a tunnel from your old cave to your new hideout—the academy itself."

"Bravo."

Daniel tried glancing around the bunker without *looking* like he was glancing around the bunker. If they were underneath the academy, then the door must lead up. Herman probably had some kind of hidden passage into the school. If Daniel could reach that door, he was fairly sure he was quick enough to outpace Herman's bodyguards. They looked tough, but not particularly nimble.

First, Daniel wanted to know what Herman was doing here. To accomplish that, he'd have to play Herman's game. The old villain loved matching wits with Daniel, testing him to see how much of his plans Daniel had already figured out. If Daniel played along, he might just find the opportunity to make for the door.

"Your new hideout is a lot more high-tech," said Daniel.

Herman shrugged. "One changes with the times."

Daniel made as if he were admiring the place, but as he wandered, he kept his eye on the door. Meanwhile, he felt the bodyguards' eyes on him.

"I know you control Plunkett Industries again," said Daniel.

"That's easy," said Herman. "I figured my nephew couldn't keep it a secret forever."

"And I know you designed the academy."

"Which makes sense once you learned that I paid for it. Go on."

"I guess this little room of yours isn't on the official blueprints, though."

"Special job," said Herman, nodding. "Private contractor and strictly off the books, you see."

"I also know you've been waging a public opinion war against the Supers. I know you used Drake and his Nobles to turn the town against them."

Herman nodded. "Finally. There's a bit of real detective work."

"They're not being mind-controlled or anything like that, so what did you offer them?" asked Daniel.

Herman shrugged. "Mostly money. Same as Lawrence and Hector here. Poor Skye's TV show isn't doing so well in the ratings. Drake and Hunter want to get rich without having to work for it. And Mutt, well, he just wants an excuse to tear things up."

"But Clay's never been in on it," said Daniel. "Because there is no way he would join them if he knew *you* were their benefactor. He remembers what you were."

"Clay was a nuisance, that's all," said Herman. "But this is very good so far. Keep going! I love it!"

"I'm guessing you put the mayor up to that little show out there," said Daniel. "It was easy for him to act after the mansion fire."

Herman chuckled. "Quite a good performance I gave, don't you think? *Please, someone save my family!*"

"But you would've let them burn," said Daniel. "Your own flesh and blood."

Herman leaned forward in his chair. Daniel searched those glassy eyes for any trace of humanity, of remorse. He didn't find either.

"I had a pretty good idea one of the town Boy Scouts would fly in and save the day. Lucky me, I got both of them."

"But you couldn't be sure," said Daniel. "You were still putting your family's lives at risk."

"I am willing to make sacrifices for the greater good!" Herman said. "Something you were never able to do."

Herman's words trailed off into a fit of ragged coughing, and he clutched at his chest until it had passed.

"I hate being old," he said after the coughing jag finally stopped.

"I figured out something else," said Daniel.

"Oh?"

"I figured out that the Witch Fire Comet is coming back tonight."

"So you read the papers. Big deal."

"And I know it's going to hit the academy."

Herman stared at Daniel, his eyes glinting. He reached

over and punched a few buttons on the console keyboard, changing the display on one of the monitors from a view of the academy gate to an image of a glowing green ball of ice and dust hurtling past a field of stars. It looked like a giant fireball, but that was impossible—fires don't burn in space.

"This is a live feed coming from the observatory telescope," said Herman. "I own that too."

"So you've built this place to prepare for it. The academy is ground zero, and you'll be safe down here in your bunker." As Daniel gestured to the computer screen, he positioned himself just a few feet closer to the door.

"Of course."

"And the spire. It's a lightning rod. You think it's going to attract the meteor? That's insane, Herman."

With obvious difficulty, Herman stood. "Don't believe it, eh? Well, let me help you. I spent decades studying a fragment of that comet. I even wore it around my neck for over seventy-five years. You could say the Witch Fire Comet and I have become intimately related."

Herman began to unbutton his high-necked jacket. Then he opened his shirt down to his stomach, and where Daniel had expected to see the sallow chest of a man near a hundred years old, he saw instead cracked and blackened skin. The wound was centered over his breastbone, and spread up his neck and down his chest. It didn't even look like flesh anymore; it was hard and scabbed. It looked more like rock.

Daniel couldn't hide his gasp of surprise and revulsion. Even Lawrence looked away.

"What's happened to you?" asked Daniel.

"Wearing the meteorite stone next to my skin for all those years exacted its price, it would seem. This"—he pointed to his ruined body—"began as soon as you crushed my pendant. At the rate it's spreading, I imagine I'll be dead in a few months."

He buttoned his shirt back up. "Like is attracted to like," he said, closing his eyes. "I can feel it, you know. Getting closer. It is coming for me. The spire won't attract the comet—*I will!*"

His eyes popped open. "And this time I'll be ready! There's a reason the comet keeps returning, why the meteorites keep falling here on Mount Noble. This spot has long been associated with anomalies after all—with so many unusual atmospheric conditions, the cell phone interference. . . . Heh, I guess flying children could be called anomalies, couldn't they?"

Then he doubled over in another spasm of coughing. Lawrence gave Herman his arm to lean on while Hector dug into his pockets for a handkerchief for his boss to spit out whatever it was that was choking him.

Daniel could run for it now. Nobody's attention was on him. Daniel could bolt for the door, and assuming it wasn't locked, be through it before they'd taken barely a step.

He could run now. He *should* run now. But he just had to

know. "What is it, Herman?" asked Daniel, remaining where he was.

The old man wiped the spittle—tar-black—from his chin with Hector's handkerchief and smiled at Daniel. His teeth were gray. "You'd like to know, at last, eh?"

Lawrence helped Herman into his seat and took a place behind his chair. Hector resumed his post a few feet to the side. The door out had never looked so far away.

"What is the Witch Fire Comet?" asked Daniel.

"There are those who would say it's a gift," said Herman. "After all, look at the wondrous powers it bestows. We know it's extraterrestrial, but I believe that it is not just a hunk of space rock. It's an alien intelligence."

"It's intelligent?" repeated Daniel.

"Why not?" said Herman. "Space is vast and the idea that alien life-forms will look like little green versions of us is the stuff of fiction."

"Then why is it here? Why does it keep coming back and giving these powers? Why doesn't it try to communicate?"

Herman took a deep, rattling breath. With gritted teeth, he resisted another coughing fit, then spoke. "I said some would consider the powers gifts, but not all gifts are given freely, or with the best of intentions."

"What do you mean?"

"White men once gave gifts to the Native Americans in this area. Gifts of blankets, infected with smallpox. Because the natives had never been exposed to the disease, they had no immunity to it. They died."

"What does that have to do with—"

"I used to think the powers were a test," interrupted Herman, "to see if we were worthy. I thought that the comet was waiting for us to do something with those powers. Something wonderful.

"But now I know better. The power of the Witch Fire Comet is a smallpox blanket. We have no experience with it. No immunity to its corrupting effects. Give us mere mortals the abilities of the gods and watch us tear ourselves apart."

As Daniel listened to the old man talk, he couldn't help but picture the night sky, the vastness of space above and the greenish light in the distance growing closer. Daniel had always assumed the comet was a natural phenomenon, a source of extraterrestrial energy that by pure chance had changed first a sleepy little Pennsylvania town, then the world.

But if it wasn't, and if Herman was right, then Daniel felt a new fear creeping up inside his gut that he'd never experienced before. It was a fear of that night sky, of the unknown. Daniel felt suddenly very small.

"So, even if you're right," said Daniel, "even if that comet isn't a comet, why are you doing all this? If another meteor falls, it will kill everyone up there! Are you just here to enjoy the show?"

Herman leaned back in his chair, his eyes mere slits.

"Hector, Lawrence, why don't you give us the room for a minute?"

Lawrence did an actual double take. "You sure? You want us to leave you alone with him?"

"Daniel Corrigan is not likely to murder me," said Herman. "Wait outside."

The two bodyguards exchanged looks, then stepped through the door, which Daniel was happy to see was not locked. The only problem now was that about four hundred pounds of thuggish muscle was standing on the other side of it. He could always make a run back toward the tunnel, but that would just put him farther away from the one place he was trying to get to—the academy right above his head. Still, if it was his only way out . . .

"Not thinking of leaving that way, are you?" said Herman as if reading Daniel's mind. The old man typed in a code on the control panel, and Daniel felt a sudden pressure change in his ears as a door somewhere in the tunnel sealed shut.

"You'll be going home soon enough," said Herman. "Don't worry."

"You expect me to believe that you are just going to send me home?" asked Daniel.

"Yes," said Herman. "Lawrence was only supposed to detain you. Since he botched even that, I'm sure the authorities will be out looking for you before long. By morning you'll be home. You have my word."

"Like that means anything," said Daniel. "Why go

through all this trouble and then just let me go? Aren't you afraid I'll tell everyone what you're doing here? Even if you get away with it, I'll still know the truth!"

"Come morning it won't matter what you know, or who you tell," said Herman. "Haven't you solved the last mystery, Daniel? Haven't you figured out why I'm here?"

"You're crazy and you want to see Johnny and the Supers destroyed."

"Johnny? Johnny?" The old man practically spat out the name. "He could have done anything. No one can hurt him, no one can stop him. The world would have had no choice but to do what he said. Instead, he walked away. He was a coward. I am not.

"When I was a little boy, I stood by as the Witch Fire Comet turned an orphanage of children and one ignorant trapper into gods. I missed my chance because I was hiding in the outhouse, crying with fear! Well, tonight I fix that mistake.

"One touch of the Witch Fire and you can become powerful. A second touch takes it all away. Tonight the Witch Fire will strike the academy and make Johnny and all the rest of your Supers mortal again. As powerless as yourself. But I . . . At last I will be what I was always meant to be."

"But the fire," said Daniel. "The destruction. People will die up there!"

"Regrettable. But things cannot go on this way. You've seen what's happening to this town already—people are afraid and these Supers are out of control."

"Only because of you!" said Daniel. "Those Nobles are your creation."

"I merely poured accelerant on the flames," said Herman. "This world doesn't need a town full of super-kids—it needs a hero. One hero, to change the world. To mold it in his image."

Herman pointed at the monitor that showed the bright green comet tumbling through space. It was so large now that it filled the screen.

"Let that be a message for them," Herman said. "Someone will defend this world. Someone has been all along."

Daniel laughed. A deep belly laugh. He couldn't help it, even though he knew that it was absolutely the wrong time. It was like getting the giggles at a funeral. Sometimes something, no matter how depressing, just makes you laugh.

"What's so funny?" asked Herman, plainly annoyed. Laughter was not the reaction he'd been looking for from his victory speech.

"You," said Daniel, wiping away tears. "You're so deluded. Still the crying kid in the outhouse, who wants to be the hero so bad. You're pathetic and sad, Herman. And I'd feel sorry for you if you weren't so dangerous."

"And you are no longer a part of this story," said Herman. "You're irrelevant."

Herman pressed a button on the control panel and barked into the speaker. "Lawrence! Hector!"

The door opened and the lumbering bodyguards stepped back into the room. The two looked like they'd been arguing, and Lawrence, red-faced, was glaring once again at Herman.

Herman either didn't notice or didn't care.

"I want you to take Daniel to the safe house. Stay with him until dawn, then set him loose."

"Set him loose?" said Lawrence. "You crazy?"

Hector put up a hand in warning. "Cool it, man."

"No way," said Lawrence. "This kid can ID us. He's got me for kidnapping and you for arson. I didn't put up with all this super-villain nonsense just to get thrown back in jail!"

"You won't go to jail," said Herman. "I will protect you."

"Oh yeah?" said Lawrence. "If you haven't noticed, you're a dead man walking! You keep saying after tomorrow you'll be able to fix all our problems, but after tomorrow all I see you being is that much closer to kicking it."

"Hey, he's treated us fair so far," said Hector. "Paid us right."

"And made us put up with all his craziness," said Lawrence as he started pacing around the bunker. "Look at this place! What's it for? It has something to do with that Witch Comet or whatever, but he won't tell us!"

Herman very coolly and calmly stood up from his chair. "What happens here is my business," he said. "And your business is to do what I pay you for. Handsomely, I might add. Now take Daniel here to the safe house and keep him there until morning. *Safe* until morning."

"Stop telling me what to do!" shouted Lawrence as he

jabbed a thick finger in Herman's face. Herman didn't even blink.

"Lower your voice, you fool," said Herman.

"Why?" said Lawrence. "We're in a freaking concrete bunker! Who's gonna hear us?"

Hector put a hand on his partner's arm. "Maybe we should do like the old man says."

"Get your hands off me!" said Lawrence, turning on Hector. "No one's giving me any more orders!" The bodyguards' argument was dissolving quickly into a shoving match as Lawrence continued to yell threats.

"Shut him up!" hissed Herman as he cast a fearful gaze toward the ceiling. Daniel wondered what Herman was so afraid of, but he didn't have to wonder for very long. An alarm sounded—a chiming bell that dinged in time with a flashing light on Herman's computer console. Lawrence and Hector gave up their struggle and looked around worriedly.

"What is that?" asked Hector.

"The proximity alarm," said Herman as he leaned over the console. Peering at the monitors, the old man said, "Brace yourselves."

Daniel's first thought was that he'd been too late and the Witch Fire Comet had arrived. His second thought was he didn't want to be there when it hit. He'd just turned to make a dash for the doorway when he felt a strong hand grab his shirt collar.

"Where you going?" snarled Lawrence.

Daniel tried to pull away from the big man's grasp. "We have to get out of here!" Daniel shouted. "It's coming!"

"What's coming?" said Lawrence.

"Not *what*," answered Herman, who had grown strangely calm as he stood up straight and adjusted his glasses. "*Who*. I told you to be quiet."

It started with a distant rumble, like a far-off earthquake. Then the concrete ceiling began to buckle and crack.

"What the—" Lawrence's words were lost in an explosion of dirt and stone as the bunker burst open. Large chucks of concrete began raining down all around them, and Daniel turned just in time to see a section of the wall behind him coming loose.

Daniel shouted at Lawrence to move, but the bodyguard panicked when he saw the toppling blocks of concrete. Lawrence threw himself clear of the rubble, but in doing so shoved Daniel toward the collapsing wall.

Then Daniel was lying on the ground, unable to catch his breath. Something heavy and hard was on top of him, crushing him. There was dust in his eyes, but that didn't matter because he couldn't see anyway. There wasn't air enough in his lungs to call for help. He was losing consciousness. His last thought before darkness took him was that he didn't want to do this alone.

Chapter Twenty-Seven
Supers vs. Nobles: Round Two

The sunlight was filtering in through the attic window—burnt-orange, an autumn color. His gram looked thin, and she breathed too deeply, as if it was hard for her to catch a breath. It was strange to see her in the flesh, because she'd been dead for almost two years now. But there was something familiar about all of this, and she was smiling and looked happy, so Daniel didn't want to question it.

"By the way, I hear you met little Mollie Lee from across the street," she was saying. "Such a sweetheart. A real cutie too. Don't you think?"

At the mention of Mollie, the ball in Daniel's stomach did a small, unexpected flip. Why was Gram smiling?

"She's okay," he said quickly. "For a girl, I mean. She's fun to hang out with. Actually, she's more like a boy in a lot of ways. . . ."

Why was it so stuffy in here?

"Well," continued Gram, "I remember when she was just a chubby little thing in pigtails and frilly dresses. The poor girl's mother tried for years to dress her like one of those porcelain dolls, but it never looked right on Mollie. She dirtied up more beautiful dresses. . . . Eventually her parents must've just given up."

Daniel smiled at the thought of Mollie wearing a frilly anything. "Can't say I blame them," he said. "When Mollie gets her mind set on something, that's the end of it."

"You don't say? And what's she got her mind set on these days?"

Another stomach jump. Just what was Gram getting at?

"Nothing. I mean, she's always on about something or other, but it's never a big deal. Girl stuff, you know?"

Gram nodded and rested her chin on her hands as she twirled her cane between her fingers. Her bent shape was silhouetted against the attic window, and just over her shoulder, Daniel could see the sun drooping low through the trees. In the pink evening glow, she looked like she had before the cancer—rosy and full of health.

"I'm glad that you're making friends, Daniel. I know that coming here couldn't have been easy on you—a new town, a new school. There's a lot of grown-up stuff going on here with my being sick and all, but I don't want you to forget to be a kid—at least for a little while longer."

Daniel nodded.

She reached over and pinched Daniel on the arm. Her eyes looked a little moist, but Daniel couldn't be sure in the fading light.

"Don't grow up too fast, Daniel. No matter what else happens, promise me that."

"I promise, Gram," he said. "I promise."

"Give him room, Mol. Let him work."

"You've got to do more! You've got to try harder!"

"Hey, look at that! Something's happening."

The first thing Daniel saw when he opened his eyes was Mollie's face. She was crying. Not some pretty, movie kind of crying—Mollie didn't do that. This was ugly, heaving, sobbing crying with tears and snot bubbles. The real deal.

She was also squeezing Daniel's hand so hard his fingers had gone numb.

"Mollie?"

"I got your text," she said, wiping her nose on her sleeve.

"Where am I?" he asked, and as he tried to sit up, he gasped in pain. Every muscle in his body ached. He was lying amid a pile of rubble and he felt terrible.

"You can thank him," said Rohan, appearing next to him and pointing to Johnny, who was lying beside him. Johnny looked awful. Sweaty and pale, he was taking deep breaths, as if he couldn't get quite enough air.

"You . . . ," said Daniel. He was still having trouble

focusing. He'd been talking to his gram, a conversation that they'd had years ago, and yet just then it had seemed like she was talking about the here and now.

The now. Daniel remembered the wall collapsing. He remembered the struggle to breathe. There shouldn't have been a now.

"It was you?" asked Daniel, and Johnny gave a weak nod.

"Look what happens when I play hero," said Johnny. "I almost brought the whole ceiling down. I'm sorry."

"But you healed me," said Daniel. "I thought you could do that only with small things."

"Me too," whispered Johnny. "But . . . I had to try."

"It wiped him out," said Rohan. "For a minute there, I thought we were going to lose both of you."

Daniel pushed himself up to sitting and looked around. They were still in the bunker, although most of it was now in ruins. There was no sign of Herman, or Lawrence and Hector, but there was a hole in the ceiling big enough to drop a car through.

"We were up top trying to convince Johnny to evacuate the school when I heard shouting," said Rohan. "It sounded like it came from below us, and then Gerald McNally—you remember that Peeping Tom kid with the X-ray vision? He started looking through the ground and said he saw people under there and that one of them looked like you."

"Then Johnny did that," said Mollie, pointing at the massive hole in the ceiling.

"Herman ran through there," said Rohan, pointing to the door. "His thugs escaped through the tunnel."

"Help me up," said Daniel, and Mollie put her arm around him for support.

Rohan had helped Johnny to sit up, but the old hero, for once, looked his age. Daniel examined the hole Johnny had created. He'd broken through at least six feet of earth and another two of solid concrete. He'd torn this bunker open like it was a wrapped present. Now he was so weak he could barely sit up.

From somewhere up top, through the jagged hole, came the sound of fighting.

"What's going on up there?" Daniel asked, worried.

"It's Eric and the rest of our friends," said Mollie. "Fighting the Nobles."

"What?"

"When I got your message, I contacted Michael and Louisa. I figured I might need help getting everyone out of here."

"It's a good thing too," said Rohan. "After Johnny crashed into Herman's hideout, the Nobles tried to stop us from following him. I think they're working for Herman!"

"Yeah, I kind of figured that out already," said Daniel. "So Eric and Michael and Louisa are alone against the Nobles?"

"No," said Mollie. "You won't believe it but Bud and Simon are helping too."

"Simon?" That was twice now that Simon had been there

when needed. Once a Super, always a Super. And Bud . . . Well, apparently people really could change.

"But you came down here to be with me, Mol," said Daniel.

Mollie nodded.

Daniel was afraid she might start to cry again. "You feel like hitting someone?"

"It's about time," she sniffed.

"Can you get me up top, first? I want to see what's going on."

"Sure."

"Rohan," said Daniel, "you keep an eye on Johnny until he gets his strength back."

"Be careful," said Rohan.

"I will."

Daniel looked at Johnny and found himself at a loss for words. Johnny Noble—the man who'd disappointed him, who'd frustrated and, at times, even frightened him—had just saved his life. A simple thanks wouldn't begin to cover all of what needed to be said.

"Go," said Johnny. "I'll be along in a . . . in a minute."

Daniel nodded, then put his arms around Mollie as she leaned into him. "Okay, let's go."

Mollie flew them up through the hole and into the night air. And directly into the middle of a war zone.

It was the Supers versus the Nobles all over again, only this time the odds were more even. Not only did the Supers have a few extra fighters on their side, but they knew what the Nobles could do. There would be no surprises this time.

Nevertheless, the Nobles were putting up a brutal fight. Daniel couldn't actually spot Drake in all the chaos, but the signs of his passing were everywhere. Large swaths of the lawn were aflame, and the immaculately trimmed hedges had gone up like kindling. Automatic building sprinklers were already spraying water and foam everywhere to combat the blaze.

Simon was locked in a duel with Mutt, and he was barely keeping the savage kid at bay with his bolts of electricity as Mutt dodged his blasts with superhuman agility. But whenever he got close enough to try and swipe at Simon, Mutt would leap back with a yowl of pain—touching Simon when he was charged up like that was a bad idea.

Daniel had been more worried about Hunter, however. The teleporter had taken Eric out of the fight last time with a touch, but this time he hadn't been so lucky. Hunter was lying on the grass, clutching his stomach and getting violently sick all over himself. Apparently, Hunter needed to concentrate to teleport, and it was hard to concentrate when you were busy retching up everything you'd eaten in the last week. A cloud of greenish fog clung to him, and whenever he tried to crawl away, the noxious vapor followed him. Bud was standing a few feet away, the boy's round face twisted up in concentration. Bud had learned to control his power after all, and at exactly the right time.

"We're doing okay for once," said Daniel, but the words had barely escaped his lips when Mollie yelled, "LOOK OUT!"

She shoved him to the ground just as a fireball went soaring past, right where Daniel's head had been.

Skye was walking toward them. Her face was all twisted in anger as she used her telekinesis to tear up flaming bushes around her to serve as missiles. Daniel and Mollie barely had time to roll out of the way before a fiery stump slammed into the ground and tumbled past them.

Skye had lifted three more burning branches into the air, and was preparing to launch them at Mollie and Daniel. Despite her expression of absolute malice, the girl was laughing as she stalked toward them. That cruel, heartless laugh of hers.

"Get out of here!" Daniel yelled.

"Not without you!" Mollie shouted back.

But then, as Skye took another step, she tripped. She was practically cackling, then she fell face-first onto the concrete sidewalk. The burning shrubbery fell with her and rolled harmlessly away.

Skye quickly scrambled up onto her hands and knees, obviously confused. She was holding her head where she'd smacked into the ground. She looked around, but there was nothing to trip over except empty air.

Then her head jerked back as if she'd been bashed in the face, or perhaps kicked with a very small invisible shoe.

Rose appeared just feet away and kicked at her again.

Skye avoided this one, but as she did so, she backed right into a ghostly image rising out of the ground, holding what appeared to be Rohan's overstuffed book bag. For a moment Louisa looked almost transparent as the smoke blew harmlessly through her, but then she solidified, the heavy bag in her hands solidifying with her just in time to be brought down onto Skye's head.

One good thing about the academy course load—a pile of books can sometimes make an excellent club.

Skye sank to the ground, dazed.

"Are you two okay?" asked Louisa.

Mollie nodded, and Daniel said, "Thanks to you, yes."

Louisa smiled and looked like she was close to saying something else, but didn't.

Rose spoke up instead. "Where's Eric?" she asked.

"We don't know," said Daniel. "We haven't seen him or Drake— Uh-oh! Incoming!"

The four of them scattered in time to avoid being squashed by Eric, who, at that precise moment, came out of the sky like a falling star. He gouged a crater thirty feet long into the earth as he skidded to a halt.

As the dust settled, he stood up on wobbly legs. His shirt was little more than charred scraps and his skin was still smoking. "Ouch," he said.

"What happened?" asked Mollie. "Did Drake do that to you?"

Eric nodded. "With help from his new buddy, Clay. Think he finally got the invite to join their club."

Then Drake and Clay emerged from the flames. Drake's eyes were glowing a bright red as wisps of flame trailed out of his mouth, and Clay was cracking his big knuckles together as they stalked forward.

"Good!" snarled Clay. "More Supers to beat down!"

"Wait!" said Daniel. "You two don't know what you're doing!"

"Really?" asked Drake. "I know exactly what I'm doing."

"It's the Witch Fire Comet!" shouted Daniel, pointing up at the sky. "It's coming and this whole school's going to be destroyed. He's just using you, Drake!"

"Nice try, kid," said Drake. "But Herman said you'd try to fill our heads with garbage. His orders were clear: no one leaves the academy tonight. He's got something special planned, and as long as he keeps paying, I don't care what it is!"

Drake began taking a deep breath, and whatever it was inside him that converted oxygen to flame was powering up.

But Clay had dropped his fists to his sides, and he was looking at Drake with a new expression.

"Wait a minute," Clay said. "Did you say you're working for Herman? Herman Plunkett?"

"Huh?" said Drake, and a gout of fire escaped his lips. "I told you if you helped us tonight, you'd get to be one of us! Don't you want to be a Noble, Clay?"

From where he stood, Daniel could see the veins in Clay's neck bulge. "Herman Plunkett is the Shroud, you moron!"

"What's a Shroud?" asked Drake, but the only answer he got was Clay's fist.

One punch, that's all it took. And Daniel knew that Drake wouldn't be getting up for a very long time.

"That's it!" Clay howled. "No more Nobles! No more Supers! No more Shroud or Bud or new kids—I've had it, you hear me? From now on, it's just me on my own. I'm sick of you all."

Then Clay turned his back on the Supers, the Nobles, and the world and stalked off alone into the night.

"He's really mad," said Rose.

"Yeah, I'd almost feel sorry for him if he wasn't, you know, Clay," said Eric.

"Maybe I should go after him," said Bud. "I don't think that Hunter kid is going to bother you all anymore."

True enough, Hunter was lying on the grass, sweaty and exhausted from his marathon puking session. He was in no shape to hurt anyone.

"After the way Clay treated you?" said Daniel. "Shouldn't you just let him go?"

"Yeah, but . . . ," said Bud, searching for the words. "We're friends. That's it, ain't it?"

With that, Bud started jogging after Clay, huffing and puffing as he ran to catch up with the retreating bully.

"Well, there's no accounting for taste," said Eric. "But,

Daniel, what's all that stuff you said about the Witch Fire Comet and Herman? You were bluffing, right?"

Daniel shook his head. "I wish I was. It's coming here, tonight."

"Oh my God," whispered Louisa.

"All of this—the academy, the attacks on the town—it was just part of Herman's plan to get you here on this night. He's trying to re-create the disaster at St. Alban's. He thinks he'll get the powers this time and you all will be—"

"Powerless?" asked Eric.

"I was going to say *dead*," said Daniel. "He's gone totally insane."

"Do you think he's right?" asked Mollie.

Daniel looked up at the spire near the center of the academy campus. It was dark against the night sky, and the only illumination came from the fires burning themselves out on the ground below. The effect was haunting. The flickering shadows that played along the spire's base reminded Daniel of the Shroud-Cave, of shadows and Shades slithering in the dark.

Was Herman right? Could they take the risk?

"We have to assume that as crazy as he is, there's a chance his plan will work," said Daniel. "Which means you have to get everyone out of here. You all open the gate and start evacuating the students."

"*You* all?" said Mollie. "What do you mean? You're coming with us, Daniel! You're not running off after Herman this time, not when this whole place might become a crater!"

Daniel held up his hands. "I'm coming, I'm coming. But we left Rohan and Johnny in the bunker, remember? Eric can help me get them out, and we'll meet you all outside the gate. But in the meantime, start getting kids out of here, okay?"

Daniel took Mollie's hand in his. "I'll catch up in a few minutes, okay?"

She nodded, and giving his hand a squeeze, Mollie turned and flew off. Rose and Louisa waved and ran after her.

Eric watched them go, and then said, "Man, are you a bad liar. I don't know why she keeps believing you."

Daniel looked at his friend.

"We're going after Herman, right?" said Eric. "We can't let him get away."

Daniel shook his head. "You're going to save Rohan and Johnny. Just like I said."

"Wait a minute," said Eric. "I'm not letting you go after him by yourself!"

Daniel started to argue, but then he saw the sky. In the distance was a bank of clouds. It looked like an approaching thunderstorm, only thunderstorms didn't produce green lightning. And it was getting bigger. Eric followed his gaze.

"Comets don't move like that," Eric whispered. "What is it?"

"That settles it!" said Daniel. "I need you to get me to

the top of that spire—that's where Herman will be. Then you need to get Rohan and Johnny out of here."

"Daniel—"

"I can't carry them. You can. It's that simple."

"All right," Eric said. "But I'll come back for you. Be on the lookout!"

Chapter Twenty-Eight
Witch Fire

Daniel couldn't get the specter of the academy in flames out of his mind; he couldn't shake the picture of Herman rising up out of the ashes. The wisest thing to do would be to flee the school with the students. If Herman's plan worked, the Shroud would return stronger than ever before. He'd have all the powers Johnny possessed, with none of that man's restraint.

That couldn't be allowed to happen. The world couldn't handle such a being. If Herman was right, and the Witch Fire Comet was some sort of stealth attack from another planet, then the Shroud would be its ultimate weapon.

Herman would destroy the world while convincing himself he was saving it.

Alone now atop the spire, Daniel could see all the academy laid out below him, and above, the sky was a blanket of roiling clouds aglow with ghostly green fire. Daniel had seen that color of light before, emanating from Herman's old pendant—the Shroud's light. Witch Fire. Tonight they were in for a storm unlike any other.

Herman's bunker was no longer safe now that the roof had been torn off, so where was the next best place to be when the meteorite hit? The spire looked solid enough to withstand an earthquake, but what about a meteorite strike?

There had to be a door up here, a hidden way into the spire. As Daniel circled the walkway, he stayed well back from the edge, where a single guardrail stood between him and a six-story drop.

Around the rear, Daniel found the door. It was standing ajar, and a quick glance inside revealed a spiral stairwell that led straight down into blackness.

Daniel glanced up just in time to avoid the cane blow aimed at his head. He brought his hands up and braced himself as Herman lunged out of the dark. The old man was frail, but he possessed the strength of someone who had nothing to lose. He clawed at Daniel's face, and threw his weight into him, nearly knocking both of them over the railing.

But Daniel kept his balance, while Herman's lunge had been wild, driven by insanity. Daniel slid to one side as he shoved Herman into the railing. The railing caught the old man in the stomach, and Herman let out a wheezing cough as he slid to his knees. He tumbled toward the walkway's edge, his cane clattering off the side and shattering on the ground far below.

And Daniel caught him. With one hand on the railing and the other on Herman's jacket, he stopped the old man from rolling off the ledge. Slowly, and with every bit of strength he could muster in his skinny frame, Daniel hauled Herman onto the walkway. Then the two of them lay there—Daniel with his back up against the spire, and Herman just inches from the edge.

The old man looked up at Daniel, exhausted. The fight was over; what little strength he had left was spent.

"You may find it hard to believe . . . ," Herman wheezed, "but I'm glad you're not dead."

"It's over, Herman," said Daniel. "The school's being evacuated. It won't be like St. Alban's."

Herman laughed. A sickly, bubbling laugh. He spit out a glob of something dark onto his jacket front.

"It's not over!" he said. "It's just beginning. When the Witch Fire comes, I wonder if we will survive."

Herman pulled himself up on one elbow, even though the effort was obviously painful. He clutched at his chest, at the wound the Witch Fire pendant had left him with.

"Will we rise as gods born out of the meteor's destruction? Two new gods, at each others' throats for the next hundred years because you won't do what needs to be done."

Herman grinned.

"Or you can just give me a little shove over the side. It's only fair. If I die, you can have all the power to yourself. Assuming you don't die in the fire first. Assuming you're as strong as good old Johnny was."

"I won't do it," said Daniel. "And we're not staying here."

"You will!" cried Herman. "Because I will not move from this spot. I will not hide from the fire this time! So, if you don't kill me, there's no telling what I'll do. What will I do with all that power, Daniel?"

For a moment, only for a moment, the sheen of insanity and rage fell away from the old man's face, and Daniel saw something else in his eyes—sorrow. Then Daniel remembered that Herman had been just a boy when this had started, all those years ago. Like Daniel had been when he'd come to Noble's Green. Just a boy.

Something Herman had once said came back to Daniel, though it had been spoken in a very different context.

It's not fair, really, Herman had said. *The boy dreams his whole life of being Johnny Noble, only to wake up one day alone in the knowledge that he is something else entirely. He's quite the opposite. He's the Shroud.*

Daniel hadn't properly understood what the old man had meant, or who he'd really been talking about, until that very moment.

Above them, the heavens glowed. In the clouds, there were shadows dancing behind the flashes of green lightning. Whatever was on its way, it would be here soon. Looking

out over the school, Daniel saw Drake's fires burning themselves out; he saw the lights of the town twinkling in the distance. And something else, familiar silhouettes coming this
way.

"I won't make it easy for you," said Herman. "Either
have the guts to kill me now or I win. There's no other way."

Daniel placed a foot on the old man's chest.

"You're wrong, Herman. There's always another way,"
Daniel said. Then he called out into the night, "Catch!"

With that, he kicked Herman off the platform . . . and
into Michael's waiting arms.

"Got him!" shouted Michael as he soared past. And
there was Eric, with Mollie right behind. Eric had promised
he'd come back for him, and Eric always kept his promises.

Eric snatched Daniel up from the platform and took off
into the air.

"Now what do I do with Plunkett?" called Michael.

"Get him far away from here!" shouted Daniel. "Prefer-
ably to a jail!"

Michael nodded and sped off toward the town, Herman
in his arms. The old man was either laughing or crying, Daniel couldn't be sure which.

"Let's round up the others and get out of here," said Eric
as he landed in the courtyard with Mollie close behind.

Louisa, Rose, Simon, Rohan, and Johnny were waiting
for them twenty feet from the gate. Simon was holding his
arm close to his chest, and Daniel could see blood soaking

through his sleeve; Louisa had a fat lip. His friends were dirty and beat-up, but they were still standing. The Nobles were nowhere in sight, and it looked like the Supers had won round two.

Of everyone, Johnny looked the worst off. He'd recovered much of his strength, but was still several shades too pale. Whatever he'd done to save Daniel had cost him.

"Everyone else is out," said Johnny. "But when your friends realized what you were up to, they wouldn't leave without you—"

Johnny's words were swallowed by the massive rumble above their heads. A flash of light lit the heavens, followed this time by a sharp crack of thunder. The clouds parted to reveal a streak of green fire heading right toward them. It hurtled through the sky, burning brighter and brighter as it drew near. They wouldn't make it out in time. No one was that fast except . . .

"Mollie, run!" At least she could save herself.

But she didn't run. Instead, he felt her fingers entwine with his.

Daniel closed his eyes. They had seconds.

"It's Johnny!" someone shouted, and Daniel opened his eyes to see that Johnny was flying straight for the meteor. It was too bright to look at directly, so Daniel had trouble seeing what happened next. Johnny's shadow against the fiery meteor burned afterimages into Daniel's eyes.

"It's slowing down," said Rohan. "Wait . . . Where's Eric?"

Eric was missing too.

Daniel had never in his life been quicker than Mollie Lee, but in that instant, perhaps because he knew what she was going to do even before she did, he was faster. She started to go after Eric, but Daniel had her by the arm.

In that moment, the irrational, selfish part of Daniel—the part that needed Mollie—held on to her and wouldn't let go.

"You can't help them," said Daniel. Mollie was fast, but she wasn't strong, and she wasn't invulnerable like Johnny and Eric. She'd be burned alive before she even touched the meteor. After a second's struggle, Mollie accepted the truth of it, and arm in arm, they watched the sky explode.

Both Johnny and Eric had disappeared in the meteor's fiery glare. It kept falling, but it had changed course. As Daniel and his friends watched helplessly, the hurtling hunk of space rock veered away from the earth and, like a slingshot, ricocheted back up into the sky. Whoever or whatever had sent the meteor was about to get it back.

No one said anything until Rohan whispered to Daniel and Mollie.

"But that meteor rock is the same stuff the Shroud's pendant was made out of, isn't it?" he asked.

"Yeah," said Daniel. "I think so."

"So when Johnny and Eric touch it," said Rohan, "what'll happen?"

Rohan was right. Johnny and Eric had taken off as supermen, but they wouldn't stay that way.

"Their powers will start to disappear; they'll get weaker and weaker until . . ."

Realization dawned on them all. Eric and Johnny weren't coming back.

"Rohan," said Daniel, "search the sky. Tell us what you see."

Rohan took off his glasses and squinted up into the night. He'd once mentioned to Daniel that he could see the footprints the astronauts had left on the moon. It was time to put that power to the ultimate test.

"There," he said, pointing up at the sky. "Something's falling. Something small."

Now Daniel let go of Mollie.

"Go!" he shouted.

"Follow that line of trees," Rohan was saying as he pointed. "And then straight up!"

Mollie disappeared in a flash and a gust of wind.

It was only seconds before she reappeared overhead with Eric in her arms. She was struggling to hold on to his limp body, but she didn't let him go until they'd landed, more or less safely, on the ground.

"Is he alive?" asked Rohan as they all rushed to her side.

Daniel knelt down next to his friend and put his ear to Eric's chest. What had remained of Eric's clothing had been entirely burned off, along with most of his hair, and his skin was a nasty shade of red, as if he'd been lying in the sun for days. But he was breathing, and his heartbeat was strong.

"He's alive," said Daniel. Then, to Mollie, he said, "That was amazing."

Mollie grinned back at him. "Yeah, it was."

Daniel looked around at the faces of his friends.

"We all accounted for?"

"Everyone except Johnny," said Rohan, still watching the stars. "I don't see him."

The Witch Fire Comet had moved on, either retreating or just following whatever course it sailed, to whatever mysterious purpose. If Herman had been right, and that thing up there really was hostile, then the Supers had just sent it a very clear message.

Don't mess with planet earth.

But most importantly, Herman's plan had failed, and Daniel's friends were all safe.

Except Johnny Noble was gone.

Epilogue

Faced with evidence supplied by several young witnesses, ex–academy students Drake Masterson, Hunter Daniels, Lester Muttles, and Janey Levine pleaded guilty to the attacks on Mr. Lemon's soda shop and Noble High School. Several of them also turned state's evidence and implicated Herman Plunkett in the burning of his own estate.

Along with recently captured ex-convicts Lawrence Jones and Hector Martin, Herman Plunkett was found guilty on counts of arson, attempted murder, and conspiracy.

While waiting for his sentence, Plunkett was admitted to Mercy General and kept there under armed guard, as he was reportedly suffering from a rare terminal cancer and expected to die in a matter of weeks.

After journalists uncovered sizable contributions from Plunkett to the mayor's political campaign, the mayor chose to resign rather than stand for reelection.

The Parmar family, having been wrongly convicted of terrorism in the press and the court of public opinion, was offered apologies by the editorial boards of the major papers. In response, the Parmars' son, Rohan, wrote his own editorial critiquing not only the content of the apologies, which he felt were too weak by far, but also the grammar.

Control of Plunkett Industries was handed back to Theo Plunkett Sr. The day of the announcement, his son, Theo Jr., bought himself a brand-new Lamborghini Veneno to celebrate.

And the Noble Academy for the Gifted was repaired and reopened with a new mission statement—to be a place of learning devoted to integrating students both with powers and without.

It was a day in early November, and two friends were getting off the bus.

"She not meeting you today?" asked Eric.

"Nah," said Daniel. "She's got band practice. She's competing with Rohan for first chair."

"You poor guy."

"Hey, it's not like we need to spend every minute together. I like a little space."

"Sure," said Eric, smirking. "Who would want to spend all their time making out with the prettiest girl in school? Awful."

"Better not let Louisa hear you say that," said Daniel.

"I meant next to her, of course!" said Eric, blushing. "That always goes without saying! It's just a good thing she doesn't have super-hearing. I'd be a dead man."

"Tell me about it."

Daniel chuckled at his friend's awkwardness, but he could sympathize. They were both trying to navigate unfamiliar territory—first-girlfriend territory—without hitting an iceberg.

"So, you finish Emerson's project yet?" asked Daniel, changing the subject to something a little less treacherous.

"You kidding? Twenty pages on an important historical figure? I have never written twenty pages on anything. Ever. In my life! I mean, who has twenty pages worth of things to say about anything?"

"They're called writers, and they make these things called books," said Daniel.

"Whatever," said Eric. "Emerson's evil."

As they walked along Elm, the wind picked up and Eric pulled his jacket close around him, shivering against the chill air. Daniel had remembered to wear a scarf that morning—the academy jackets were not very warm—but Daniel had

had fourteen years to get used to the cold. Eric had only had about three months. And though his hair had grown back, it was still so short as to be little use against the chill.

Most of the trees along this street were already bare, and Daniel and Eric passed by a yard where neighborhood kids were raking the fallen leaves into piles and then jumping in. Daniel felt a small pang of jealousy. If he and his friends tried that, someone would call the cops and complain that teenagers were messing up someone's lawn. Fourteen was a brutal age.

"So," said Eric, "who are you writing your biography paper on? I was going to do Lincoln, but half the class is doing him."

Daniel hesitated. He had a person in mind, but he wasn't sure how Eric would take it.

"I'm thinking of writing about Johnny," he said.

Eric stopped walking. "Really? Wow, I wasn't expecting that."

"I don't know if Emerson will go for it, but I figure there was no more important person in this town's history, at least."

"Oh, I can think of one," said Eric, winking at Daniel.

"Get real."

"It's going to be hard to find stuff on Johnny, though," said Eric. "I heard all sorts of people have been trying to piece together what he was doing all those years and no one's been able to."

"Johnny told me things," said Daniel. "He dropped hints

about where he'd been. He fought in World War II, you know."

"Wow," said Eric. "Just like in the comics."

Daniel shook his head. "No, not like in the comics. He wasn't dressed up in tights and a mask. He was a regular enlisted soldier. I'm a detective. I figured I'll start there and see where it takes me."

"Cool," said Eric. "On second thought, I think I *will* do Lincoln. With everyone else doing him, someone's bound to let me copy."

The wind was really getting cold now, but Daniel didn't mind. Someone in the neighborhood had a fire going, and the crisp autumn air smelled of woodsmoke. He loved this time of year.

When Daniel's home came into view, Eric pointed and said, "Look."

Daniel thought at first that his friend was pointing at his house, and immediately worried that Georgie had punched another hole in the wall. But Eric wasn't pointing at the house; he was pointing above it.

There were shapes in the distance. Three figures playing in the sky near Mount Noble.

"Michael?" Daniel asked.

"Gotta be," answered Eric. "Probably Martin and Sasha too."

Eric just stood there and stared, watching the three figures twirl and dive through the air. They played for a few more minutes and then sped away, off to soar through a different patch of sky.

Daniel knew exactly what Eric was feeling, because whenever he saw those shapes in the sky, he felt it too. He had ever since he'd moved to Noble's Green. It was hard not to envy freedom like that.

"You miss it," said Daniel. He was stating the obvious, but he honestly didn't know what else to say.

Eric nodded. "I do. I really do. And you know the worst part? Sometimes I wake up in the morning, and for a few seconds I forget. I think that I can just step outside and reach up toward the clouds and . . . Then I remember all the things that I can't do anymore, and it's like losing them all over again." He tore his eyes away from the sky and turned to Daniel. "But I don't regret what I did. Not even a little."

Daniel smiled. "You were a hero."

"So were you. So were a lot of people that night, especially Johnny. We can be proud of that."

Eric put a hand on Daniel's shoulder and gave it a squeeze. There was a time when Daniel would've winced under the strength of Eric's vise-like grip. Now it was just like any other.

"Besides," said Eric, "who's to say our hero days are over?"

"What? No way. Herman's locked up and probably won't last the month. And the Nobles are in a heap of trouble."

"C'mon. This is Noble's Green! *Weirdest Town on Earth.*"

"I think you got the slogan wrong."

"You might be needed again, Sherlock," said Eric. "And when you are, you'll need a Watson."

Eric stood back and pretended to hook his thumbs through imaginary suspenders. "I'm very good at asking you to explain stuff."

Daniel laughed and shook his head. The last thing he wanted was more excitement. The mystery, he loved; it was the danger he could do without.

"Sorry, but I'm done," said Daniel. "Finished."

"Says you," said Eric. "Anyway, I better get going. I have a paper not to write."

Daniel waved. "See you tomorrow."

He watched Eric go as his friend turned off Elm toward Briarwood, where his own house was waiting for him. It took Eric an extra half hour to get home when he got off at Daniel's bus stop, but he always did it anyway. He said it was because he liked to walk.

Then Daniel hoisted his book bag over his shoulder, took a deep breath of the bracing autumn air, and went home.